DEATH ON A PLATTER

JOSIE MARCUS, MYSTERY SHOPPER

Elaine Viets

OBSIDIAN
Published by New American Library, a division of
Penguin Group (USA) Inc., 375 Hudson Street,
New York, New York 10014, USA
Penguin Group (Canada), 90 Eglinton Avenue East, Suite 700, Toronto,
Ontario M4P 2Y3, Canada (a division of Pearson Penguin Canada Inc.)
Penguin Books Ltd., 80 Strand, London WC2R 0RL, England
Penguin Ireland, 25 St. Stephen's Green, Dublin 2,
Ireland (a division of Penguin Books Ltd.)
Penguin Group (Australia), 250 Camberwell Road, Camberwell, Victoria 3124,
Australia (a division of Pearson Australia Group Pty. Ltd.)
Penguin Books India Pvt. Ltd., 11 Community Centre, Panchsheel Park,
New Delhi - 110 017, India
Penguin Group (NZ), 67 Apollo Drive, Rosedale, Auckland 0632,
New Zealand (a division of Pearson New Zealand Ltd.)
Penguin Books (South Africa) (Pty.) Ltd., 24 Sturdee Avenue,
Rosebank, Johannesburg 2196, South Africa

Penguin Books Ltd., Registered Offices:
80 Strand, London WC2R 0RL, England

First published by Obsidian, an imprint of New American Library,
a division of Penguin Group (USA) Inc.

First Printing, November 2011
10 9 8 7 6 5 4 3 2 1

Printed in the United States of America

Praise for the
Josie Marcus, Mystery Shopper Series

An Uplifting Murder

"Entertaining . . . As always, Viets creates a heroine replete with wit, intelligence, and a sense of humor and entwines her in complicated plot strands." —*Mystery Scene*

"Viets designs a flashy murder with just the right amounts of sparkle and shine." —Fresh Fiction

"Fans will laugh at the predicaments this mystery shopper finds herself in on the job and [while] sleuthing."
—The Mystery Gazette

The Fashion Hound Murders

"I've read most of Ms. Viets's work. All of it is good, most of it excellent. This one is superb, maybe the best she's written so far. My attention was caught from the first page, and stayed caught the entire book. It is a wonderful cozy read. The characters are great, as are the relationships between the characters." —Gumshoe

"Elaine Viets does it again! . . . *The Fashion Hound Murders* is a hilarious story . . . [and] a fun-filled adventure. . . . Pick this book up if you are looking for a lighthearted read with great shopping tips!"
—The Romance Readers Connection

Murder with All the Trimmings

"Viets milks much holiday humor in her novel, pulling out all the wonderfully garish stops."
—*Pittsburgh Tribune-Review*

"Elaine Viets writes exciting amateur sleuth mysteries filled with believable characters; the recurring cast, starting with Josie, adds a sense of friendship that in turn embellishes the feeling of realism." —*Midwest Book Review*

"[A] wonderful holiday read. . . . a book to be savored by a cozy fire with a good cup of hot chocolate."
—Gumshoe

continued . . .

Accessory to Murder

"Elaine Viets knows how to orchestrate a flawless mystery with just the right blend of humor, intrigue, and hot romance. If you are looking to complete your wardrobe for the fall, you just found the most essential piece."

—Fresh Fiction

"The writing and plot are superb . . . no wasted words, scenes, or characters. Everything advances the plot, builds the characters, or keeps things moving. It's what her many fans have learned to expect."

—Cozy Library

"A funny, laugh-out-loud who-done-it. Elaine Viets has created characters that you can identify with. . . . This is one book you don't want to miss."

—The Romance Readers Connection

High Heels Are Murder

"Laugh-out-loud comedic murder mystery guaranteed to keep you entertained for any number of hours—the perfect read for a rainy day . . . Shopping, St. Louis culinary treats, and mayhem abound, providing for a satisfying read."

—Front Street Reviews

"*High Heels Are Murder* takes Josie into the wicked world of murder, mayhem, and toe-cleavage . . . Viets spans the female psyche with panache and wit."

—*South Florida Sun-Sentinel*

"Viets has written one of the funniest amateur sleuth mysteries to come along in ages. Her protagonist is a thoroughly likeable person, a great mother, daughter, and friend. . . . The strength and the freshness of the tale lies in the characters."

—*Midwest Book Review*

Dying in Style

"Finally, a protagonist we can relate to."

—*St. Louis Riverfront Times*

"Laugh-out-loud humor adds to the brisk action."

—*South Florida Sun-Sentinel*

"A fine, unique espionage, murder-in-the-mall thriller."

—The Best Reviews

For my grandpa, Edward Vierling,
a real South Side storyteller

Acknowledgments

This novel about St. Louis food reminded me how much I miss the good food, good friends, and good conversations I've had in my hometown.

Thanks to Liz Aton, Valerie Cannata, Mary Garrett, Jinny Gender, Kay Gordy, Alan Portman, Molly Portman, Jack Klobnak, Bob Levine, Sue Schlueter, Janet Smith, Jennifer Snethen, Anne Watts, and Emma, my expert on eleven-year-olds. Thanks to Facebook friends Judy Merrill Moticka, Rich Zellich, and Jessica Hribar.

Rachelle L'Ecuyer, Community Development Director for the City of Maplewood, helped with information about Rocketship Park and other Maplewood landmarks and businesses.

Big Dave, the pizza delivery man, is Dave Kellogg, a pizza driver and reservist who is now a contractor in Afghanistan.

Carole Wantz introduced me to Winslow's Home.

Special thanks to Detective R. C. White, Fort Lauderdale Police Department (retired), and to the law enforcement men and women who answered my questions on police procedure. Some police and medical sources have to remain nameless, but I'm grateful for their help. Any mistakes are mine.

My husband, Don Crinklaw, is the definition of supportive. My agent, David Hendin, earns every nickel.

Thanks to my editor, Sandra Harding. Your critique made this a better novel. I appreciate the efforts of assistant Elizabeth Bistrow, hard-working publicist Kaitlyn Kennedy, and the Signet copy editor and production staff.

Many booksellers help keep this series alive. I wish I could thank them all.

Thank you to the librarians at the Broward County Library, the St. Louis Public Library, and St. Louis County Library. Librarians are the original search engines.

Amelia's cat is based on my cat, Harry. Dina Willner has a cat named Kinsey who as a kitten morphed into a raging furball. Becky Hutchison has a chocoholic poodle named Mikey.

Stuart Little is a real shih tzu. His owner, Bill Litchtenberger of Palm City, Florida, made a generous contribution to the Humane Society of the Treasure Coast auction to see Stuart's name in my novels. Harry and Stuart's photos are on my Web site, www.elaineviets.com.

Chapter 1

"You want me to eat brains? Do I look like a zombie?" Josie Marcus asked.

"Not raw brains," Harry the Horrible said. "Or people brains. These are cow brains. I want you to eat fried brain sandwiches. You're supposed to mystery-shop restaurants for a food tour. Brains are real St. Louis food."

"They're disgusting," Josie said.

So was Harry, Josie's boss and the head of Suttin Services in St. Louis. Harry loved to give Josie awful mystery-shopping assignments. He had never forgiven her for reporting a rude saleswoman who turned out to be Harry's niece.

Rudeness seemed to run in the family. Harry was barely visible over the mound of yellowing papers on his desk. More papers were piled on his guest chair. He didn't move them.

Outside, it was a golden September day where autumn leaves danced in a playful breeze. Inside, Harry's office was a frosty February where dust motes circled in the dead air. Harry kept his cave chilly.

"Brains are a delicacy." Harry bared his teeth in a smile that made Josie want to back away. "You only have to go to one brain sandwich place. And look at all the other good food you get to eat—toasted ravioli, St. Louis pizza."

"I'm still trying to wrap my mind around the brains," Josie said. "Did you ever eat brain sandwiches?"

"Sure," Harry said. "If you cover them with ketchup, they're not half bad."

That wasn't reassuring. Harry would eat Alpo with ketchup. The wastebasket beside his desk looked like a culinary crime scene heaped with red-spattered takeout bags.

Harry looked like a case for the fashion police. Bunches of coarse brown hair sprouted from his fingers, ears, nostrils, and at the base of his dingy collar—everywhere but his scalp. Mother Nature had had a sense of humor when she'd made Harry. His mother had cooperated when she gave him a name that was both a description and a joke.

Harry switched gears from gloating to righteous. "Last time, you complained when I asked you to mystery-shop a salad restaurant. Now you're upset because I want you to eat good old St. Louis grease. Choke down the brains and then enjoy the rest."

Choke was right, Josie thought. "Why do I have to eat brains? St. Louis has so many good restaurants. We're a city of foodies, a mini–San Francisco. St. Louisans love to go out to dinner. Our restaurants are known for their menus. They serve organic and locally grown food."

"So what did you have for dinner last night, Miz Foodie?" Harry asked.

"Macaroni and cheese," Josie said.

"Made from specially aged cheddar?" Harry asked. "And that macaroni? Did you whip it up in your kitchen from organic wheat?"

"Kraft makes a quality product," Josie said.

"I thought so. Josie, this is a big deal for the city. This is a TAG Tour—that's Travel America Guided Tours, the biggie out of New York City. TAG Tours are designed for sophisticated travelers who want to explore cities beyond the usual tourist sites. St. Louis has been selected as one of ten cities for a TAG Tour. Their New York scouts identified toasted ravioli, pizza, pig ear sandwiches, and brain sandwiches as the exotic local dishes."

"Pig ears, too?" Josie's stomach fell like an elevator with snapped cables.

"That's a specialty in African-American neighborhoods," Harry said. "When touring celebrities, including actors, rap singers, and big-league basketball players, come to St. Louis, they drive up in limos to eat pig ear sandwiches. White-bread America needs to discover them. TAG is asking you to eat at these restaurants. If you give the okay, you only have to visit one. If their first choice fails, you'll have to eat at two places. Do you want the job or not?"

Josie had to worry about her own weekly food tour at the supermarket. She had to support Amelia, her eleven-year-old daughter. This was supposed to be a cold winter. Josie had barely been able to pay her air-conditioning bill during the record-breaking summer heat. The heating bills would devour the last scraps of her bank account.

Josie had no rich relatives or wealthy husband to rescue her. She was a single mom and barely made a living as a mystery shopper. She could afford housing in a good neighborhood, thanks to her mother. Jane rented Josie and Amelia the first floor of her two-family flat and never raised the rent. But Josie's mom wasn't rich, either. Jane made do with a small bank pension and Social Security.

Mystery-shopping jobs were growing scarcer as businesses died in the ailing economy. Josie couldn't afford the luxury of refusing any job, no matter how distasteful. She'd close her eyes, pour ketchup on the brain sandwich, and eat her way to the good stuff. Josie thought toasted ravioli was worth a special trip to St. Louis and the city's pizza was like no other in the country.

"I'll do it," Josie said. She wondered if her daughter would appreciate this sacrifice on her behalf.

"Good girl." Harry bared his teeth again. He pulled a paper out of the printer near his desk and said, "Here's the list. Make one visit at the specified time, either for lunch or dinner. The restaurants that make the cut will be on the tour. That guarantees them anywhere from fifty to two hundred prepaid meals once a week. Twice a week during the peak tour season."

Josie felt a surge of pride—and power. Thanks to her, visitors from around the world would be dining in selected local restaurants. She thought St. Louis was an underrated city and wanted to show it off to strangers. As a mystery shopper, she could dole out fat rewards to the restaurants who met TAG's standards.

She studied the list and recognized most of the names as small, family-owned businesses. A guaranteed clientele would be a big perk for them. They could use the cash infusion and notoriety from a TAG Tour.

"You can bring one other person," Harry said.

"Can I take my friend Alyce?" Josie asked.

"No age or gender restrictions," Harry said. "You can take a friend—or an enemy, for all I care."

Josie figured Alyce would enjoy the toasted ravioli and pizza. Her generous proportions reflected her personality. Josie's blond friend was addicted to cooking, so Alyce would give Josie accurate details about ingredients and preparation.

Their friendship was unusual. Alyce was a stay-at-home mom married to a lawyer. Her suburban mansion looked perfect, but Josie always felt at home there. Alyce planned the dinner parties that advanced Jake's career and belonged to the committees that helped him. She didn't need a job outside the home, but mystery-shopping with Josie gave Alyce the feeling she was walking on the wild side.

Some of the places on Josie's list might be a little too wild. She couldn't see Alyce in a city bar or a café in a marginal neighborhood. Ted Scottsmeyer, Josie's veterinarian boyfriend, would enjoy those assignments. He'd definitely like the brain sandwiches and probably the pig ears. The last four names on the TAG list looked out of place. "Why is a bakery here?" Josie asked. "And a chocolate maker?"

"Didn't I tell you?" Harry said. "You have to eat our chocolate. And gooey butter cake, too. It's another St. Louis specialty."

"Sweet," Josie said, then realized she sounded like her daughter.

Chapter 2

"This frittata is scrumptious," Josie said. "Amelia, you've aced another cooking lesson."

"Hey, no biggie," her daughter said. "A frittata is like flat scrambled eggs. I just added potatoes and cheese."

"I can't make anything like this," Josie said. "Once I get past basic scrambling, my eggs taste like rubber."

Jane, Josie's mom, put down her fork to add a dollop of advice. "You turn up the heat too high," she said.

"I'm thirty-one, Mom," Josie said. "You keep trying to turn me into a domestic diva. The cooking gene skipped me, but my daughter has it in spades."

"The talent is there, Josie," her mother said. "You never use it. But I never give up hope. I prayed for years that you would meet a fine young man, and my prayers were answered."

"I'm not sure Ted is the answer to *my* prayers, Mom," Josie said.

"I like him," Amelia said.

"My love life is not up for discussion," Josie said. "Understood?"

"As you wish," Jane said. Those three words were tinged with frost. She gave her daughter a regal nod. Jane wasn't wearing a gold crown, but a silver helmet. Today was her weekly visit to the beauty parlor. Jane had a small bald spot and her stylist hid it with careful combing, then sprayed the hair to withstand gale-force winds.

Josie was touched that her mother had put on lipstick, her good pink pantsuit, and earrings for dinner with her and Amelia.

"We can discuss cooking if you'd like," Jane said.

Anything, Josie thought.

"Eggs have to be cooked slowly or they get tough," her mother continued. "Scrambled eggs should be done on medium heat. They take thirty minutes or more."

"I don't have that much time," Josie said. "Don't they have tenderizer for tough eggs?"

"You make everything into a joke, Josie." Jane's carefully powdered forehead was creased with a frown. She seemed to regret her sharp words and switched to a neutral subject spiced with a smile. "Did you get a new mystery-shopping assignment today?"

"A good one," Josie said. "Well, mostly good. TAG is doing a St. Louis food tour. I'm getting paid to eat pizza, toasted ravioli, gooey butter cake, and chocolate."

"Cool! I'll help you eat the pizza," Amelia said through a mouthful of frittata.

"Wait till you hear the other choices," Josie said. "I also have to eat brain sandwiches and pig ear sandwiches."

"Gross," Amelia said. "Who eats those?"

"Pig ears are popular in older African-American neighborhoods," Josie said.

"That's not food," Amelia said. "That's garbage."

"Wrong," Josie said. "Singapore chefs, who are some of the finest cooks in the world, consider pig ears a delicacy."

"It's wrong to eat pigs," Amelia said. "That's why I

didn't put ham in the frittata." She slipped a cheesy morsel of frittata to her striped cat. Harry was rubbing his forehead against her leg.

"Don't feed Harry people food," Josie said.

"But, Mom, he loves it," Amelia said. Harry licked his chops with a bright pink tongue.

Josie used her ultimate weapon. "Ted says cats should eat cat food and he's a vet. He knows what's best for Harry."

"Sorry, Harry," Amelia said. "Mom says you can't have any more."

The brown tabby stared at Josie with green eyes.

"Look how sad he is, Mom. See. He's smart enough to know what we're saying. Animals are smarter than we think," Amelia said. "We learned about pigs being smart in science class. Pigs are so smart they can use computers."

So could Harry the Horrible, Josie thought, then stopped herself before she set off verbal land mines about eating her boss.

"But you eat hamburgers," Josie said. "Are cows stupid enough to eat? Do you only believe in intelligent animals' rights?"

"Mom!" Amelia said. "You know what I mean. I was trying to explain why I won't eat pigs."

Josie grinned. Amelia did not. She stuck out her lower lip in a childish pout. Josie noticed her daughter no longer had a little girl's face. The childlike roundness was giving way to the planes and angles of young womanhood. Amelia had let her dark brown hair grow to her shoulders. She pulled it back with a green headband. Josie liked her daughter's elegant nose. Amelia insisted it was "too big" and longed for a trite little button.

"I'll eat pizza with you, if it doesn't have ham or bacon," Amelia said, as if granting Josie a favor.

Josie could see Amelia was sticking to the no-pork

platform. How long before my daughter is embarrassed to be seen with me? she wondered.

"Then pizza it is," Josie said. "No ham or bacon."

"I'd like to go with you for toasted ravioli," Jane said. "Which restaurants are you testing for the tours?"

Josie showed Jane the list.

"Tillie's Off the Hill is on here," Jane said. "Did you know I went to grade school with the owner, Tillie Minnelli?"

"She sure must have loved Mr. Minnelli to take his name," Josie said.

"She did," Jane said. "Tillie was one of the first girls in my group to marry. It was a June wedding, right after high school graduation. Girls did that more when I was young. Tillie was madly in love with Zack. Such a beautiful wedding." Jane gave a little sigh.

"Zack had worked as a waiter and a busboy and he knew the restaurant business. He got a loan from his parents and opened the restaurant in 1954, the year after they married. Zack called it Tillie's Off the Hill in honor of his bride."

"Off what hill?" Amelia asked.

"That's what we used to call St. Louis's Italian section," Jane said. "Actually, that was only half the real name. People said words then that we'd never use. They called the Italian section Dago Hill."

"A word we never use in this house," Josie said.

"I just said that," Jane said, her voice tinged with acid. She looked like a hen with ruffled feathers. "I was trying to explain history, the way things used to be. Of course we wouldn't talk that way now, any more than civilized people would use the N-word. But Amelia is too young to know that some nationalities used to live in certain neighborhoods. The old-time Germans lived in South St. Louis. Italians lived on the Hill. Tillie's was in River

Bluff, way north, near the airport. That was a bold move before interstate highways. St. Louis has so many Italian restaurants it was hard to tell them apart. Zack called theirs Tillie's Off the Hill. It helped people remember their place."

"'Get toasted at Tillie's!'" Amelia said. "I saw the billboards."

"And the TV ads," Josie said. "And the magazines and the newspapers. Tillie's ads are everywhere."

"You know someone famous, Grandma," Amelia said.

"Tillie is famous for her ravioli, but she deserves to be," Jane said. "That woman has worked all her life. She started waiting tables at the restaurant when she was a bride of nineteen. Now she's a widow and still working. Tillie's daughter—Lorena, I think her name is—is a waitress at the restaurant. Tillie cooks and tends bar, even though she's my age, seventy-six. Restaurant work is hard at her age, but Tillie keeps on going. She's proud of her place."

"Sounds like you've kept in touch with your friend," Josie said.

"Of course," Jane said, as if there was no other possible answer. "This is St. Louis. We're loyal. Most of the girls from my grade school still come to our class reunions. We keep in touch by phone, but I haven't been to her restaurant in ages. I'd like to see Tillie again. When are we going there?"

We? Josie had her doubts about taking Jane on this eating expedition.

"I could go there tomorrow for lunch," Josie said. She checked the sheet of instructions. "Between noon and three o'clock." She finished the last bite of her frittata, savoring the melted cheese, then said, "Uh, Mom, do you think you can be an unbiased eater?"

Once those words left her mouth, Josie knew she was in for trouble.

"Of course I can!" Jane stuck out her chin. "This is St. Louis. It would be hard to find a locally owned restaurant where we didn't know the owner. I know good toasted ravioli, Josie. This city's reputation is at stake. I wouldn't let my city down, not even for a friend of seventy years."

Jane threw down her napkin and plunked her plate in the sink.

Chapter 3

Tillie's Off the Hill looked like every old-fashioned Italian restaurant and bar. Josie and Jane entered the bar side, a dark cave lined with wooden booths and lit by beer signs. Through an arched doorway Josie could see the dining room with its red checked tablecloths, candles in fat warty glass holders, and travel posters of Rome.

Jane's school friend was wiping the bar top. Tillie was a short woman in a no-nonsense white apron. She was designed for work: Her spiked gray hair required no styling. Her eyes were brown and shrewd.

"Tillie!" Jane cried.

Tillie lifted up a hinged section of the bar top and came out to greet them. "I haven't seen you in too long, Jane," Tillie said, and smiled. "Phone calls and Christmas cards aren't the same as real visits. What brings you way north?"

"I wanted Josie to try your toasted ravioli," Jane said. "I told my daughter it's the best in the city."

"It is," Tillie said. "I make it myself. The sauce, too. Nice to meet you, Josie. I haven't seen you since you were a little bit of a thing." She shook Josie's hand with a quick, firm grip. "That's my daughter, Lorena, coming out of the kitchen."

Lorena pushed through the swinging doors with porthole windows. She balanced an oval tray piled with pasta on thick white crockery, a feat of strength Josie admired. Lorena set it on a stand by a table of four and served the steaming dishes.

"Come over here, honey, and meet my friends," Tillie said.

"As soon as I get more bread, Mom." Lorena hustled through the kitchen doors, delivered a bread basket to the table, then came over to Josie and Jane.

Tillie's daughter was nearly a foot taller than her mother and looked to be in her early fifties. Lorena had a harried prettiness. She wore a uniform of black pants, a white shirt, and sensible shoes. Her shoulder-length hair was a gentle brown.

"We're here to try your toasted ravioli, Tillie," Jane said.

"You want a seat in the bar or the restaurant?"

"The bar's fine," Jane said.

"I'll join you as soon as I finish up here," Tillie said. "Want anything besides toasted ravioli?"

"Two Chiantis," Jane said.

They took a booth by a window overlooking a vacant lot. Wedged between the booths along the back wall was an old-fashioned bowling machine with grapefruit-sized balls and a claw machine with garish plush animals and plastic toys. A thick-shouldered man in his midthirties was trying to capture a Pepto-Bismol–pink teddy bear. The man softly cussed the machine, took a swig of beer, and fed the machine another dollar.

Lorena delivered the drinks and ice water, then went

back into the kitchen. Tillie came to their table with a platter. "Scootch over," she said. "I've got your ravioli. I'll join you for my lunch."

She set a blue platter with two dozen breaded, fried ravioli in the center of the table. The plump golden brown squares were heaped around a glass dipping bowl of red sauce.

Josie dredged a ravioli through the sauce and took a bite. "Delicious."

"Horseradish gives my sauce a little kick," Tillie said. "And cayenne pepper. I grow my own. If the sauce is too hot, I can make it milder."

"It's perfect," Josie said.

"Mm," Jane agreed, her mouth full.

"I love the name toasted ravioli," Josie said, reaching for another one. "It sounds so healthy. I can almost forget that I'm eating fried food."

"Toasted ravioli was invented when people enjoyed eating," Tillie said. "They didn't count calories and carry on about cholesterol. They were grateful they had something good to eat.

"Take my daughter, now. Lorena's a good girl and a hard worker, but she bores me to tears talking about her weight. She lives on rabbit food: salads with low-cal dressing, grilled chicken, and fish. Talks about the calories in everything. Won't touch my toasted ravioli. Calls them fat bombs." She bit into her ravioli as if she were angry at it.

"I wonder if my granddaughter, Amelia, is ready to make toasted ravioli," Jane said.

"It's a complicated recipe, even for an experienced cook," Tillie said. "You have to make the dough, grind the meat, and stuff the ravioli. You still live in Maplewood, right? You're close to the Hill. Buy some from Mama Toscano's and teach your granddaughter to make a good sauce. Most toasted ravioli in the local restaurants comes from that store."

Jane and Tillie discussed cooking. This allowed Josie to get more than her share of ravioli while they talked.

"This platter's empty. I'll fix us another," Tillie said.

"Sit down and relax," Jane said. "We're fine."

"Nobody leaves here hungry," Tillie said. "I have another batch going. I'll be right back." She bustled off to the kitchen with the empty platter.

"Those ravioli were good, even if she is my friend," Jane whispered.

"*Sh!* We can't discuss business here," Josie said. "Wonder why the city doesn't cut those weeds next door." The lot alongside the restaurant was choked with scarlet poison ivy and castor bean plants with broad green-black leaves.

"Makes me itch just looking at that poison ivy," Jane said.

"It's pretty poison," Josie said. "I hope no children live around here."

"Not anymore," Tillie said, setting another platter on the table. "The families all moved away. That's why you see so many vacant buildings, like that one." She nodded toward a crumbling two-story brick bordering the lot. "The owners took their fat buy-out check and moved to a fancy suburb."

Josie studied the building's leaning chimneys and boarded windows. "They got good money for that building?" She couldn't hide her surprise.

"For that land," Tillie said. "Lorena wants me to sell out and retire. Says we could get a nice condo in Florida. I keep telling her no. I'd be lost without my work."

"She does have a hard job," Josie said.

"You don't have to tell me," Tillie said. "I worked as a waitress for thirty-some years before I started cooking and tending bar. I get tired being on my feet all day, but not tired enough to quit. My husband started this restaurant. Together we built it into a St. Louis landmark. I don't want to leave it.

"All that money is making Lorena restless," Tillie said. "So is her age. She's divorced and turning fifty-five. Lorena says she wants to find another husband while she's still pretty. She says all she'll meet here are barflies."

"Damn!" the man at the claw machine shouted. He had thick brown hair, regular features, and a muscular body beginning to turn to fat. He whacked the glass, then shoved in another dollar with one hand while he hung on to his beer with the other.

Lorena might have a point, Josie thought. Jane frowned at her daughter, as if she could read Josie's thoughts, and speared another ravioli.

"For years, this neighborhood was the middle of nowhere," Tillie said. "Businesses were dying right and left. Now that the casinos moved next door into Maryland Heights, we're hot property. A new gambling casino wants my land. A developer is offering me a million dollars for this broken-down building. Can you believe it?"

Josie looked at the tired tile floors, sagging plaster ceiling, yellowing paint, and decided silence was the most tactful response.

"Which developer?" Jane asked.

"A big one. With Vegas connections. Won't come out and make an honest deal. That's their man sitting in the corner there," Tillie said, lowering her voice. "Says his name is Desmond. I'm not sure I believe that. His British accent sounds phony."

Josie turned and pretended to straighten her coat. She saw a slender, dark-haired man in an expensive dark suit nursing a club soda. Desmond's eyebrows were dark wings. His nose was long and elegant. On his right hand was a ring with a diamond the size of an ice cube. The other customers wore jeans or work uniforms.

"He's no barfly," Josie said. "Is he wearing a diamond pinkie ring?"

"I don't think it's a cubic zirconia," Tillie said. "At least that seems genuine. Desmond says he admires our architecture, but we don't have any. This is a beat-up two-story brick that needs tuck-pointing.

"Kathleen, the secretary at the local real estate office, comes here for lunch. She told me Desmond is acting as a straw party buyer for that big casino. He won't say so, but nearly every bit of land on these six blocks has been bought up. I'm one of the last holdouts. He doesn't know I know what he is.

"My daughter, Lorena, flirts with him. He's dating her, but I think he's only interested in her real estate, and I'm not talking about her rosy rear end."

Jane frowned at her friend's language and reached for another toasted ravioli. "Lorena is an attractive young woman," she said.

"Not that young," her mother said. "Not young enough for the likes of Desmond. Lorena thinks if she quits hustling plates he'd marry her, but she's dreaming. Sometimes he comes up to the bar and stares at me. Creeps me out. I shoo him off when I can. He's here nearly every day, watching, waiting. Maybe he's expecting me to drop dead. Well, I got news for him. My mother lived to be ninety-three and my grandmother passed at ninety-seven. This old girl isn't checking out anytime soon."

Their talk was interrupted by the man at the claw machine yelling, "Son of a bitch. Thirty dollars and I can't win a thing." The light from the machine was bright enough to show the broken veins on his nose.

A wide-bottomed brunette wrapped her arms around him. "Now, Clay, honey," she said in a baby-doll voice, "don't get upset. We can go to the casinos and have fun and win real prizes—money and cars, not stupid stuffed animals."

Clay shook her away. "I like stuffed animals, Gemma Lynn. I take them home to my wife."

"You don't have to mention her now." Gemma Lynn stuck out her lower lip.

Clay kicked the machine, then slammed it again.

Tillie stood up. "Excuse me, ladies," she said. "I'd better deal with Clay."

She marched over to the claw machine and confronted its attacker. "Clay! You behave yourself." Tillie barely came up to his biceps.

"God d—," Clay said.

"Watch your language," Tillie interrupted, "or I'll call your wife, Henrietta."

She hit the word "wife" hard and glared at Gemma Lynn. Gemma backed away from Clay.

"Go ahead," Clay said defiantly. "She's probably with her boyfriend." He kicked the machine with his work boot again.

"That's it," Tillie said. She punched a number into the phone and said, "It's me. You want to come get that man you married? Yes, I know you're at work, Henrietta, but you've got to do something about Clay."

There was a pause; then Tillie said, "Okay, if that's what you want."

She slammed down the phone and said, "Clay, for your information, your wife is at work, selling insurance while you drink up her paycheck. And I'm calling the cops."

Clay kicked the claw machine again, hard enough to dent the side. He kept kicking it while he drank the rest of his beer. Tillie dialed 911, then reached under the counter by the cash register for a tape-wrapped metal pipe. Gemma Lynn slipped out the door.

"I said stop it." Tillie held the pipe, ready to swing it.

Clay laughed at her, grabbed the pipe out of her hands, and threw it on the bar as two River Bluff police cars pulled up. A pair of officers cuffed the surly Clay and hauled him off for drunk and disorderly conduct.

Two more officers stayed behind to talk to Tillie. She served them toasted ravioli. One uniformed officer had a face like worn mahogany. He was about six-two with weary eyes. His dark hair was just starting to go gray. Josie suspected he'd been on the job a long time—maybe too long. His younger partner looked like he'd stepped off a recruiting poster: blond hair, blue eyes, square jaw. He was fresh-faced and unlined.

"Third time this month, Tillie," the older cop said, as he ate a ravioli. "You're going to have to eighty-six him." His partner ate two.

"I did ban him, Officer Harris," Tillie said, "but Clay keeps coming back. He won't listen to me. He comes in here at the height of the lunch hour. I don't want a scene when this place is packed with customers. That's why I called you."

Six more ravioli disappeared in quick succession while Harris listened. He looked down and saw all but two of the ravioli had disappeared.

"Are you going to leave me those last two ravioli, Zellman?"

"How about if we split them?" Zellman said.

"And speaking of serve, Tillie, if you're worried about a scene and don't want to call us," Officer Harris said, “then don’t serve him more beer.” He ate the last ravioli.

“I didn’t. Gemma Lynn sneaked him a beer when my back was turned.”

“You need to get your old chef back,” Officer Harris said. “Jeff will scare him off good.”

Chapter 4

"Can I speak to Mel?" The girl sounded young enough to be a friend of Amelia's, but Josie didn't recognize her voice.

"There's no Mel here," Josie said and hung up the kitchen phone.

She heard Amelia shriek, "Mom! What did you do?" Her daughter raced into the kitchen. Harry the cat slid on the tile floor, scrambling to keep up with her.

"It was a wrong number, Amelia. Some girl wanted to speak to Mel."

"That's me," Amelia said.

"Since when?"

"Since I went to middle school. Amelia is a baby name. Mel is more sophisticated."

Sophisticated? Her little girl? Amelia had just started wearing a bra.

"Do you know who it was?" Amelia said. "Did she say?"

"I know it wasn't Emma," Josie said.

"That's a big help." Sarcasm dripped off her words. Amelia flounced off to her room, Harry trotting behind her.

"Maybe Emma knows," Josie called after her.

Amelia didn't answer. Most of her friends texted one another. Calls to home phones were for major announcements, the way Josie's mom saved her engraved stationery for special occasions.

"Hey, if you're going to change your name, you could let your mother know," Josie added.

No answer.

Josie scrubbed furiously at the kitchen countertop, as if she could wash away her feelings. She was hurt that her daughter had rejected the name Josie had given her. Amelia's late father had been a dashing helicopter pilot. Josie was sure her daughter would only inherit his best qualities. She'd named her for Amelia Earhart, the woman explorer. Now her child didn't like that name.

No point in brooding, Josie decided, rinsing out the dishcloth and hanging it up to dry. She had to write a mystery-shopping report. Tillie's Off the Hill deserved a rave, even if her mother was friends with the owner.

Josie went to her office. That's what she called the corner of her bedroom that had a computer and a fax machine. Josie gave the restaurant high marks for cleanliness, prompt service, and quality food. The sauce was tangy and the toasted ravioli freshly made.

Atmosphere? "Casually comfortable," Josie wrote in the "remarks" section. These travelers wanted to see the real St. Louis. They might enjoy relaxing in a booth polished by generations of diners instead of sitting in a stiff restaurant with white tablecloths and six forks.

"Recommended for visitors who enjoy local color and the unexpected," she added.

She hoped Tillie could keep the too-colorful Clay out of her restaurant. She wanted to alert the tour company to a possible problem. Josie took mystery-shopping seriously. She didn't lie or exaggerate. Those tourists had a right to an enjoyable meal without listening to an angry drunk. On the other hand, Clay might stay away after he spent a little time in the local lockup.

Josie was finishing the report's last section when her mother called. "Josie, did you give my friend's restaurant a good rating?" It wasn't a question. It was a demand.

"I gave the ravioli and the service the highest possible marks." Josie didn't mention her reservations about customers like Clay.

"Good," Jane said. "Is anything wrong? You sound a little off."

"Amelia wants me to call her Mel," Josie said.

Jane snickered.

"What's so funny?" Josie asked.

"I love it when chickens come home to roost," Jane said. "You've forgotten how many times you changed your name when you were her age. Remember when you wanted to be called Josephine?"

"I did?" Josie asked.

"And you were quite the little empress. I even made you an empire-waist gown for Halloween."

Josie had a vague memory of a long high-waisted yellow dress with puffed sleeves and a crown with plastic jewels.

"Your Highness left the throne when you couldn't learn French."

"I never was good at languages," Josie said.

The yellow empire dress was the good part of that memory. She hoped her mother wouldn't recall Josie draping herself languidly on the living room couch like the real Josephine. She'd asked her mother to serve her dinner. Jane had had a few choice words about that stunt.

"After Josephine, you tried on Jo for size," her mother said. "That was your *Little Women* phase."

"I liked Louisa May Alcott," Josie said. "Jo was the smart sister. Amy was pretty, but a simp."

Jane continued relentlessly. "That phase lasted a couple of months. Next you were Joey."

"I wanted to be called Joey?"

"You said Josie was too girly." Jane was enjoying this way too much.

Josie thought she heard a chicken clucking. Yep, the bird was definitely roosting in her home. She felt embarrassed for her eleven-year-old self.

"Then it was Jay-Jay." Jane was really piling on the guilt.

Josie remembered practicing two versions of that name on a lined tablet. She'd written Jay-Jay and J.J. with blimplike *J*s that she'd thought looked elegant.

"You told me that Josie was old and boring," Jane said. "Like those were the two worst things anyone could be."

Please stop, Josie begged mentally. "What made me go back to Josie?"

"You read a history of the Wild West that said Josie Marcus was the woman Wyatt Earp loved," Jane said. "There was some doubt that Josie Marcus had even married the lawman. That's when you decided your name was romantic, even dangerous."

Josie felt a hot blush burn her cheeks. Josie hadn't married Amelia's father. She'd planned to tell him she was pregnant and get married, but he'd been arrested on drug charges.

Trust me to pick a woman with an uncertain reputation, she thought.

"Amelia is acting like a normal girl her age, Josie." Jane's voice was crisp. "She's trying on identities the way we try on clothes. When she finds a name that fits her, she'll keep it, just like you did."

"Thanks, Mom. That's smart advice."

"I get smarter as *you* get older," Jane said.

Ouch, Josie thought. It was true. Once she'd become a mother, she'd had more appreciation for Jane's parenting skills. Her father had abandoned them when Josie was nine and moved to Chicago to start another family. Jane, who'd expected to be a well-off full-time mother and club woman, had had to take a dreary job in a bank.

"Looks like I got my wish," Jane said cheerfully. "I wanted you to have a daughter exactly like yourself. I'm taking Stuart Little for a walk. Bye."

Jane hung up before Josie could answer. She heard her mother's footsteps on the back stairs, the clink of the shih tzu's collar tags and the patter of his paws.

Josie faxed her report to Suttin Services. "Mom, I'm hungry." Amelia stood in the doorway to Josie's room, her cat balanced on her shoulder. "What's for supper?"

"Want to help me eat a St. Louis pizza for my mystery-shopping report?" Josie asked. "It's Imo's. Big Dave can deliver it." Like most frugal St. Louisans, she used coupons. Imo's had a dozen or so specials going at any one time. She also had the Imo's number on speed dial.

"I want a double cheese," Amelia said.

Josie started to order a pepperoni and mushroom, then remembered Amelia's anti-pork campaign. "Cheese and mushroom for me."

She ordered two twelve-inch pizzas. "This is no ordinary pizza. We're testing for the whole world."

"Awesome," Amelia said.

"I wonder what outsiders will make of St. Louis pizza," Josie said.

"George Clooney ate pizza from Pi when he filmed *Up in the Air* here," Amelia said. "President Obama liked Pi pizza, too. He had it when he campaigned in St. Louis. He even invited the restaurant owners to come to Washington to make pizza. It was in the news."

"Pi's pizza is good," Josie said. "It has the St. Louis

thin crust. But does it count as real St. Louis pizza? It doesn't have Provel cheese."

"What's Provel?" Amelia said. "I thought all pizzas had the same cheese."

The doorbell rang. Josie peeked through the mini-blind slats and saw Big Dave on the front porch with the telltale flat boxes.

"We'll continue this conversation over our pizza," Josie said.

She handed Big Dave her Imo's coupon, the pizza money, and a generous tip. Meanwhile, Amelia cleared the kitchen table, poured their drinks, and put out a pile of paper napkins.

Josie opened the flat boxes and they inhaled the smell of sweet, spicy tomato sauce. Both pizzas were crispy-brown at the edges, pooled with melted orange cheese and cut into squares about the size of Post-it notes.

"Back to our pizza cheese lesson," Josie said. "Most pizzas are made with mozzarella, a gooey white cheese that stretches into long bubble-gum strings when you bite into it."

Josie helped herself to a slice of her orange pizza. "This is Provel cheese, a mix of provolone, Swiss, and white cheddar. It's sort of Italian Velveeta. Technically, Provel is 'cheese food.' Most people outside of St. Louis have never heard of Provel. Looks like TAG Tours is going for old-school St. Louis pizza."

"I've never eaten pizza in another city," Amelia said.

"I have," Josie said. "Your daddy liked to go flying on the spur of the moment. On our first date, we flew along the Mississippi River in the moonlight. The Arch shone like pure silver."

Josie still remembered the wild early days of her romance with Nate, before things went wrong. She'd dumped her safe, serious fiancé. She was not going to have a drab life like her mother. Josie Marcus would know passion. She would see the world.

"Another time we dashed down to the Cayman Islands to scuba dive. Once, he flew me to Manhattan and we had dinner at the Four Seasons. Your daddy was very romantic."

Josie tried not to think about the sad drunk that Nate became. Or that she couldn't marry Nate when she discovered he was dealing drugs. Now she was sitting in a suburban kitchen with an eleven-year-old daughter. Josie couldn't imagine—or want—a life without Amelia.

"You were telling me about pizza," Amelia prompted.

"Sometimes we'd get pizza instead of an expensive dinner," Josie said. "Your daddy liked Chicago-style, but I thought the thick crust was too bready. New York pizza has a thin crust, but they use yeast. St. Louis crust is more like a cracker."

"That's what Rachel said," Amelia said. "She's the new girl at school from New York. She doesn't like St. Louis pizza. Rachel called it orange matzo and said square pizza was stupid. I said our pizza was round."

"It is round," Josie said. "But we cut it into squares. In other cities, most places cut pizza into wedges. St. Louis pizzas are piled with gravity-defying amounts of toppings. A deluxe pizza here may have sausage, mushroom, green pepper, onion, bacon, and more. The St. Louis thin crust can't support a big wedge with so many ingredients. That's why we cut our pizzas into smaller squares."

"I think our pizza is the best," Amelia said.

"So do I," Josie said. "But we'll try those other cities' pizzas someday. Let's rate this one for TAG."

"That's easy," Amelia said. "It should get an A."

"You're prejudiced," Josie said.

"Will the tour people have Imo's delivered to their hotel rooms?" Amelia asked.

"They could," Josie said. "But they could also go to Imo's restaurants. They're not fancy, but the tourists could sit down and eat."

"I like this job," Amelia said. "You get paid to eat pizza."

"I also get paid to walk miles in the malls," Josie said. "It's not the best way to make a living."

"Then why do it?" Amelia asked.

"Because the hours are flexible and I get to be with you. That's important to me." She kissed her daughter. Mel or Amelia, she loved her. "Now, do the dishes, please."

Amelia threw away the pizza boxes and napkins and put their drink glasses in the dishwasher. Josie signed the report and faxed it to Suttin Services.

She'd barely finished when her boss called. "TAG liked your toasted ravioli report," Harry said. "They want you to go back to see if the restaurant is people-friendly."

"What's that mean?" Josie asked.

"You're supposed to see if the owner will give you a tour, ask how she makes the food, and describe the customers. TAG wants you to take someone else and they want it tomorrow."

"I could ask my friend Alyce," Josie said.

"Just do it quick," he said.

Josie felt worried and excited. If all went well, Tillie's lifetime of hard work would pay off. Or it could be ruined by one loud drunk.

Chapter 5

"Are you sure this neighborhood is safe?" Alyce eyed the abandoned buildings warily.

"Of course," Josie said, with more confidence than she felt. She'd insisted on driving her beat-up car. She didn't tell Alyce that her black Cadillac Escalade was an invitation to a carjacking.

Josie was relieved that her friend was dressed sensibly for an iffy neighborhood. Alyce wore a plain blue sweater and no jewelry except a gold wedding band.

Alyce kept her purse close to her when she climbed out of the car. "I wish it wasn't so deserted," she said.

Josie locked the doors and said, "That's good. There are no street people or panhandlers around. And we're not alone. It's the lunch hour and Tillie's is packed. Look at all the cars on this street."

"Empty cars," Alyce said. "Their drivers are in the restaurant."

"We're only two blocks away," Josie said. "There are two of us."

The women picked their way carefully across the broken sidewalk, then marched down the middle of the street, away from the shadowy doorways.

A thin wind rattled the rusty chain-link fences. Dead leaves drifted sadly into the trash-clogged gutters. Alyce's baby-fine blond hair wafted on the wind. Josie's stylish chin-length bob blew across her face. She pulled her sweater tighter. She could feel winter coming, despite the weak autumn sun.

They rounded the corner and Tillie's Off the Hill burst into view. A giant red sign screamed GET TOASTED AT TILLIE'S! The fireplug in front of the building was painted red, white, and green, the colors of the Italian flag.

Inside, the restaurant felt cheerfully warm and welcoming. Alyce sniffed the air. "Tomato sauce and garlic," she said. "This is more like it."

Every table and booth was filled with customers. Lorena was carrying a steaming tray to a table of six. An older dark-skinned man was clearing a booth, loading dirty dishes and silverware into a gray plastic tub.

Tillie was pouring drinks behind the bar. She waved a strong, stubby arm at Josie and called, "We'll have that booth for you in a few minutes, as soon as Mitchell sets it."

Josie's heart sank when she saw Clay at the bar. He was loud and drunk. "My wife says I should get off my ass and work," he said, slurring his words.

"She doesn't appreciate how hard it is to find a job, sweetie," Gemma Lynn said in that annoying childish voice. Her impossibly black hair was in soft curls, but her dark eyes were hard as black marble.

"Tha's what I said," Clay told her. "It's work finding work."

Josie whispered to Alyce, "That's Clay, the troublemaker I told you about. The brunette sitting next to him is Gemma Lynn, his girlfriend."

"Sitting?" Alyce said. "She's wrapped around him

like a boa constrictor. How come he's drunk? That looks like a club soda in front of him."

"I'm guessing Gemma Lynn is helping—or enabling—him," Josie said.

Gemma giggled at Clay and tucked a black curl behind her ear. When Tillie turned to get a bourbon bottle from the back bar, Clay gulped down Gemma's beer. Gemma Lynn slurped his ear and Clay rubbed her bottom.

"Tillie, my beer's gone," Gemma Lynn said.

"Then quit giving it to Clay," Tillie said. "He's drunk."

"He's happy," Gemma said, pouting.

"Happy, my aunt Fanny." Tillie twisted the cap off a bottle of Busch and set it in front of the man next to Clay, along with a clean glass. "Clay won't find a job on that bar stool. You two stop making out in my restaurant. Get a motel room. Or go to your antique shop, Gemma Lynn. You've got plenty of beds there."

Clay's handsome mouth was twisted into a surly smile. "You can't make me leave. Don' wanna scene in your precious restaurant."

"Then I'm calling your wife." Tillie twisted open four beers and put them on Lorena's tray. "She'll get you out of here."

"Go ahead," Clay taunted.

Alyce watched the trio like a live soap opera. "This conversation sounds like high school," she whispered to Josie.

Tillie dialed the phone under the counter, talked briefly, then said, "Henrietta's on her way here, Clay. She says she's had it with you."

Clay repeated Tillie's words, mocking her.

"Shut up, Clay," said the fat man in a white chef's coat and pants on the next bar stool. "We're sick of you and your bimbo."

"Hey!" Gemma Lynn said. "That's no way to speak about a lady, Jeff."

"I wasn't," Jeff the chef said. "I was talking about you."

"Well, you're . . . you're . . ." Gemma paused, searching for an insult. "You're fat."

"Won't argue with you about that, sweet cheeks." Jeff patted his doughy belly. "Never trust a thin chef."

Gemma turned away from him and cuddled with Clay.

"Tillie, can I talk to you?" Jeff asked.

Tillie was pouring red wine into a glass. "I'm busy," she said. "In case you hadn't noticed."

"That's why you need me," Jeff said. "I want my old job back."

"Why, Jeff? So you can rob me blind again?" Tillie set the wineglass down so hard the contents slopped over the side. "Whenever you worked this bar, the take was always short twenty or thirty dollars. After you quit here to start your own restaurant, I didn't have any more shortages."

"You wouldn't give me a raise," Jeff said, not denying her accusation. "I only wanted twenty-five cents an hour more."

"I didn't give me a raise, either," Tillie said. "Or my daughter, Lorena. Every year, we take home a little less. I didn't cut any staff. I kept your job and that's how you repaid me. Then you up and quit and started your own restaurant three blocks away. Now, when it's not working out, you come crawling back."

"I'll be honest with you," Jeff said.

"That's a first," Tillie snapped.

"My place is in trouble." Jeff took a drink of beer. "I can keep Chef Jeff's open for dinner if I have a job at lunch. If you take me back, I could save my restaurant. I'm asking you for a favor."

"You already used up your favor," Tillie said. "Two favors. I didn't call the police when I knew you were stealing from me. I can't afford to have you around, Jeff. I hired another cook. Nancy's good and she's honest. I'm not letting her go because you want your job back. If you need money, sell your property to Desmond. That's him taking up space at the four-top in the corner."

Josie looked in the bar mirror. Desmond's gray suit blended with the shadows in the dark corner. His diamond pinkie ring glittered.

"Can't," Jeff said. "My place is outside the magic circle. I'm stuck."

"Shoulda thought of that before you put your sticky fingers in my cash register." Tillie slammed an open beer in front of a customer three stools down. Foam oozed out of the top.

Jeff the chef turned sullen. He poured his beer into the glass and gave it to Clay. The drunk gulped it down.

"Tillie," Clay shouted. "Another beer."

"I'm not serving you or anyone near you," Tillie said. "You're drunk."

"You need some food, buddy," Jeff said, his voice soft and sly.

"Right. Get me some food." Clay's voice was nearly a shout. "Toasted ravioli. I'm already toasted at Tillie's, so I'll be double toasted."

He laughed loudly. Only Gemma laughed with him. Tillie ignored the man, rinsing glasses in the bar sink with expert movements.

"What about your lady, Clay?" Jeff asked. "She hungry?"

"Nothing for me," Gemma Lynn said coyly. "I'm watching my figure."

"So am I, baby." Clay leered at her.

"Tillie, give me some ravioli and I'll give you your heart's desire: I'll leave. That's what you want, isn't it? For me to go away?"

"Yes," Tillie said.

"Make that new chef put some spice in the sauce," Clay said. "She makes it too mild."

"I'll personally spice it up, if you promise to eat and get out." Tillie pushed open the swinging kitchen doors and called, "Nancy, will you watch the bar for me a minute?"

The new chef was thin and gray as an old dishrag. Josie saw Nancy strip off her hairnet, wipe her hands, tie on a fresh apron, and slip behind the bar.

"Club soda only for Clay," Tillie told her. "I'm making him a quick order of toasted ravioli and then he's leaving.

"Josie, your booth is ready, honey." Tillie seated Josie and Alyce in the freshly cleared booth, then powered through the swinging kitchen doors like a little tank.

Jeff waved at someone on the restaurant side and left his bar stool. A brunette in a navy business suit and dark pumps burst through the door. She spotted Clay with Gemma Lynn and shrieked, "I'm working all day while you're chasing this slut?"

"How dare you!" Gemma Lynn cried. "He's going to marry me."

"Good," Henrietta said. "You can have him. I'm sick of supporting that lazy no-good."

The restaurant had gone so quiet it might have been under a spell. Food-loaded forks stopped in midair. Conversations died. Drinks were left untouched.

Lorena rushed over and put her arm around Henrietta. "Don't get upset, honey. He's not worth it." Clay's wife was wide-hipped and bosomy. Her face was round and pretty, with pale skin and fine features. Lorena steered Henrietta to a quiet table in the far corner. "Mom's fixing him toasted ravioli and then he'll leave with you. Can I get you something?"

"No." Henrietta's eyes bored into her husband's back.

Gemma Lynn shifted in her seat and pulled away from Clay as if she felt his wife's angry glare. She sat primly upright.

Desmond watched the scene, eyes sparkling like his diamond. Lorena stopped for a moment to flirt with the developer's spy, then sashayed into the kitchen, a little extra swing in her hips.

"How can Clay like Gemma Lynn?" Alyce asked. "She seems so coarse compared to his wife."

"Maybe that's her attraction," Josie said.

"This is an exciting lunch," Alyce said.

"Too exciting," Josie said. "I can't recommend Tillie's to TAG Tours after that scene."

"Maybe the tourists will enjoy the show," Alyce said.

"They're supposed to enjoy the food," Josie said. "Domestic dramas are dangerous. Ask any cop. Clay attracts too many angry people. This restaurant is a recipe for trouble."

"They're not here now," Alyce said. "It's just Gemma Lynn and Clay, and they're both behaving."

She was right. Desmond and Henrietta had disappeared. Josie saw no sign of Jeff. Clay was quiet. Gemma Lynn sedately sipped her club soda. The normal restaurant sounds had resumed: the clank of plates, the clink of cutlery, and the quiet hum of conversation.

Lorena appeared at Josie and Alyce's booth. "What can I get you, ladies?"

"I want to try your famous toasted ravioli," Alyce said.

"Me, too," Josie said. It was probably the last time she would ever eat at Tillie's. She dreaded telling Jane about today.

Tillie barged through the kitchen door and set a platter in front of Clay. "I made this specially for you."

Clay dredged a ravioli through the sauce and swallowed it in two bites. Then he ate a second. The third was so loaded with sauce, he could hardly get it in his mouth. Josie thought he looked like a snake swallowing its meal whole. When Clay finished the seventh ravioli he said, "Sauce is still too bland."

"You sure as heck ate those ravioli fast enough," Tillie said.

"I've got almost a dozen and a half to go. I'm outta sauce. Put some kick in that dipping sauce so I can eat and leave. I like spice, Tillie." He squeezed Gemma Lynn and she giggled again.

Josie looked around and was relieved to see Clay's angry wife had deserted her corner table.

"You want kick, you'll get kick," Tillie said. "I'll give you so much kick it will knock you flat." She passed Josie's table on the way back to the kitchen and said, "Watch this. I'm going to get rid of Clay once and for all."

"I don't like this," Alyce said.

Five minutes later, Tillie pushed through the swinging doors carrying a soup bowl brimming with red sauce. She set it on the bar next to Clay. "If this isn't hot enough, then you've got a mouth lined with asbestos. Eat and leave." Gemma Lynn was crunching the ice in her glass.

Clay dragged the ravioli through the sauce until it looked like a bloody lump. He took a big bite, chewed, then screamed, "I'm burning, I'm burning! My mouth is burning. Oh my God."

Clay grabbed his club soda and gulped it. "It hurts! It hurts! I can't breathe!"

"Here, have my ice," Gemma said.

Clay brushed her hand away. Desmond, Henrietta, and Tillie came running from the back.

Josie heard cries of "Try milk!" "Make him chew bread!" "Give him air!" "Get a doctor!"

"She killed me." Clay's voice was a wheeze. His face was flushed red. "She—"

Clay tried to say something, but he could make only strangled noises. He slid from the bar stool and collapsed on the floor.

Gemma Lynn screamed.

Chapter 6

"You killed my husband!" Henrietta howled as sirens shrieked toward the restaurant. "You killed the only man I ever loved."

Josie could not tear her eyes away from Clay's wife. Fury was etched in her face. A blue vein throbbed under the pale skin on Henrietta's high forehead and the tendons in her neck stood out like architectural supports.

"You didn't love him. I did!" Gemma Lynn shouted. She was louder than Henrietta, as if shouting was proof of her devotion. She did look distraught, Josie decided. Black mascara streaks smeared her cheeks. Her girlish curls stuck out at insane angles. She wondered if Gemma Lynn was sincerely worried or enjoying the drama.

"You had no right to him," Henrietta cried.

"You didn't want him," Gemma Lynn said. "I did."

The two women argued over Clay while he lay on the floor. Tillie pushed the warring women aside and kneeled next to him. She cradled his head on her lap, pushed his brown hair off his sweating forehead, and gently slapped his face, trying to bring him back. "Clay," she said. "Clay, please wake up. I didn't mean it." Her voice shook as she pleaded with the unconscious Clay.

He didn't respond. His skin was flushed. His eyes stayed shut. Tillie was as pale as her apron as she tried to revive Clay. Henrietta and Gemma Lynn didn't notice her distress—or Clay's obvious illness.

Customers were shaking off their shock and rushing for the entrance. A thin woman stepped over Clay's outstretched legs and nearly tripped. She was saved from a fall by her lunch companion, a man in a business suit. He pushed her toward the door. Josie heard car engines starting as the sirens grew closer.

Tillie's restaurant was nearly empty by the time four paramedics sprinted through the door carrying bright orange bags of emergency equipment. They loaded Clay onto a gurney and swiftly carried him to the waiting ambulance. By that time, Jeff the chef had forced his way through the escaping crowd and folded the weeping Henrietta into his arms.

"He's dead. He's dead," she cried on his shoulder.

"No, he's not," Jeff said, kissing away her tears. "The ambulance lights and siren were on. That means he's alive. Let me take you to the hospital so you can be with him."

"What about me?" Gemma Lynn demanded, like a whiny child. "I loved him. And she hated him." She pointed a rhinestone-tipped talon at Tillie. "And she killed him. After Clay promised to leave. What am I going to do?"

"Go," Tillie said. "Gemma Lynn Rae, get out of my restaurant right now."

Ordering Gemma Lynn to leave helped Tillie recover. Her color was returning, but she was still shaky. Tillie used a bar stool to help herself up off the floor.

Josie ran forward and folded her mother's friend into her arms. "It will be okay, Tillie," she said. "Would you like me to call Jane?"

"No, no, I'm fine," Tillie said and burst into tears. She wiped her eyes with her grease-stained apron and said, "I'm sorry. I'm sorry. I didn't mean to kill him."

"He's not dead," Josie said.

"I didn't want to hurt him," Tillie said. "I just wanted him to go away and not come back. He's costing me business."

You have no idea what that man cost you, Josie thought. She hoped Tillie would never find out that Josie had been mystery-shopping her restaurant for TAG Tours.

"He complained my sauce wasn't hot enough," Tillie said. "I grow my own cayenne peppers in my kitchen. I figured if he wanted it hot, he'd get it. I took two whole peppers and chopped them up. I wanted that sauce to blister his mouth. But I'd never kill him."

"I know that," Josie said. "Clay will be okay." Josie had her doubts. The man had been the color of putty when the paramedics rolled him out of the restaurant. She rocked Tillie in her arms. The little woman felt so much like Jane. She seemed fearless, but Josie could feel the frail old bones under that tough exterior.

Lorena stayed in the back of the restaurant. Why didn't she come up front to help her mother? Josie wondered. Then she saw Lorena talking to Desmond. The developer's spy said something and Lorena laughed. What could she find funny now? Was Lorena using Clay's illness as an opportunity to be with Desmond? Or was that simply nervous laughter? Josie couldn't see their expressions clearly in the shadows.

She did notice Gemma Lynn searching for her purse by the bar. Clay's girlfriend reached under the bar stool and pulled out what looked like a black plastic trash bag with a gold handle. The monstrous bag's sides were studded with rhinestones and patches of silver and patent leather. Gemma slung it over her shoulder and retreated toward the door.

She never got out of the restaurant. Two uniformed River Bluff police officers rushed in. Josie recognized the pair. They'd been there when Clay was arrested for drunk and disorderly conduct on her first mystery-shopping visit. They'd eaten Tillie's ravioli. Officer Harris had advised her to rehire Jeff.

"Someone called nine-one-one and said a man had been poisoned," the tall, brown-skinned cop said. "They said he was dead."

"We don't know if he's dead," Josie said. "The paramedics just took him to the hospital."

"Who are you?" Officer Harris demanded. He looked even more tired today. Now he had dark circles and pouches under his eyes.

"A friend of the family," Josie said. "I stopped by for lunch at noon."

"Did you call nine-one-one and say he was poisoned?" Officer Harris was abrupt, as if he didn't have time for polite discussion.

"No," Josie said. "Someone else must have. This restaurant was full when the trouble started. Most of the customers ran away."

"He wasn't poisoned," Tillie said. "He wanted extra hot sauce and he got it." Like Jane, Tillie had a lot of attitude, but this was the wrong time to show it. Josie wished the restaurant owner still looked pale and frightened instead of pugnacious.

"Who got the poison?" Officer Harris asked.

"It wasn't poison," Tillie said.

"I'm not standing here like a damned owl calling who," Officer Harris said. "I'm asking you, Tillie. What is the name of the person who was taken to the hospital?"

"Clay Oreck." Tillie dragged out the name, reluctant to say it.

Officer Zellman raised one eyebrow. "Tillie, that man has been a thorn in your side for months. My partner and I were here yesterday, when Oreck was arrested. He just got out of the drunk tank. Now suddenly he's so sick he has to go to the hospital? You know I like you, Tillie, but I can't play favorites. We have to treat this as a potential assault."

"With what?" Tillie asked. "A deadly pepper?"

Josie winced. That was exactly the wrong answer.

"I hope for your sake you're still joking about this tomorrow," Officer Harris said. "Meanwhile, this restaurant is a potential crime scene. Nobody leaves here until they've been questioned by a detective."

Josie heard more sirens. Three police cars were parked haphazardly outside the restaurant and more River Bluff uniforms flowed through the door. Officer Harris gave them orders.

Gemma Lynn was arguing with a uniformed officer at the door. "What do you mean, I can't go? The man I love is dying. I have to be with him. *She* got to go with him in the ambulance."

"If you're talking about Mrs. Oreck, she is his wife," the officer said. "She's entitled. And she wasn't in the ambulance. She followed behind in her car."

So Jeff didn't drive her to the hospital, Josie thought. She saw the chef hovering by the front door, as if he wanted to leave, too.

"Everyone go back to your seats," Officer Harris said. "And no talking. A River Bluff detective is on the way."

Josie and Alyce slid into their booth. The half-finished plate of toasted ravioli was still there. The ice was melting in their drinks.

"I can't believe this," Alyce said. Her skin looked like

she'd powdered it with flour. "I had a bad feeling about coming here. What are we going to do?"

"Nothing we can do but wait it out," Josie said.

"Why did Clay's wife say he was the only man she ever loved?" Alyce asked. "A few minutes ago, she told Gemma Lynn she could have him."

"Haven't you ever hated your husband enough to leave him?" Josie asked.

Alyce flushed and Josie regretted that question. She knew the answer: Alyce and Jake had gone through a bad patch a year or so ago. Josie thought Jake had cheated on his wife, but she never knew the details. A romantic cruise and a more matronly nanny had restored Alyce's marriage.

"Sorry," Josie said. "What a stupid question. Every woman feels like killing a man some time or another."

She found a toasted ravioli congealing in a pool of oil and popped it into her mouth. It tasted cold and greasy, but at least she couldn't say anything else embarrassing.

"Josie!" Alyce said. "How can you eat that?"

"I didn't touch the sauce," Josie said. "And it tastes better than my foot."

There was a shadow over their booth. It was Officer Harris's partner, the blond poster boy. "You were asked not to talk, ladies." Officer Zellman's skin looked steam-cleaned and his uniform starched. "I'm going to ask you to move to separate booths."

"We need to call our families," Josie said. "I have an eleven-year-old daughter. She'll be getting off school soon and I can't go pick her up. I want to ask my mom. Please?"

"I need to call my nanny and ask her to stay longer," Alyce said. "I have a three-year-old boy at home."

"I'll stay here while you make the calls. You—" He pointed at Josie. "Take this booth here."

Josie got up quickly, before Officer Zellman changed his mind about that call. Now she was sitting with her back to Alyce. She could hear her friend negotiating with Justin's nanny. Josie speed-dialed Jane's phone, then braced herself for her mother's questions.

Jane sounded surprised and suspicious. "What do you mean, a little problem at Tillie's?"

"I can't discuss it, Mom. The police asked me not to."

"The police!" Her mother's voice was louder and shriller.

Josie tried to soothe her. She glanced uneasily at the blond cop. Officer Zellman was staring straight at her. "Mom, I'll tell you as much as I can when I get home." Her words tumbled out and Josie felt she was talking faster than a tobacco auctioneer. "Mom, please call Ted and tell him I can't see him this evening."

"Josie, it's not polite to cancel on such short—"

Josie interrupted her mother midlecture. "The officer is standing right here. He's going to take my phone away. Can you pick up Amelia for me this afternoon?"

"Of course, Josie, but I'd like to know what's going on."

"Me, too, Mom." Josie hung up on her mother.

Chapter 7

"I'm not saying Tillie killed Clay or anything," Jeff said, his voice earnest and oily. "But I did hear her say she wanted him out of her restaurant permanently."

Brian Mullanphy, the River Bluff detective, wrote down every treacherous word.

That rat, Josie thought. No, pig. That was a better description. The chubby chef with his pink face looked like a pig with a tattoo. His skin was shiny, as if he'd slathered it with cooking oil. The barbed-wire tat twisted around his wrist, turning Jeff's plump hand into a no man's land.

Josie could see the chef sitting at a table near the entrance to the dining room side of Tillie's. She could hear him, too. Sometimes. Other times, his voice trailed off.

Josie got Jeff's message loud and clear. He was setting Tillie up for attempted murder.

She knew Jeff wanted his old job back. She'd heard him ask Tillie if he could work here again. Tillie had turned him down and Jeff had been furious. Of course he didn't mention that to Detective Mullanphy.

Mullanphy wasn't a homicide detective. He'd explained that the River Bluff force was too small to have a full-time homicide division. He investigated crimes against persons, from assaults to murder. Now he was interviewing the handful of people who'd remained after Clay was rushed to the hospital.

Jeff was the first. He leaned forward on his well-cushioned elbows as if confiding to the detective and said, "You know Clay drank a little too much. How often did Tillie call your department when Clay was drunk and loud?"

The detective ignored Jeff's question. "Where were you at the time of the incident, Mr. Bartlett-Smith?"

"Jeff, please," he said. "No need for the double-barreled name. Mom combined her maiden name and my dad's name. She thought it sounded classy. I'm just plain old Jeff the chef."

"Where were you at the time of the incident?" Mullanphy repeated.

"I was next to Clay at the bar, having a beer. I thought I saw someone I recognized sitting at that table there." He pointed across the aisle. "I came back here to say hello to Rick. But it wasn't him after all. Then I talked to a few other people on the restaurant side. A lot of Tillie's customers know me because I used to work here. I was chatting with someone when I heard Clay screaming that his mouth was burning and I ran up front."

That was close to what really happened, Josie thought. She remembered that Jeff had hung back until after the ambulance left with Clay. Then he went up front to comfort the man's wife.

"Tillie grows her own peppers in the kitchen here," Jeff said. "She keeps the plants on the windows over the sink. Says they give her sauce its kick. The horseradish helps, too. Did you know the best horseradish is grown right across from St. Louis in Belleville, Illinois?"

Detective Mullanphy wasn't interested in the secret

to Tillie's sauce. "What is your relationship to Mrs. Minnelli?"

"Relationship?" Jeff looked puzzled. "None. She's an old lady."

"You said you used to work here."

"Oh, right. I did. I cooked here for about three years and tended bar for Tillie. Then it was time for me to move on. I've started my own restaurant, Chef Jeff's. But we're still on good terms. I stopped by to see her at lunchtime."

Liar! Josie heard the words in her head so loud she was surprised Detective Mullanphy didn't turn around and look at her.

But Jeff continued, blithely lying about how he offered to help "the old girl" out at lunch. "Tillie's not as young as she used to be and she needs help. I guess she won't be needing it now. Word gets out about this and her business is probably going to drop off."

And you'd like that just fine, wouldn't you? Josie thought. She was angry at how Jeff had twisted the truth, like that barbed-wire tat twisting around his wrist. After Jeff finished, he was directed to a table in a back booth, where he wrote a statement and signed it while a uniformed officer stood nearby and watched.

Mitchell, the older man who'd bussed tables that afternoon, was called in next. Mitchell's voice was a deep rumble and Josie had a hard time hearing him. She caught phrases: "Didn't see anything . . . running in and out of the kitchen . . . I saw a lot of people in the kitchen, but there always are when it's busy. . . . Yes, sir, Tillie did say she was going to make that sauce extra hot."

Josie glanced at her watch. It was 2:52, nearly three hours after Clay's lunch. Amelia would be home from school soon. Her plans to see Ted were gone. She hoped Ted would understand why she'd canceled their dinner tonight. She really did like the vet. No, this was more than like. She loved him and she'd told him so. Josie had finally found a good man after some bad choices. Amelia liked Ted. So did Jane. And their cat, Harry. Everyone liked Ted so much, it made Josie nervous. She worried that he was too good to be true.

On the bar side she could see the customers and staff watching the clock on the wall. The hands seemed to crawl around the neon-lit face. She felt Alyce shift in the hard booth behind her. Desmond stared at the wall. Lorena sat in a booth near her mother, nodding off. She must be exhausted from hauling those heavy trays around, Josie thought. Gemma Lynn was still weeping. She sounded like a whining puppy. Josie found her tears almost as annoying as her talking.

A uniformed officer went up and down the aisles. She was a stern-faced woman who reminded Josie of a hall monitor.

Tillie waved her hand tentatively. "Officer, is there any word on Clay Oreck?" she asked.

"Sorry, ma'am. I can't say. All I know is he's still at the hospital."

The young blond poster cop burst through the door holding a stainless-steel mixing bowl in his gloved hands. He carried it back to Mullanphy. "Uh, Detective, I found this in the kitchen trash," he said. "It's got traces of a white substance in it and what looks like cooked ground meat."

"Bag it," the detective said.

White? And ground meat? That would be the ravioli filling, wouldn't it? The white was probably horseradish. Did you put horseradish in the ravioli filling? Not for the first time, Josie wished she knew more about cooking.

But why would Tillie throw away a good mixing bowl?

"There's more," the young cop said. He held up a pair of yellow rubber gloves. "These were in the trash with the bowl. They look like they've been used, but I don't see any holes."

The gloves looked fine to Josie, too—at least from across the room. Tillie was watching her money. She wouldn't throw them away. Unless she really was mixing up poison. Now Josie felt sick—and not from the greasy ravioli.

Tillie saw the gloves and the bowl.

"The gloves look like mine," she said. "They must have been thrown away by accident. I didn't use that metal bowl to make Clay's sauce. I used a glass bowl. You can find it in the dishwasher. I turned it on when . . ."

She stopped. Tillie was upset, but she must have realized if she turned on the dishwasher, then she'd washed the evidence that could save her down the drain.

The afternoon crawled forward like a wounded animal. While Detective Mullanphy interviewed customers and staff, Josie had plenty of time to study the man. His face just missed being handsome. He had a strong jaw, thick brown hair, and a nose like a new potato. That lump of a nose didn't belong on his square-cut face. She tried to focus on the interviews.

She heard Desmond confirm that Tillie wanted rid of Clay. He didn't mention that she was one of the last holdouts for the casino deal and he was trying to buy her building.

Gemma Lynn wept and whined about her love for Clay. She might seem on the edge of hysteria, but she was calm enough to knife Tillie every chance she could to Detective Mullanphy.

Lorena told him she didn't hear or see anything. "I was too busy running in and out of the kitchen and waiting on tables."

After each person finished, they wrote and signed a statement in the back booth.

At 4:35, Alyce was called. Josie heard her mention that Chef Jeff wanted to be rehired by Tillie. She also said that Clay had complained the dipping sauce was too bland and demanded Tillie spice it up. Fifteen minutes later, Alyce was writing out her statement and it was Josie's turn to talk.

"What is your relationship with the victim?" Detective Mullanphy asked.

"None," Josie said. "This is my second time at Tillie's. I was in a few days ago with my mother. Mom went to grade school with Tillie."

"Why did you come back so soon? You don't live in this area. You told me you live in Maplewood. That's a long way to drive for toasted ravioli."

Good question, Josie thought. She was not going to mention the TAG Tours. "I wanted my friend Alyce to try Tillie's ravioli. It's famous, and Alyce lives way out in the burbs. She never comes to River Bluff and the nanny could watch her little boy today."

She held her breath, hoping Alyce had given a similar answer. She studied the detective's face for some reaction. Nothing. The man would make a good poker player.

"How did the victim behave?" he asked.

"Clay seemed pretty drunk," Josie said. "Tillie quit serving him beer. Chef Jeff asked Tillie if he could work lunches for her, but she refused. She implied that he'd been helping himself to twenty or thirty dollars every time he worked. He said he needed a job now to keep his new restaurant going."

No reaction from Detective Mullanphy again. But at least he'd heard about Jeff's treachery from two sources.

"Chef Jeff seemed angry when Tillie refused to rehire him. That's when he slipped Clay some of his beer."

She repeated the whole saga—including Tillie's threat to make Clay leave permanently. She figured it couldn't do Tillie any more harm. The detective had already heard it.

When the detective finished with his questions, Josie sat in the corner booth to write her statement while Alyce waited. A subdued Tillie was called in next for an interview. It was just after five o'clock.

Officer Harris, the African-American with the weary eyes, was at the door. "Detective, may I see you a moment? There's a message for you."

Tillie sat unmoving at the interview table. All traces of her attitude were gone. Josie thought she looked older than her seventy-six years. Her eyes were sunken. The skin along her jawline hung in loose folds. Her back was bent.

Josie could hear the detective and Officer Harris whispering outside the door. The detective seemed more subdued when he returned.

"Mrs. Minnelli, Mr. Clay Oreck is gravely ill."

"I know pepper juice can blister—" Tillie said.

"This isn't damage from pepper juice. The man has been poisoned. He's vomiting. He has severe abdominal pain and convulsions. His kidneys are shutting down. You used that hot pepper to disguise the taste of poison."

"No!" Tillie said.

"Tell us what kind of poison you used, Mrs. Minnelli, and the doctors may have a chance to save him."

"I can't," Tillie said. She looked desperate. "I would if I could, but I don't know. I don't keep any poison in my kitchen, not even rat poison."

"If he dies," the detective said, "it's murder."

Chapter 8

When Josie got home at seven o'clock that night, she felt like she'd been doing hard labor. Why did her back and shoulders ache? How could she be so tired? All she'd done was sit in a restaurant booth.

And watch a man collapse and nearly die. And wait to be questioned by the police. Each tense minute had ticked by, while Josie wondered if the detective would discover the real reason she was at the restaurant. If he found out Josie was mystery-shopping for TAG Tours, she would have handed the police Tillie's motive on a platter.

After Josie had been interviewed by the police, she'd face another tough interrogator—her mother. Jane knew her daughter well. Josie had called her mother from her cell phone in the car. Her mother could tell that Josie was trying to downplay the seriousness of the situation. Talking to Jane had been an ordeal. Josie wanted to leave the neighborhood and so did Alyce, but she wouldn't try to drive while delivering this news to her mother.

Alyce eyed the deserted street uneasily, while Josie tried to calm Jane. Her mother was upset that Tillie had lost out on a TAG Tour. "She's worked all her life, Josie, and now it's gone," she kept repeating.

"Maybe not, Mom. Clay is still alive."

"If he dies, she could lose her restaurant," Jane said. "She could be arrested for—what's that thing when you didn't mean to kill someone but you do anyway?"

"Manslaughter," Josie said.

"I'm going to call her right now," Jane said. "She needs my support."

"That's what friends are for," Josie said. "Did you call Ted and tell him I couldn't go out to dinner with him tonight?"

"I did as I was told. Now you tell me: Is something wrong between you two?" Jane didn't bother hiding her alarm. She wanted Ted to be her son-in-law.

"No, Mom, I'm just wrung out. I wouldn't be good company. I want to go to bed early."

"You're too young to feel like that, Josie. I worry about you driving in rush hour traffic if you're that tired."

"I'll be fine, Mom. I have to take Alyce home first. I'll call you after I get to her house, then come straight home."

"Well, then," Jane said, "get off the phone. You can't drive right if you're talking to me."

Josie hung up and started laughing. She loved her tough little mom, every irrational ounce of her. She started the car and told Alyce, "I hope Ted won't be upset because I've canceled our dinner date."

"He's too good a guy not to understand, Josie. Are you really that tired?"

"Tired and bedraggled. Besides, I don't want to sit in another restaurant after spending all afternoon at Tillie's. I'm looking forward to a soothing hot shower, a bowl of soup, and an early bedtime."

"You are?" Alyce asked.

"I sound one step away from the nursing home, don't I?" Josie said.

"A hot man is no match for hot soup," Alyce said. "But I don't feel much perkier."

"At least you have the excuse of an active toddler and a dog," Josie said.

"Bruiser is active, all right," Alyce said. "But that little dog runs around so much he helps tire out Justin. Bruiser does me a favor. I never thought I'd own a Chihuahua, but he's a good addition to our family."

The two women waved to the guard at the entrance to the Estates at Wood Winds and Josie drove into Alyce's subdivision. They passed an Italian palace, a French château, and a Victorian Gothic horror. Alyce lived in a Tudor mansion with a half-timbered garage.

"Do you want to come in?" Alyce asked.

"I'd better get home," Josie said. "I'll call Mom from the driveway."

She waved to her friend as she speed-dialed her mother.

"I'll expect you home in twenty minutes," Jane said. "The sooner you get here, the sooner I can spend time with Tillie. She needs me."

Jane's two-story flat looked good in the gathering dusk. The red brick was mellowed with age. Jane had brightened the front porch with pots of fat bronze mums. Josie parked her car in front, then walked quickly to the house, crunching the fall leaves. She took childish delight in stomping dinner-plate-sized sycamore leaves and the bright maple leaves that gave her town its name.

Josie sniffed the evening breeze. The air smelled like . . . steak.

Steak?

She inhaled again. Definitely steak. The rich aroma of broiling meat came from her home. Josie unlocked the front door and caught the scent of steak with top notes of baked potato. Where did Amelia get money for steak? Maybe Jane had decided to surprise Josie.

The surprise was waiting in Josie's living room. Ted folded her into his arms. The vet was so tall her head only reached his chest. He bent down to kiss her and Josie felt his slightly scratchy beard. Ted had a sexy five o'clock shadow.

"What are you doing here?" she asked. "Mom was going to cancel our date."

"She did," he said. "I figured you'd be too tired to go to dinner, but you'd like some good food. You were planning to open a can of soup, weren't you?"

"Am I that predictable?" Josie asked.

"Yep. You need something heartier. The filet mignon will be ready shortly. The baked potatoes are done. I made green beans with slivered almonds, but you don't have to eat them. You don't like vegetables."

"I love almonds," Josie said, kissing him again. "And I love you for thinking about me."

"I figured you wouldn't be in the mood for Italian food after spending all day at Tillie's," Ted said.

"You figured right," Josie said.

She saw Amelia in the kitchen, setting the table. "I made brownies for dessert, Mom."

"This is too good to be true," Josie said.

That's when the cat made a flying leap onto the table and started lapping coffee cream from a fat pitcher.

"Harry!" Amelia cried. "You know better."

"Time-out for the cat," Josie said. "Harry is confined to your bathroom until after dinner."

Amelia didn't argue. She picked up the feline and carried him down the hall to her purple bathroom. Harry's big ears drooped. He knew he was in disgrace. Amelia dropped him in the bathroom and shut the door.

Josie dumped the cream down the drain, washed the pitcher and refilled it.

"Maybe you'd like to wash up before dinner," Jane said. "Does she have time, Ted?"

"Dinner will be on the table by the time you're ready," he said.

Now that Ted was here, Josie felt suddenly energized. She could see why her mother sent her to freshen up. She washed her face, put on fresh lipstick, then combed her brown hair. Her bob still had bounce. There. That looked better. She'd finished buttoning a clean white blouse when she heard Jane knock on the back door. Ted must have opened it. She hurried out and saw Jane carrying her new red purse and wearing a matching raincoat and red-and-blue scarf.

"You look nice in that color," Ted told her.

"Thank you." Jane flushed at the compliment. "I wanted to tell Josie I'm leaving now to be with Tillie. She's a wreck and that daughter of hers is no help."

"Any word on how Clay is doing?" Josie asked. "That's the man who got sick, Ted."

"Ted knows," Jane said. "I already told him. Clay is not well, from what Tillie said. His symptoms are too disgusting to mention at dinnertime, but his system seems to be shutting down."

"How does Tillie know this?" Josie said.

"After more than fifty years in the restaurant business, Tillie has friends everywhere, including the hospital ER."

Apparently patient confidentiality crumbled before toasted ravioli, Josie thought.

"I'm worried, Josie. I think she's in serious trouble. The police told Tillie not to leave town, like in the movies. What do they think she'll do—escape to Brazil? She's seventy-six years old. She's lived in St. Louis all her life. She has a successful business here. I just hope her restaurant survives this."

"It will," Josie said. "Tillie has lots of friends. Do you want us to walk Stuart Little?"

"I've already walked the dog. He's asleep," Jane said. "I'll call you if I stay with Tillie all night. I'd better go. I'll see you when I see you."

Jane marched to the backyard garage. Her small, determined figure seemed prepared to fight the entire River Bluff force.

"Your mom is unstoppable," Ted said.

"I pity the River Bluff police," Josie said.

She surveyed the kitchen table, carefully set with the good dishes and cloth napkins. A fat bronze mum floated in a shallow bowl as a centerpiece. Josie hugged her daughter. "Good job on the table. Your new pink jeggings look nice. You're slender enough to wear them, Amelia."

"Mel," her daughter corrected.

Josie also noticed Amelia had attempted to cover the freckles on her nose with Josie's makeup. She'd talk to her about that later.

Ted set a plate with a grilled filet in front of Josie and said, "Sit down. You must be exhausted."

"Not too tired to admire this dinner," Josie said. "It's like a magazine photo. See how the melted butter drips down the brown skin of the baked potato. The green beans add contrasting color on the blue plate."

"Red wine or iced tea to complete the picture?" Ted asked.

"Wine," Josie said as she cut a triangle out of her filet. It was medium rare, just the way she liked it.

Between bites, she told Ted about Clay, Gemma Lynn, Tillie, Lorena, and the other characters in the restaurant drama. She toned down Clay's affair with Gemma Lynn. Amelia didn't need to hear every sordid detail.

"Enough about me," Josie said. "Tell me about your day. What happened at the clinic, Ted?"

"I should talk to the animals," Ted said. "I don't do as well with humans. One of my regulars, Ryan, brought in his bichon. Brie is a sweet dog, but she weighs twenty-seven pounds."

"Isn't that a little hefty for a bichon?" Josie asked.

"A little? The dog is fat and Ryan knows it. I've told him so often he's sensitive about his dog's weight. He's a good owner, except he overfeeds her. He brought in Brie because she had a lump on her thigh. I examined it and said, 'It's just a fatty tumor. Nothing to worry about.'

"Ryan looked stricken and said, 'But she's on a diet.' I had to explain that fatty tumors have nothing to do with weight."

"You must have really scared him," Josie said.

"I have to," Ted said. "People think it's cute to overfeed their pets; then they're devastated when the poor animals die. They eat and eat until they ruin their health."

"Sort of like people," Josie said. "Like this person, anyway. I've cleaned up everything on my plate."

"Good," Ted said. "You're not overweight. You need to keep up your strength. I hope you've saved room for Mel's brownies."

Amelia rewarded him with a dazzling smile for remembering her name.

"No way I'll miss those," Josie said.

She made coffee while Amelia dished out the brownies. Josie and Ted said no to vanilla ice cream on the side, but gave Amelia heaping helpings of praise for her baking.

After dinner, Ted and Amelia cleared the table while Josie loaded the dishwasher.

"Are we finished?" Amelia asked, hanging up her dish towel. "I have to do homework and let Harry out of the bathroom."

"I'm impressed," Ted said, when she disappeared down the hall. "Mel went straight to her homework after dinner."

"I suspect she's really texting her friends," Josie said. "But she'll do homework in between. More coffee? More wine?"

"Just coffee," Ted said.

They settled in on the living room sofa with their cups. Josie rested in the crook of Ted's arm, sipping her coffee. She felt content.

"This isn't such a bad day after all," she said. "Thanks for being so thoughtful." She kissed his cheek.

He kissed her back, a deeper kiss. Josie glanced down the hall to make sure that Amelia's bedroom door was shut and settled back into the comfortable couch for more kisses.

"I'm glad you wanted to spend time with me," Ted said. "Did I ever tell you that white blouses are sexy?"

His fingers were unbuttoning the buttons and he was kissing Josie's neck when the front door burst open.

Josie sat up, pulled her blouse shut, and stared at a wild-eyed Jane standing in her living room.

"Mom, what's wrong?"

"It's Tillie," Jane said. "Clay died an hour ago. The police arrested Tillie."

Chapter 9

"Arrested!" Ted said. "What for?"

Josie was scrambling to arrange her clothes. Jane was so distraught she hadn't bothered to knock. She'd opened Josie's front door and charged straight into the living room. She was too upset to notice that Josie and Ted had been making out on the couch like teenagers.

Ted smoothed down his tousled brown hair and tucked in his shirt.

"The police say she committed a felony," Jane said. "They arrested her for reckless endangerment."

"What's that?" Josie asked. She fastened a crucial button on her blouse.

"As I understand it, that means Tillie showed a—" Jane stopped for a moment, as if searching her memory, then recited, "A heedless disregard for potential results. Because she put cayenne pepper in Clay's sauce."

"But he asked her to," Josie said. "No, he demanded it. I heard him say it."

"It's still reckless endangerment," Jane said. "Cayenne pepper juice is strong. Tillie has to wear gloves when she chops up those peppers. The juice burns if it gets into any cuts in her hands. A young waiter got some in his eye and had to go to the ER to have it flushed out. That juice is like acid. The cops don't know this, but Tillie told me she doubled the pepper juice.

"Tillie didn't mean to hurt him, but the law says that doesn't make any difference," Jane said. "He's dead, just the same."

"But Clay wanted his sauce extra hot," Josie repeated.

"Doesn't matter," Jane said. "All the police have to do is prove Tillie didn't care about the damage she could cause."

Josie tucked in her blouse while Jane paced the living room. "Tillie wouldn't kill anyone," her mother said. "She's been my friend since she was six years old. She's a good, careful cook."

Who desperately wanted rid of a bad customer, Josie thought.

Josie's agitated mother kept running her fingers through her short hair. She used enough hairspray to keep her hair in place during a tornado. Now, instead of her usual silver helmet, Jane's hair stood up in stiff spikes, as if she'd stuck her finger in a light socket.

"Mom, sit and try to calm down."

To stop her mother's frantic movements, Josie held her. She could feel the rigid muscles in Jane's shoulders. Josie feared she would worry herself sick. She smoothed her mother's hair back in place. Jane would have been mortified if she knew that the small bald spot at the top of her head was exposed.

Jane shook herself free and asked, "How can the police be so stupid?"

She marched around the coffee table. Ted pulled in his long legs and Jane completed her circuit. "How could they possibly think Tillie would poison that man?" she asked. "This will kill her. Just kill her."

Josie blocked her mother's next lap around the living

room. She saw tears in Jane's eyes. "Tillie's smart and tough, Mom. Let's have some coffee and talk about it."

"I don't want more coffee," Jane said sharply. "I've had enough."

"Some wine?"

"No!" Jane was as wired as a stadium scoreboard.

Josie glanced at Ted and raised an eyebrow. He saw Josie's silent signal for help and disappeared into the kitchen.

Josie was relieved to see that Ted's clothes were now in place. Maybe it wasn't so bad that Jane had interrupted them. Amelia was right down the hall. What if her daughter had opened her bedroom door and caught her mother on the couch? An eleven-year-old didn't need to see that scene.

"At least sit down, Mom," Josie said. "You're wearing yourself out pacing around."

"All I've done is sit!" Jane said. But she plopped down in the easy chair, unwound her scarf, and unbuttoned her coat. Her hands trembled slightly with the buttons.

"No, you didn't sit," Josie said. "You helped Tillie when she needed you. That's hard work."

"Helped, my eye," Jane said. "Tillie was arrested anyway."

Josie felt sick. She and Alyce had watched Tillie kill Clay. His death had been an accident, but Clay was never going to be in the bar again. That made it worse for Tillie.

"The police took Tillie away in a squad car like a criminal," Jane said. "At least they didn't handcuff her."

"She's in jail?" Josie asked.

"Her lawyer got her out on bail. Lorena and I had to go to the bail bondsman's place. It was a nasty little office full of criminals. They had tattoos and bad teeth. One had his beard braided."

"He might have been a biker, Mom. Some of them braid their beards so the long hair doesn't blow in their faces when they ride."

"Well, Tillie doesn't belong in a group with braided beards. We got her a bail of one thousand dollars. We had to pay one hundred to the bondsman and put up a thousand in collateral. The bail bondsman took the title to Tillie's new Cadillac. He said an old lady was a safe bet.

"I got mad and said she wasn't old. She's only seventy-six. That's my age." Jane stuck out her jaw in a gesture of defiance. She looked as tough as a teddy bear.

Josie fought to hide a smile. She'd learned not to underestimate her mother. "I don't think of you as old, Mom—or Tillie, either. She has to be strong to work those long hours in that restaurant. Who is her lawyer?"

"Some character called Renzo Fischer," Jane said. "Tillie says he's an old customer."

"Good," Josie said. "He's the best."

"At what? Eating ravioli?" Jane was still wound up. "He looked odd to me. Tillie called him as soon as she heard that Clay was in a bad way. Mr. Fischer came over to her house an hour later. I know that's a nice thing for a big deal lawyer to do. He talked to Tillie before the police arrived and advised her to give herself up, which she was going to do anyway. I hope he doesn't charge her for that advice."

"Can Tillie afford him, Mom?" Josie asked. "Did Renzo want her to mortgage the restaurant?"

"That was the first question out of Lorena's mouth. That girl is useless, even if she is Tillie's daughter. No, Mr. Fischer wouldn't hear of her mortgaging anything. He said he expected to eat free there for the rest of his life."

"Then he'd better live to be a very old man," Josie

said. "Good defense lawyers aren't cheap. Renzo sounds like a good guy. What's wrong with him?"

"I don't like his looks," Jane said. "He dresses like a clown in cowboy boots, a string tie, and a ten-gallon hat. This is St. Louis, not the Wild West."

"He's an old-school trial lawyer, Mom. They're theatrical. They dress for a part. Renzo has cast himself as John Wayne riding in on his white horse to save innocent clients. Juries love Renzo. He's different from the dull corporate lawyers in suits. Renzo will make the jury root for Tillie. If anyone can save her, he can."

"I hope so, Josie. I can't believe the way she's being treated. Everybody in St. Louis knows Tillie. She's fed the police for years. None of them died from her food, not even the ones who wanted her sauce extra hot. Now the cops have turned on her."

"They're doing their job," Josie said. "If they gave her special treatment, it could be worse for her. Do the cops know what killed Clay?"

"No," Jane said. "It's too early for the autopsy results."

"Too bad Tillie said she wanted rid of Clay," Josie said. She heard Ted moving around in the kitchen.

"You didn't tell the police Tillie said that, did you?" Jane asked.

"I had to," Josie said. "The whole restaurant heard her. The police wouldn't have believed me if I didn't mention it. But I also told the detective that Chef Jeff wanted his job back and Tillie said he'd been helping himself to her cash, so he knows Jeff was angry at her. And I mentioned that Desmond wanted to buy Tillie's restaurant for a new casino. I gave the police two more killers to consider."

"Well, they didn't," Jane said. "They arrested her anyway. They said neither one would use Tillie's pepper juice."

Ted appeared with a cup, a plate, and a napkin. "I know you're a coffee drinker, Jane," he said. "But I've made you some chamomile tea. It's caffeine-free and supposed to be soothing. You should have some of Amelia's brownies, too. You need sugar after your ordeal."

Jane smiled at Ted. "Thank you. Most doctors tell me *not* to eat sugar."

"My patients are animals," Ted said. "But I don't need a medical degree to see you've had a rough time."

Jane took a ladylike bite of a brownie, then wolfed down the rest of it. Three brownies and half a cup of tea later, she patted her lips daintily with the paper napkin and was ready to resume the conversation.

"There. That's better. Josie, I don't understand why you're defending the police."

Josie warned herself to tread carefully. She knew she'd stepped into dangerous territory. "Mom, Tillie admitted putting cayenne pepper juice in Clay's dipping sauce and now he's dead."

"Tillie didn't mean to kill him," Jane said. "She called his wife because she knew Henrietta would drag him out of there."

"It doesn't matter," Josie said. "He's still dead, Mom."

"That's what Renzo said," Jane told her. "I expected better from you. My friend has a police record. A rap sheet!"

"That's why I'm glad she has a good lawyer," Josie said.

"She shouldn't have been arrested at all. Someone else killed Clay."

"I sure hope so," Josie said.

"That's why I want you to find who did it."

"Me! I'm not a professional investigator." Josie saw she'd missed a button on her chest and fastened it before Jane noticed.

"You'll still do a better job than those so-called pros."

"But, Mom—," Josie said.

"Don't 'but, Mom' me. The police aren't going to help clear Tillie's name. They think they've got their killer. It's up to you to find the real murderer."

"I—"

"You need a babysitter and a chauffeur to pick up your daughter. And you've got one. I'm on call twenty-four hours a day. I'm happy to help you, Josie. Now it's your turn to help me. Are you going to save Tillie or not?"

Josie had called her mother for help that very afternoon. She needed Jane.

"Well?" Jane demanded. "What's your answer?"

"I'll do it, Mom. But it's a high price to pay for a sitter."

Chapter 10

The crushed couch cushions and flattened pillows on Josie's couch looked like accusations. Josie knew she'd been guilty of reckless behavior. She and Ted had gotten carried away last night. Josie blushed at the memory of their passionate scene.

Josie whacked a throw pillow as if punishing it, then tossed it on the couch. She sprayed lemon furniture polish on a cloth and dusted the end table and the coffee table. The harsh morning light revealed the wear on her garage sale finds. At least her old furniture was clean, she thought.

She had stepped back to admire her work when the phone rang.

"How are you this morning, Josie?" Ted's voice was warm and sexy.

"Just fine," she said. "Especially since you called."

Josie wasn't fine. She was worried—about her mother, about Tillie, about her and Ted.

"How's your mom?" Ted asked. "Jane seemed pretty shaken up last night."

"She's better this morning," Josie said. "She woke me

up early taking the dog for a walk. I'm sure she's still worried about her friend, but Mom is a survivor."

"I've got some news that's going to worry her more," Ted said. "My ten o'clock brought in a bug for his shots."

"You treat insects?" Josie asked.

Ted laughed. "No, a bug is Kate's name for her type of dog. It's a Boston terrier–pug mix. Cute little guy she calls a 'bug.' Kate is an ER nurse at Holy Redeemer. She was on duty when that guy from the restaurant was brought in."

"Clay Oreck?" Josie asked.

"She didn't tell me his name. Just said he'd eaten some toasted ravioli from Tillie's. Everybody in the ER knows the restaurant. They were really surprised a customer would have food poisoning."

"Food poisoning is good, isn't it?" Josie asked. "I mean for Tillie. It beats being charged with reckless endangerment."

"Sorry," Ted said. "I should have said they thought Clay had food poisoning when he first showed up. It's only natural when someone arrives by ambulance from a restaurant. What killed him may be worse. Kate thinks he ingested a toxic plant."

"He what?" Josie asked. That didn't sound good. She poured herself more coffee and plopped onto the sofa. This sounded like news she should take sitting down.

"Kate said the man was poisoned and it wasn't pretty. The ER kept some of the— This is gross. Do you want to hear it?"

"I'm a mom," Josie said. "I've changed diapers." She took a sip of coffee and burned her tongue.

"Okay. The guy was throwing up and they saved some of it. The ER doc thought he recognized bits of castor beans in the vomit and sent it for testing."

"Castor beans grow wild in the vacant lot next to Tillie's restaurant," Josie said. "If that's what really made Clay sick."

"The doctor was fairly sure," Ted said. "The beans have a distinctive look—they're dark brown with pretty patterns. He'd treated a castor bean poisoning in the ER in August. A toddler had chewed a bean. Fortunately, the mom caught her kid in the act and rushed him straight to the hospital. The boy survived. Clay wasn't so lucky."

"Why would a child survive, but not a grown man?" Josie asked.

"Who knows?" Ted said. "The boy only chewed on one bean and his mom made him spit it out. The doc found quite a few pieces coarsely chopped when Clay got sick. He estimates the man ate several beans, but he's not sure how many. Plus Clay had liver damage."

"He was drunk at the bar that afternoon," Josie said. "He was turning into an alcoholic."

"That could make the reaction worse," Ted said. "Too bad there's no antidote for castor bean poisoning. I thought you'd want to tell your mom that Clay was probably poisoned, so she can warn Tillie. Her lawyer will want to know."

"Poor Tillie," Josie said, then stopped. "If Kate is a nurse, why is she blabbing Clay's medical history to you?"

"Clay is dead, and a reporter was at the hospital," Ted said. "Kate expects the story will be on television as soon as the tests confirm it's castor beans. Tillie should brace herself for some bad publicity."

Josie groaned. "And maybe a murder charge. I listened to the TV news this morning while I was getting dressed and didn't see anything about the story. I thought Tillie was safe."

"I think it's going to hit like a tornado," Ted said. "You've got everything for a perfect media storm: a beloved St. Louis restaurant, the city's favorite food, a high-profile lawyer, and his cute old lady client."

"Better call her an old*er* woman if you value your life," Josie said. "Tillie is Mom's age and neither sees herself as an old lady."

"You're right," Ted said. "Your mom didn't like it when I said that last night. I have more bad news. Kate said the dead guy's wife was at the ER."

"Henrietta?" Josie said.

"Sounds right, but I'm not sure. When Clay died, Nurse Kate said she didn't act like a grieving widow. There were no tears, no shocked silence, no request to be alone with her husband. Henrietta started screaming that she was going to sue Tillie. She called a lawyer before they wheeled her husband's body out of the ER. The lawyer ran straight to the hospital."

"Talk about an ambulance chaser," Josie said.

"It was pretty shameless, according to Kate," Ted said. "The lawyer was wandering around the emergency room, trying to get information, taking the names of potential witnesses and interfering with the staff. Security had to throw him out. Now everyone is waiting to find out what killed Clay. Kate swears it's going to be castor bean poisoning."

"This just gets worse, Ted. I'd better hang up so I can call Mom."

"I'm worried about you, Josie. Do you still have more TAG Tour assignments?" Ted asked.

"Several," Josie said. "Why?"

"I don't like you going on these mystery-shopping assignments alone, eating at strange restaurants."

Josie felt uneasy. She didn't like anyone questioning

her independence, no matter how well-meant. "Ted, you don't have to worry. I wasn't alone. I'm supposed to take someone with me to each place. This is a dream job. I'm getting paid to eat at restaurants."

"Where a man was poisoned," Ted said.

"An obnoxious man," Josie said. "Clay's death was different. He was as welcome as a roach at Tillie's. None of the places on my list know who I am or what I'm doing. That's the good part about being a mystery shopper—I'm a nobody, representing other nobodies."

"You're not a nobody," Ted said.

"Okay, an ordinary person who makes sure other ordinary customers get extraordinary service."

"That's better, but I'm still worried about you," Ted said.

"Then come with me," Josie said. "I'd really like company today. I'm mystery-shopping pig ear and snoot sandwiches at the C & K Barbecue. I don't want to eat exotic pig parts." Josie shuddered at the thought of biting into a pig's nose.

Ted laughed. "You don't know what you're missing. I love snoots and ears."

"You do? I thought they were African-American food."

"They are," he said. "But high-powered foodies have discovered barbecue. Some big-time barbecue chef in Manhattan is from St. Louis. You'll never guess where I read that."

"*Bon Appétit*?"

"The *Economist*," Ted said. "And how did you know the name of a gourmet cooking magazine?"

"My friend Alyce gets it. When did you start getting the *Economist*?"

"A client complained my office magazines were older

than his dog and brought over his magazines," he said. "I read some before I put them in the waiting room. Thanks to that article, I am a fount of barbecue information. Plus I've had years of hands-on research. That makes me a qualified expert."

Josie laughed. "Are you free for a lunch?"

"I'm free the rest of the day," Ted said. "I see my last patient at eleven thirty. How about if I pick you up at twelve thirty? And where do you want to eat your barbecue? C & K is carryout only."

"We could come back here," Josie said.

"Might not make it all the way to your house," Ted said. "That barbecue is incredible. Besides, it's too messy to eat in your kitchen. This is a ten-napkin sandwich. We're talking crunchy ears on pillowy white bread piled with mayonnaise potato salad and slathered with sweet red barbecue sauce. It's a perfect fall day. How about a picnic? I was thinking Deer Creek Park."

Josie could name nearly a dozen nearby parks, but not that one. "Where's Deer Creek?"

"Not too far from your house," Ted said, "on Laclede Station Road near I-44. By Cousin Hugo's bar."

"Oh, you mean Rocket Ship Park! Every kid in Maplewood knows it. Amelia loved the old rocket ship slide when she was little."

"We dog owners know it as Disc Dog Park. The St. Louis Disc Dog Club has practice there most Saturdays. I take my Lab for Frisbee practice. The park has picnic tables."

"I'll bring the napkins, paper towels, and wipes," Josie said.

"I'll bring the beer," Ted said.

"How about Festus? Can he go with us?" Josie asked.

"He's on a diet," Ted said. "I have to practice what I preach about fat animals. It would be cruel to eat barbecue in front of him. I'll pick you up. Don't wear anything you don't want to see covered in barbecue sauce. And prepare to meet a St. Louis institution."

Josie hoped this meeting would be less deadly than the last.

Chapter 11

What can I wear that would look cute covered in barbecue sauce? Josie wondered.

She settled on a tomato-colored shirt that brought out the natural reddish highlights in her brown hair. Any dripped sauce would match the shirt. The day was warm enough for her strappy red sandals.

She combed her hair, put on makeup, and looked in the mirror. She felt ready to tackle any pig part. Josie had barely finished dressing for her date when her phone rang.

"Josie!" Jane's frantic cry shattered Josie's calm.

"Mom, what happened?"

"It's Tillie. She's been arrested for murder. It's going to be on television after the commercial." Jane's voice changed from slashing anxiety to an old woman's quaver. "What is she going to do?"

"I'll be right up."

Josie skimmed upstairs to her mother's kitchen. She was greeted at the back door by a joyously playful Stuart Little. She scratched the shih tzu's ears while he pranced and wagged his tail.

Jane didn't greet her. She was glued to the small

television on the counter, staring at a used car commercial. Josie thought Jane must have been in the midst of making an omelet. She saw two eggs and a bag of shredded American cheese on the counter. On the stove, chopped green pepper and onions were starting to smoke in a skillet. Josie grabbed the skillet and put it on a cool burner.

The normally kitchen-careful Jane didn't see that, either. She watched the car dealer's "unbelievable deals" as if they were promises of salvation.

"Mom?" Josie said.

"Sh!" Jane said. "They're back."

The blond anchorwoman and her dark-haired cohost had the plastic perfection of a couple on a wedding cake. The blonde put on her serious face and read the news story on the teleprompter: "Tillie Minnelli, owner of the landmark Italian restaurant, Tillie's Off the Hill, was charged with first-degree murder today in the death of Clay Oreck."

A shot of Tillie's restaurant flashed on the screen, followed by a photograph of Clay, brown-haired and lean. It must have been taken long before the alcohol left him bloated and broken-veined. The photograph was blurry, as if foretelling Clay's future as a drunk.

"Mr. Oreck, a thirty-two-year-old unemployed roofer, died after eating toasted ravioli at the restaurant," the anchorwoman said. "Police say the ravioli and the sauce were laced with lethal castor beans, a poisonous plant that grows wild in Missouri.

"Police say Mr. Oreck had an altercation with the restaurant owner and Mrs. Minnelli said she wanted rid of the victim permanently. The day before, she had brandished a weapon and threatened him."

"Threatened him!" Jane shouted at the television. "He was drunk! She brought out a lead pipe from under the cash register and he took it away from her. Some threat!"

The anchorwoman continued her relentless reading. "Mr. Oreck collapsed while eating ravioli personally prepared by Mrs. Minnelli. He was taken to Holy Redeemer Hospital. Efforts to revive him failed and he was pronounced dead later that evening.

"Mrs. Minnelli was originally charged with reckless endangerment and released on bail, but after a massive dose of chopped castor beans was found in the victim's vomit"—the anchorwoman paused slightly but continued—"the charges were changed to first-degree murder. If Mrs. Minnelli is convicted, she faces the death penalty."

"That's not what happened," Jane told the television screen. "You forgot the dipping sauce. Tillie wanted Clay to leave and he wouldn't. That's why she made the sauce hotter." Jane waved the knife she'd been using to chop onions at the oblivious anchor.

Josie gently pried the knife out of her mother's hand. "It's okay, Mom. That's why Tillie has a lawyer. Renzo will tell the whole story to the jury."

The anchor said, "River Bluff police arrested Mrs. Minnelli this morning."

Jane shrieked when she saw Tillie being escorted to a waiting police car by two hulking uniformed officers. The small, sturdy woman seemed to have shrunk. Her face was hidden by a pale blue hoodie. Her pantsuit flapped pathetically around her limbs. She looked like an abandoned scarecrow.

"Big bullies!" Jane cried. "They should be ashamed."

Now a prosecuting attorney with a face like a bilious fish told the TV audience, "The River Bluff police recovered enough forensic evidence to charge Mrs. Minnelli with murder in the first degree. Her fingerprints were on the inside of a pair of rubber kitchen gloves that had traces of castor beans. The police also recovered a mixing bowl that had traces of mashed castor beans. The bowl was found in a trash can in the restaurant kitchen."

Jane kept a seething silence.

Attorney Renzo Fischer was interviewed outside the Clayton County jail, wearing his trademark white Stetson, bolo tie, and ostrich-skin cowboy boots.

"My client is innocent," Renzo said. "One look at that little lady and you know she's no killer. I eat at Tillie's all the time. Lots of people want to see me dead, but I'm healthy as a horse." He patted his stomach and preened for the camera.

"Tillie has promised to make me more of that ravioli as soon as she's free. I'm gonna suggest you eat it, too. Lots of it. I need her to pay my bill."

"That son of a buzzard," Jane said. "He told Tillie he wouldn't charge her."

"He can't announce on television that he's working for free food," Josie said. "Once Tillie was charged with first-degree murder, Mom, the terms changed."

"They shouldn't," Jane said. Josie hoped the beaten Tillie would be able to show some of her mother's spirit.

"Well, Josie, what are you going to do about this?" Jane said. "You're supposed to be investigating that man's murder. Now you've let Tillie get arrested."

"Me?" Josie said. "I haven't done a thing."

"Exactly," Jane said.

"I mean it isn't my fault Tillie was arrested." Josie scrambled to find a satisfactory answer. She didn't want to lose her built-in babysitter. "I've already found out something. I talked with Ted this morning."

Josie felt a flash of guilt. Ted had warned her that Tillie would be arrested. I should have called Mom immediately and prepared her for this bad news, Josie thought.

Instead, I got ready for my date. I need to pull my head out of the clouds and start helping.

"I'm going to visit Tillie in jail tonight. She was just arrested this morning."

"And what are you doing the rest of today?" Jane asked.

"My job, Mom. Ted and I are going to eat pig ear sandwiches for TAG Tours."

"That's all! You're doing nothing else today?"

"I've found out something already, Mom," Josie said. "One of Ted's clients is an ER nurse. She was there when Clay was brought in. Henrietta called a lawyer before his body was even cold."

"That's disgusting!" Jane said.

"It sure shocked the ER nurse," Josie said.

"In the meantime, you're going to enjoy yourself while my friend is in jail." Jane's face was dark pink with outrage.

"Mom, there's nothing else I can do. Besides, I'm not going to enjoy myself. I'm going to eat pig ears. Please tell Renzo about Clay's wife. Tillie's lawyer has an investigator. He's on the case, too."

"He's useless," Jane said. "He and his investigators. That lawyer was so busy hamming it up for the cameras, he didn't mention any of the evidence in Tillie's favor."

"What evidence?" Josie asked.

"The prosecutor said he had evidence against Tillie," Jane said. "*Humph!* Her fingerprints were inside the rubber gloves. Big deal. That's where they're supposed to be."

"Her prints were also on the bowl the cops found in the trash," Josie said.

"So what? That bowl was from Tillie's kitchen," Jane said. "Tillie wouldn't throw away a perfectly good mixing bowl."

"She might consider it a small sacrifice to get rid of Clay," Josie said. "I was only there twice and I thought he was obnoxious."

"Whose side are you on?" Jane asked.

"Tillie's," Josie said. "I'm just pointing out how the police could build a case on what they found. Castor beans grow right outside her restaurant's kitchen door. She could grab enough poison to put Clay out of her misery. You know that, Mom. We saw the castor bean plants and the poison ivy. We talked about how pretty they looked growing wild in the vacant lot next door."

"Where anyone could have picked them," Jane said.

"But, Mom, only Tillie had a good reason to get rid of Clay."

"Exactly," Jane said. "That's why she wouldn't kill him. It's too obvious."

"I think that explanation only works on television," Josie said.

Chapter 12

Josie stared at the massive pig ear sandwich in front of her, a mound of food nearly five inches high. She was grateful the pig ear did not look like it had once been part of a porker—it was simply a deep fat–fried hunk of something.

But what? Were pig ears like rubber? Gristle? They sure didn't look meaty.

Focus on the potato salad, she told herself. And the barbecue sauce. The red sauce smells delicious. The bread is plain old white. I like both of those. If I close my eyes, I can do this.

Josie wished she could enjoy their picnic at Deer Creek Park. The sky was a blue china bowl and the trees were blazing with fiery color. But Josie didn't notice the fall beauty. She didn't even see Ted, who looked absurdly handsome with his square jaw and broad chest.

All she saw was that pig ear sandwich. It seemed to get bigger by the second, throbbing, morphing into a red-spattered monster. Josie had to eat it. She had a duty as a mystery shopper. Maybe she should just take Ted's word that the sandwich was good. No, Josie wouldn't chicken out. She would pork out or else. She lived by her code, and her code said she had to taste the sandwich. One small bite for the honor of St. Louis.

"What's the matter?" Ted asked. They sat side by side at the picnic table. Ted was ready for his snoot.

"I'm trying to get up the nerve to eat a pig ear," Josie said.

"Just take a bite. You'll love it. I promise. Doesn't that barbecue sauce make your mouth water?"

"Yes."

"And the potato salad is amazing. Here, try that. We'll approach the wild sandwich one step at a time." He scooped some potato salad with a plastic fork.

Josie allowed herself to be fed like a toddler. "That is good," she said. "I'm trying to get up the nerve to bite a pig ear."

"Please don't keep me waiting," Ted said. "I want my snoot. We'll dig in on a count of three. Come on. One."

Josie picked up the huge sandwich with both hands. Bright sauce dripped on the newspapers she and Ted had spread on the table. A clump of potato salad plopped out onto her paper plate.

"Two," Ted said. "Three!"

Josie bit. *Yum!* She took another bite. It was even better. By the third bite, she was painted with barbecue sauce and splashed with potato salad, but she didn't care.

"Fabulous," she said. "You were right. I thought a pig ear would taste rubbery, but it's crunchy. Kind of like those pork rind snacks, only better."

"I told you." Ted chomped his sandwich with a resounding crunch. "Wanna try some of my snoot?"

"No, thanks," Josie said. "But you have barbecue sauce on your snoot." She wiped a red smear off the tip of his nose.

"Before I finish, I'll be basted in barbecue sauce," he said. "That's why I wore this red shirt."

"Plaid shirts are chic," Josie said.

"So is barbecue," Ted said. "Barbecue experts say the snoot sandwich is St. Louis's contribution to barbecue."

"I thought it was our sweet spicy sauce," Josie said, licking her fingers.

"That actually comes here by way of Kansas City," Ted said. "Sweet tomato barbecue sauce is served throughout most of the Midwest. Barbecue is different in other parts of the country. North Carolina 'cue is mostly pork. They wait and add the sauce when they sit down to eat. They may use a vinegar sauce with pepper flakes. Or it might have some tomato. Some eat the barbecue plain.

"Memphis likes its barbecue with a rub of spices but no sauce. Texas goes for thick spicy tomato sauce and beef brisket. That's cattle country."

Ted took a big bite of his snoot sandwich.

"And this is based on your hands-on knowledge," Josie said.

Ted chewed thoughtfully, then said, "Along with a solid intellectual foundation."

"From that magazine in your waiting room," she said.

He winked at Josie. "I'm prejudiced, but I like St. Louis barbecue best," Ted said. "We've been undiscovered and unappreciated for decades. Thanks to your work for TAG Tours, the whole world will know how good it is."

Josie finished the last of her pig ear sandwich. "I had no idea I could lead a crusade just by stuffing my face."

"You'd think there would be a shortage of food this good," Ted said. "Pigs only have two ears."

"Do you really think anyone in Alyce's neighborhood is going to demand pig ear sandwiches?" Josie asked.

"Why not?" Ted said. "Too snooty?"

Josie groaned. "I can't see McDonald's serving a McSnoot."

"They don't know what they're missing," Ted said.

"I wonder why TAG didn't choose St. Louis ribs," Josie said.

"Too easy," Ted said. "Ears and snoots are unique. C & K has the city's sweet spicy sauce."

The wind ruffled the edges of their newspaper tablecloth and sent a paper napkin flying. Ted retrieved it while Josie gathered the barbecue-soaked picnic remains and tossed them in the trash. It took ten minutes to scrub off the sauce with wipes and wet towels.

Dark clouds appeared from the west, but the fall air still felt warm. "Now that your ordeal is over, want to go for a walk?" Ted asked.

Josie took his hand and they strolled over to the rocket ship slide that gave the park its name. The colorful playground also had a "launch pad," plus ladders, tunnels, bridges, and walkways.

"Is this the slide Amelia used to play on?" Ted asked.

"No, the one she used was smaller," Josie said. "My girl is too old for slides now. Besides, she's transferred her affections to the giant turtles at Turtle Park. I used to enjoy taking her to this park. She was about the age of that little girl."

A thin, dark-skinned child with her hair in pink ribbons blazed her way down the rocket ship slide, while her mother waited to catch her at the bottom.

"I want to fly!" the girl shouted. She ran to a kid-sized plane and jumped in the open cockpit.

“For a while, Amelia wanted to be a pilot like her father,” Josie said. “But she’s changed her mind several times since then.”

“What’s the latest?” Ted asked.

“She wants to be a veterinarian.”

“She’s good with Harry and your mom’s dog. She could intern at my office.”

“Don’t reserve a place for her yet,” Josie said. “I expect her to change careers a few more times. Right now, I’m hoping she’ll finish college.”

“It must be tough being a working mom,” Ted said, “even with a kid as good as Amelia.”

“I took this job so I could spend more time with her,” Josie said. “And my mom has been a big help. She picks up Amelia at school when I can’t get there. I’m lucky to have her on call as a babysitter.”

They walked in silence—a deafening silence. Josie watched the wind create red-and-gold whirlwinds of leaves. Ted pulled Josie down on a blue park bench near two flame-red bushes and said, “Josie, it’s none of my business, but your mom pretty much blackmailed you into investigating Tillie’s case.”

“So?” Josie felt uneasy. She didn’t like Ted criticizing her mother.

“So, it’s dangerous to meddle in a murder investigation. I know you’ve had some luck in the past, but poking around in a murder can get you killed.”

“You’re right,” Josie said.

Ted smiled. His eyes crinkled. Josie wished they hadn’t. She loved his eye crinkles. “It is none of your business.”

Ted’s smile disappeared.

“I love you,” Josie said, “but Mom needs my help.”

Ted tried to put his arm around her, but she shook it off.

“But that’s why Tillie has a lawyer,” Ted said. “Renzo

will have a case investigator, a professional private eye. You shouldn't be doing this on your own."

"I didn't ask for your advice, Ted. I appreciate your concern, but I want to go now. It's time to pick up Amelia."

Angry clouds scudded overhead. The wind had a cold, slicing edge to it.

"Josie!"

"I really need to go home," Josie said. "I'm a grown woman. I can take care of myself."

Ted looked contrite. "I'm sorry. I was out of line. I had no business meddling. It's just that I love you so much. You're so beautiful and funny. Of course you can handle your own life. You're doing a terrific job. Amelia is proof of that. Can we start over, please?"

Josie nodded.

"I want to help," he said. "You've taken on a tough task, but I'll be there for you. If you need dinner, if you want me to pick up Amelia, if you need a bodyguard, I'm there."

"That's better," Josie said.

Ted kissed her. A long, lingering kiss.

"You taste like spicy tomato sauce," she said. "I forgive you. If you really want to help, go with me on my next mystery-shopping assignment as penance for your sins."

"Where?" Ted said.

"I have to eat brain sandwiches at Ferguson's Pub in South City."

"Are you kidding? That's no penance. I love brains," Ted said. "My dad used to take me there. When do we go?"

"Tomorrow afternoon," Josie said.

"Perfect," Ted said. "Do you want me to drive you to Amelia's school now?"

"No. We need to have a private mother-daughter talk," Josie said.

Dark clouds hid the sun now. The wind whipped the leaves into small fiery tornadoes. The weather was turning cold. A fat raindrop plopped on the bench as they ran toward Ted's orange Mustang.

Chapter 13

Rain slashed Josie's Honda. The wind battered its small body and nearly blew the car sideways. She clung to the steering wheel and dodged a downed tree limb. At a red light, she scrubbed her fogged windshield with a tissue, but it didn't help. Josie could hardly see through the storm.

She could hardly see where she was going with Ted, either. After their tiff at the park, Josie and Ted had run to his car, dodging raindrops. They were laughing once they were inside his '68 orange Mustang, cushioned by the leather bucket seats. Josie loved his warm man smell—coffee and cinnamon with a dash of wood smoke—in the closed car. Before he started the engine, Ted kissed her again, then licked the raindrops off her eyelids. The windows had fogged.

"No," she said. "I really do have to get to my car and pick up Amelia." It took all her strength—moral and maternal—to push him away. Josie remembered those stories of fear-maddened mothers who'd lifted whole cars to save their babies. That's what it felt like to refuse Ted. She wanted to spend the afternoon making love in that car—hot, hasty, hormonal love.

You're a mother with responsibilities, she told herself. You're too old to be lovesick.

"Josie, I really do love you," Ted said.

"I love you, too," Josie said. Her voice was a hoarse whisper.

"Are you mad at me?" he asked.

Was she? "No," she said. "I just wanted you to understand."

"I do," he said. "I needed reminding. That's all."

So do I, Josie thought. I need to remind myself my tween daughter is waiting for me at the Barrington School for Boys and Girls.

Josie wiped away the condensation on Ted's windows and he drove the few blocks to her home. By the time he reached Phelan Street, the trees whipped restlessly and fat leaves were plastered to the windshield. The sky had turned so black the streetlights came on.

"Looks like tornado weather," Ted said. "The sky is green."

"I don't hear the warning sirens," Josie said. But the storm made her feel uneasy. She was anxious to get to Amelia and protect her. Maternal instinct had trumped hormones.

"There's my car. Gotta go!" She kissed Ted lightly, then ran for her Honda. If the rain held off, she could pick up Amelia with time to spare.

The storm wasn't all that made Josie uneasy. She was in love with Ted. Soon she would have to decide if she wanted to marry him. Amelia adored Ted, but what would happen when she turned into a surly teenager? Would Ted be a steadying influence, or would he make it more difficult for Josie to bring up her daughter? What if he didn't want a teenager around? He said he liked Amelia—now—but people changed after marriage.

I'll have to make up my mind soon, she thought, or our romance will wither and die.

She was almost grateful when the storm broke about a mile from Barrington and she could no longer think about her love life. As the rain pounded down, Josie flipped on the headlights and inched up the school's semicircular drive, careful not to hit the children sprinting for their family cars. She crawled past the humpbacked shapes of SUVs, each holding a waiting mother. Luxury vehicles were second cars at the upscale school.

She made out a Hummer's blinker flashing dimly through the rain and pumped her brakes to slow her car. The dark, bulky monster powered out of its parking slot, confident it couldn't be hurt. Josie tapped her horn to let the driver know she was behind her. Another ding wouldn't make a difference on Josie's ancient Honda, but hellfire would rain down if she scratched a trophy vehicle.

Josie didn't fit in at Barrington. The other mothers never let her forget that she was a single mom who worked a low-paying, no-status job. Josie tried not to care.

Amelia was a scholarship student. Barrington prided itself on its diversity. Living in Maplewood, a red-brick suburb more than a hundred years old, made Amelia a "city kid." She was an exotic species in the rich, sheltered suburbs where women bragged that they hadn't been downtown in years.

Even with a scholarship, Amelia's schooling wasn't free. Josie used a small legacy from her aunt and occasional help from Amelia's Canadian grandfather. Jane would pick up Amelia after school in a pinch, but she disapproved of Barrington. Jane wanted Amelia in a Catholic school.

Amelia seemed to thrive at Barrington. She was

stronger and more mature than Josie had been at her age. Josie had winced when the mean girls at her high school made fun of her mother's styleless purse as a "cleaning lady's bag." When an overprivileged Barrington child had asked Amelia if their dented Honda was the maid's car, Amelia had shrugged off the insult.

"Her daddy better leave her a bunch of money, because she's too dumb to make her own," she told her mother.

Josie watched her daughter carefully for signs that she felt slighted or bullied, but Amelia seemed at home there. Josie would shrug off the petty slights to give her daughter the best possible education.

She was determined that Amelia would dress as well as the other students. Josie stalked the sale racks so her daughter was as stylish as her classmates. Her mystery-shopper skills helped her achieve that goal.

Josie pulled into the Hummer's recently vacated slot and a loudspeaker blared, "Amelia Marcus!" Barrington students didn't rush out of the school in packs. They were announced, and only when their ride had arrived. They could be picked up only by designated drivers. Anyone else needed written permission, filed at the office in advance.

She saw her daughter's yellow hoodie bobbing through the downpour. Amelia opened the car door, flopped into the passenger seat, and dumped her backpack on the floor.

"Awesome storm," she said. The rain had plastered Amelia's bangs to her forehead.

She still allowed her mother to kiss her, and Josie was grateful. Amelia no longer had the sweet smell of a little girl. Now Josie caught the strawberry scent of her shampoo.

"You're just like your father," Josie said. "He loved

bad weather. We used to go out on the balcony at his apartment and watch the wind and rain until we were drenched. Even when the tornado sirens were blaring, he didn't want to go inside. One night, a barbecue grill sailed past us on the second floor."

"Daddy was fearless," Amelia said proudly.

And reckless, Josie thought. That same disregard for risk led Nate to fly drugs into the US and get arrested and sent to a Canadian prison. It also made him an ardent and inventive lover. Josie remembered making rainy day love while thunder crashed and lightning lit up the bedroom, but she couldn't say that to her eleven-year-old.

"Am I like him?" Amelia asked.

That was the opening Josie had been waiting for. The storm had eased to a light shower. Josie turned onto the wider, safer lanes of Lindbergh Boulevard. Time for that mother-daughter talk.

"You're brave like he was," Josie said. "It takes courage to go to a school like Barrington on a scholarship. You have your father's brown hair and eyes. It's a richer color than mine."

Amelia's smile was as bright as her yellow hoodie.

"You have his freckles, too. I noticed you covered them up with my makeup when Ted made us dinner."

"Freckles are fugly," Amelia said, her face sullen.

"Please don't use that word," Josie said.

"Why?"

"You know why. It's a contraction of the F-word and ugly. And freckles are not ugly. Rashida Jones has them."

"She was Karen in *The Office.* The cute one who got dumped for Pam," Amelia said.

The cute one. That was progress, Josie thought.

"That's her," she said. "Her parents are Quincy Jones and Peggy Lipton from *Twin Peaks*. Rashida could cover up her freckles or laser them off, but she doesn't. Neither does Emma Watson. A few freckles didn't keep her out of the Harry Potter movies."

"Okay, I get it," Amelia said. "You've been surfing the Internet for ways to make me feel better about myself."

Josie stopped at a red light. A pale yellow sun peeked through the clouds.

"Busted," Josie said. "I also found out that Miley Cyrus has no freckles." She grinned at her daughter. Amelia hated Miley.

"She smoked salvia in a bong," Amelia said, her lip curling in disgust. "The light's green."

Josie figured she'd made her point. "Are you and Grandma having a cooking class at her place tonight?" Josie asked.

"I'm worried about Grandma." Amelia was talking too fast. Josie's daughter seemed eager to distract her from the uncomfortable subject of freckles, covered or uncovered. "We were supposed to make stuffed steak. Now Grandma says we're making deviled egg casserole instead."

"It sounds rich but good," Josie said.

"It's lame and disgusting," Amelia said. "We've made eggs for the last two classes, Mom. Eggs are cheap. We used to fix meat and fish. We'd make pork chops, catfish, sirloin tip roast, even stuffed peppers. Now she's teaching me about cooking on a budget."

"That's good," Josie said.

"Maybe. But we couldn't make that frittata until Grandma found twenty-seven cents in the couch cushions so she could buy a dozen eggs. I think Grandma needs money."

"I see."

Josie didn't like what she saw. Jane had had a shopping addiction, an uncontrollable urge to buy things she didn't need or want from the Home Shopping Network. Jane's closets and the spare bedroom had been crammed with lamps that switched on by clapping, collectible dolls, even ankle bracelets.

Jane had almost bankrupted herself with her addiction. She knew the UPS drivers by name and the times of their deliveries. She had neglected her home, her friends, and herself.

To Josie's relief, her mother finally realized she had a problem. She saw a counselor for more than a year. The treatment seemed to be successful. Jane had stopped seeing the counselor three months ago. Was she backsliding? Jane had been fixing herself an omelet when Josie saw her at noon.

She hadn't noticed any signs that Jane's shopping addiction had returned. She didn't see the telltale piles of UPS packages on the porch this afternoon, but she'd been running for her car.

I thought that problem was solved, Josie thought. I knew it was too easy. Or maybe Jane was just temporarily short of cash. It happened to Josie often enough.

"I don't want to take advantage of Grandma," Josie said. "Maybe we could help by buying the groceries for your class."

"I told her I could shop for the food, Mom, but Grandma said she could handle it. She sounded mad that I even brought it up. That's why I'm worried."

"Me, too," Josie said. About a lot of things.

Chapter 14

"I still think I should go with you," Jane said. She stepped in front of Josie, barring her way to her daughter's front door.

Josie neatly sidestepped around her mother, a sure sign that Jane still wasn't quite herself. A hunk of hair stuck out over her left ear. Jane had failed to tame it with hairspray. Josie wondered if her fastidious mother would wait two more days for her standing hair appointment or call for an emergency fix.

"Mom, we've been through this," Josie said. "Tillie can only have two visitors a week and she wants to see Lorena tomorrow."

"I know. I just think I could help if I was there." Jane had the stubborn bulldog look that Josie dreaded.

"I'm sure you could," Josie lied. "But I promised I'd help Tillie and I need to talk to her right away."

"I could wait in the car at the jail," Jane said.

"I need you to be here with Amelia. I still don't trust her to stay alone after she went off the reservation last winter. I'll be fine, Mom. Downtown Clayton is safe and there are police all over."

"Well, those people make me nervous," Jane said.

"What people?"

"The ones you'll be standing in line with at the jail."

"Mom, they didn't commit any crime. They're just visitors. I've been in that line before. They're tired, unlucky people."

"But they're seeing criminals," Jane said. "Drug dealers, robbers, murderers."

"Murderers like Tillie?" Josie said. "She'll attract a vicious crowd."

"You know what I mean," Jane said.

It was mean to tease Mom, Josie thought. Jane was frantic about her friend, and rightly so. Jail was a hardship and a humiliation, especially at Tillie's age. Josie wondered if a person could die of shame.

"I do know, Mom, but we can't change the county rules. You can see Tillie next week. I promise to give you a full report tonight. I'll come straight home, no stops. Now, GBH?"

Jane refused to budge.

"Family rules," Josie said. She stepped forward and folded her small, stubborn mother into her arms. GBH stood for Great Big Hug. After a disagreement, if one called GBH, a hug was required, no matter how angry the Marcus women felt.

Josie felt her mother's stiff spine soften slightly and rubbed her back.

"I'm just so worried about Tillie," Jane said. "She's not young anymore. Some of those women in that jail are vicious, and you know it. Some are guilty. They'll enjoy tormenting an old woman, like bad boys enjoy hurting cats. Those guards can't be everywhere."

Josie was touched. For her mother to call a friend her age an old woman was a huge admission.

"I'll do my best to help her. I promise." She kissed Jane and heard her mother sniffling.

Josie reached into her coat pocket. "Here's a tissue, Mom."

Jane wiped her eyes and said, "I'm not crying. I'm coming down with a cold."

"That happens in this changeable weather." Josie wanted to leave her mother with some dignity.

"I think I'll take Stuart Little for a walk," Jane said. "A brisk walk will cure a cold." She called down the hallway, "Amelia, are you coming with me? I'm walking the dog."

"I'll get my hoodie. Do I get to hold the leash?" Amelia asked.

"If you're careful," Jane said. "But you have to pick up, too."

Josie smiled. Crafty Jane had turned walking the shih tzu into a privilege. Amelia fought for the honor of scooping up after the dog.

"I'll be back as soon as I can," Josie said.

"And I expect some progress," Jane said.

Josie might have disappointed her mother by getting pregnant and dropping out of college, but Jane still had high expectations. Josie was supposed to solve Clay's murder when the police had failed.

The evening sun was shining on a freshly showered city. Josie ached all over after her day. The emotional scene with Ted made her heart ache. Her neck throbbed from driving in the fierce storm. The trip to Barrington School had been tense. And the conversation with Amelia made her head hurt. What if Jane was back in the grip of her addiction? Josie couldn't support her mother and her daughter, not on what she made. The mystery shopper's mother had a shopping addiction—it was a cosmic joke.

I'll tackle one worry at a time, Josie thought. Right

now Tillie is at the top of my list. She found a well-lit parking spot in the garage near the jail. Her optimistic view of the inmates' visitors changed when she stood in line with them. Yes, that slump-shouldered dark-skinned man in khakis seemed to have stopped by after a hard day's labor. And the woman in the fresh pink hospital scrubs was probably on her way to work that evening. But Josie suspected the slender young thing in front of her with the impressive tattoos and piercings also worked evenings—on a street corner. Miss Thing wore more costume jewelry than costume: a scrap of skirt, a bedraggled bunny-fur jacket, and ankle straps like suede stepladders. Her purple acrylic daggers were studded with rhinestones. Josie wondered if the guard would consider them lethal weapons.

At a little after seven o'clock, Josie had cleared the official hurdles and sat down in a visitor's booth opposite Tillie.

Josie tried to hide her shock. She hardly recognized the brash woman who'd ruled a popular restaurant. Tillie looked as if someone had rubbed away her edges with an eraser. This was a blurry, monochrome copy of Jane's friend.

Josie didn't bother asking Tillie how she was—she could see. She had to talk fast. They had only forty minutes. "Mom sends her love," Josie said. "She'll visit you next week. I don't want to waste any time tonight, so I'll ask you straight out. Who would want to kill Clay?"

"His wife and his girlfriend," Tillie said. She didn't hesitate.

"Both? His wife said she loved him."

"Maybe now that he's dead, but Henrietta knew he was slipping around while she was at work," Tillie said. "That man made her feel like a fool. She went on a crying jag one night and told me she was sick of his drinking and fed up with his unfaithful ways. A woman can turn a blind eye for only so long and Henrietta had had enough."

Tillie stopped and looked down at her trembling hand. "I did something really bad," she said.

Was she going to confess she'd killed Clay?

"Maybe you should tell your lawyer," Josie said uneasily. Could the guards hear their conversation?

"Not bad like that," Tillie said. "I mean I did something bad to Henrietta. I shouldn't have called her to come get Clay when he was drunk. I knew she was at the end of her rope. I did it to stir up trouble. Well, I sure stirred it, but not the way I wanted. Henrietta was supposed to confront him, not kill him."

"We don't know if she killed him," Josie said.

"I do," Tillie said. "Henrietta's trouble. Clay said she had someone on the side, but I never saw her with another man. Could be Clay was lying to justify running around with Gemma. Usually, the only time Henrietta was in my restaurant was to haul home her sorry excuse for a husband. A few weeks before he died, she broke down and said she'd had it up to here." Tillie slashed her hand across her neck.

"Why didn't she leave Clay?" Josie asked.

"Who knows? Maybe her boyfriend was married."

"It's a possibility," Josie said. It was more than a possibility, she thought. It fit with the story Nurse Kate had told Ted at the vet clinic. Kate thought the freshly widowed Henrietta had acted more greedy than grieving.

"Any other ideas?" Josie asked.

"Gemma Lynn was pressuring Clay to leave his wife and marry her," Tillie said. "They argued about it nearly every afternoon. I heard them. People think if they lower their voices I won't know what they're saying, but I caught every whisper and Gemma Lynn didn't bother whispering. They fought all the time. Those two had some doozies."

"Why didn't Clay want to marry her?"

"Gemma Lynn didn't have enough money, if you ask me," she said. There was a glint of malice in her faded eyes. "What's the word for a male gold digger?"

"Boy toy?" Josie asked.

Tillie snorted. "He was no boy—that's for sure—and I wouldn't touch him with tongs. But Gemma Lynn had it bad for that man." Tillie seemed to grow stronger and more confident as she dished the dirt. "But she likes used goods. She owns Gemma's Junktique, two blocks from my place. That name says it all—she's got more junk than real antiques.

"Her shop's so dusty you need a shower after you walk through it, and not many people do. She's barely hanging on and Clay knew it. He couldn't find work, not that he could look very hard perched on that bar stool. He liked his life just fine: He wanted to stay married so his wife would support him and he had Gemma on the side for fun.

"If he left Henrietta and Gemma's junk shop folded, he'd lose his soft life. Clay wasn't about to live on love."

"Is Gemma's shop in the golden square?" Josie asked. "If she's one of the holdouts for the casino land, then Clay had a woman with a rich future."

"Nope. The developer's scout wasn't interested in Gemma or her land. She tried batting her eyelashes at him, but he ignored her. Can't think of his last name. Can't think straight since I got in here. Desmond somebody. Sounds like a teabag. Lipton?"

"Twinings," Josie said.

"That's him," Tillie said with satisfaction. "That Desmond buzzard is another suspect. He didn't have anything against Clay personally—not that I could tell—but he'd love to see my restaurant ruined. He got his wish when Clay died and I was arrested. My business will go down the tubes. He'll grab my land cheap. I'll bet you once I sign those papers he'll dump my daughter."

"Your customers won't desert you," Josie said. "They love you."

"*Humph*. We'll see. Lorena reopens the day after tomorrow. I kept the restaurant closed out of respect for the dead."

And because it was a crime scene, Josie thought. "How's Lorena going to run Tillie's without you?" she asked.

"I told her to hire Jeff the ex-chef back and get one of those nanny cams. Lorena bought a teddy bear with a camera in it. She put it on the back bar near the liqueurs. If Jeff tries his light-fingered ways again, the camera will catch him in the act. This time I'll press charges.

"Henrietta, Gemma Lynn, and Desmond Twinings," Tillie said. "Those are the suspects."

Josie could think of one more: Lorena. How could she ask Tillie about her own daughter? There was no way around it. Tillie might lie, but her reaction might reveal something. Josie hesitated. Her question would hurt Tillie—but not as much as being locked up. Josie braced herself and said, "I know you don't want to think about this, but what about Lorena?"

"My daughter! You think my daughter is a cold-blooded killer?"

"I don't mean that she killed Clay on purpose," Josie said. "Maybe Lorena just wanted to make him so sick he'd never come back. Nothing personal. Or, if your restaurant closed, she'd be free. She's still a young woman. She's looking at years of hard labor."

Hard, loveless labor. Lorena would have to carry heavy trays of hot food, deal with dirty dishes and demanding customers while her looks faded and her romantic prospects dwindled.

"No!" Tillie's face seemed to collapse in on itself. "Not my girl." Her tears were a sad trickle, as if she'd already cried her eyes dry.

Josie felt like something that should be scraped off a shoe. She wanted to comfort Tillie, the way she'd hugged her mother, but she couldn't. There was a plastic barrier between them.

Tillie put her head down and wept, more tearless sobs torn out of her small body.

"My girl wouldn't hurt anyone," Tillie gasped out between sobs. "She's been helping me. She could have closed the restaurant, but she's trying her best to keep it open. Lorena is a good girl and I won't hear otherwise." A flash of anger dried up the last tears.

Tillie suddenly realized she'd been crying in public and looked around. The bleached blonde on her right was oblivious. She was talking to a weary older man. The coffee-skinned woman on Tillie's left was deep in conversation with a serious-faced light-skinned black man.

Josie finally realized Tillie's desperate circumstances. No one noticed tears in this place.

Chapter 15

Jane was waiting in Josie's living room like a queen ready to behead anyone who dared bring bad news. Stuart sat at her feet. He raised his head and gave Josie a friendly woof. Josie started to scratch the dog, but Jane interrupted.

"Well?" Jane said. "How's Tillie?" Her voice was deliberately neutral.

Josie didn't have bad news, not exactly. Still, she approached Jane cautiously. There's no reason for me to be afraid of my mother, Josie told herself, as she slowly unzipped her jacket and hung it up. Mom is in her mid-seventies. She's barely five feet tall.

None of that mattered. When it came to summoning moral authority, Jane was a giant.

"Tillie's doing as well as can be expected," Josie said.

"What's that mean?"

"She's holding together. Sort of." Josie's voice trailed off.

"She's not doing well," Jane said.

"She's doing better than I would," Josie said.

"That's not an answer." Jane was merciless.

"Mom, what do you want me to say? I think Tillie's doing well for a woman who's been thrown in jail and charged with murder. But she's not great, okay?" Josie didn't try to keep the impatience out of her voice.

Jane backed away after Josie showed a little spine. "That sounds more like it," Jane said. "Thank you."

"You're welcome," Josie said. "Can I get you some coffee, Mom?"

"No, thanks. Amelia and I made deviled egg casserole for dinner," Jane said. "We left some for you."

"Sounds good," Josie said. "I like eggs with diced ham."

"This recipe doesn't use ham," Jane said. "It uses cheese, sour cream, and mushroom soup."

"Still sounds good," Josie said. And cheap, she thought. Was Mom making a meatless meal again because she was pressed for cash?

"You can have a plate after you tell me what Tillie said." That was a command. Queen Jane was back. Josie obediently sat down and told her mother Tillie's top three suspects for Clay's murder: Desmond Twinings, Clay's lover, and his wife.

"Ted told me that Henrietta behaved badly at the hospital," Josie said. "One of his patients belongs to an ER nurse named Kate. She was working there the day Clay came in. She said Henrietta called a lawyer before her husband's body was cold and swore she'd sue Tillie."

"That's your motive right there," Jane said. "Henrietta killed her husband, blamed Tillie, and now she's going to sue her for big bucks."

"Filing a lawsuit doesn't guarantee instant money, Mom. If Tillie's case ever goes to court, a jury might find Henrietta's behavior cold for a new widow. Even the nurse was shocked by the way she acted—and nurses don't shock easily.

"Besides, there may not be much money for Henrietta. What if Tillie's customers don't return after the bad publicity?"

"I still say Henrietta did it," Jane said.

"I like Desmond Twinings, the casino developer's scout," Josie said.

"Maybe. That man sits in that restaurant all day like a ghoul," Jane said. "He creeps me out. It's like he's waiting for something to go wrong. Now Tillie's got problems—and those problems just happen to work in Desmond's favor. He can pick her carcass clean."

Josie heard the approval warming her mother's voice. Desmond made a good candidate for the killer. He was rich, strange—and best of all—from out of town.

"Clay's death will make it easier for Desmond to get her property cheap," Jane said. "He makes more sense than that crazy Henrietta."

"You got it," Josie said. "Tillie will need money for her lawyers. Even if Renzo really will work for ravioli, a trial is expensive. He'll have to hire expert witnesses and investigators. If Henrietta does file a wrongful death suit, Tillie will need another lawyer for that suit, too. Tillie may be forced to sell to Desmond Twinings for whatever he feels like giving her."

"I never did like that man," Jane said.

"You only saw him once," Josie said.

"Tillie doesn't like him, either," Jane said. "And I'm a good judge of character."

Josie nearly strangled herself trying not to answer. Jane had ignored Mrs. Mueller's faults for so many years. She never seemed to notice how their obnoxious neighbor bossed Jane around and ruled the major church committees like a dictator. I'll just start a fight if I go down that road, she thought.

Instead, Josie foolishly took a far more dangerous path. "There's a fourth suspect, though Tillie denies it. One other person wants to close the restaurant. And she'd be happy to help that developer."

Jane knew where her daughter was going. She made what sounded like a growl. Stuart raised his head, alert to the possible danger. Josie didn't detect it.

"Don't you even think it, Josie Marcus. Lorena did not kill Clay."

"She could have. Clay was annoying," Josie said.

"Lots of people are annoying. It's part of the restaurant business. If Lorena killed them all, she wouldn't have any customers."

Josie barged on ahead. "But if the restaurant was closed, Lorena wouldn't have to work there anymore. She could take the money and retire."

"What money?" Jane said. "First you tell me Tillie might be in financial trouble and won't get the money she expected for her property. Now you're saying there's enough money for Tillie and Lorena to retire—and Lorena is only in her fifties. What's she going to live on for the next thirty or forty years?"

"I was just tossing out ideas," Josie said.

"Well, toss that one back," Jane said. Her chin came down like a guillotine, cutting off that thought. "If Lorena is the killer, you might as well shoot poor Tillie now. That girl is all she has in the world."

Jane's voice wobbled. Was her mother going to cry? Jane wasn't a tearful type, but her friend's arrest had left her shaken. Josie didn't want to weather another tear storm today.

"I didn't say Lorena did it, Mom. I was just speculating."

"Well, speculate someplace else. You're supposed to help my friend, not make things worse."

"I thought we wanted to know the truth," Josie said.

"The right truth," Jane said. "The truth that will get Tillie out of jail, not make her life worse." Stuart Little thumped his tail. Josie still wasn't going to venture too close.

"Mom, I hope someone horrible killed Clay, like Desmond or Henrietta. But it doesn't always work that way."

"I understand that. But don't you go accusing her daughter, Josie. Tillie wouldn't raise a murderer any more than I would. I've known Lorena since she was a baby. She was always a good girl. She helped out at the restaurant on the weekends from the time she was thirteen. She went to work there after graduation."

"And she's been chained to the place ever since," Josie said.

"She's not chained. She's a loyal daughter."

"While we're talking about daughters," Josie said. "Where is mine?"

"In her room, doing her homework."

Josie heard a giggle from down the hall. "She usually doesn't find her homework so entertaining."

"Go check on Amelia, then get your dinner before it's completely dried out," Jane said.

Josie tiptoed down the hall and peeked into the room. Amelia was waving a red ribbon at Harry. The cat tried to catch it, but it remained just out of his reach. He jumped at the ribbon and flopped over on his back, then whipped around and caught his own tail. Amelia laughed out loud.

"That doesn't look like homework," Josie said.

"My homework is done," Amelia said. "Harry and I were taking a break." Josie didn't need to check her daughter's work. Amelia was good about doing her homework. Josie trusted her on that and Amelia had never disappointed her.

"Grandma showed me how to make deviled egg casserole, Mom. It's gross. We've got to start cooking meat again. Try it," Amelia said. "Looks like barf."

"Please, Amelia, don't. I'll see what I can do to help Grandma," Josie said.

Josie's stomach lurched when she saw the remains of the casserole. Amelia's description was way too accurate. She spooned out one egg, popped it into the microwave, then poured herself a soda and brought her meal back in the living room. The creamy casserole tasted bland and heavy.

"What do you think?" Jane asked.

"It's different," Josie said. Usually Jane was better at choosing new recipes.

"Our girl has a natural talent," Jane said.

"Yes, she does," Josie said. "Amelia said you're concentrating on low-cost meals. Budgeting is always a good idea, but those cooking lessons are expensive, Mom. I don't want to take advantage of you. May I buy the food for the lessons?"

"You think I can't afford a couple of eggs?" Jane was annoyed. More than annoyed. She was furious.

"No, no, Mom. I was just offering."

"I don't want your money," Jane said. "I'm perfectly capable of handling my own finances. I'm teaching my granddaughter about bargains. She's hanging around with rich kids at that fancy school. She'll never learn anything practical there. And now, if you don't mind, it's time for me to go to bed. Come along, Stuart."

Jane paraded out through the kitchen.

"Thanks, Mom, for watching Amelia," Josie said.

Jane shut the back door a little too hard.

Chapter 16

"Josie, why are you picking at your brain?" Ted asked.

Josie stared glumly at the sandwich on the thick white china plate. In the dim light at Ferguson's Pub, she could see it all too clearly.

"It's hard to work up an appetite for a deep fat–fried cow brain," she said. She'd spent last night dreading this moment.

Josie managed a slipshod smile and turned her eyes to Ted. Even in the bar's dark comfort, he seemed to glow. Maybe it was the beer sign behind him. No, Ted was special. When he loped into the bar, women watched him. Even the older ones seemed soft-eyed and dreamy. Ted had pulled out a chair for Josie. At the next table, the woman with the crinkly silver hair and worn face nodded approval. She knew most men didn't do that anymore. Josie flushed at the attention. Mystery shoppers were supposed to be anonymous.

They'd ordered two brain sandwiches with fries and beer. The waitress brought their order way too fast. Now Josie was about to bite into this nightmare on a plate.

"Put some ketchup on it like I did," Ted said.

She eyed his ketchup-slathered entrée. "That looks like an autopsy on rye."

"Wrong," Ted said, and kissed her cheek. "That looks like heaven. Tastes like it, too. Ferguson's serves some of the best brains in St. Louis. I've been eating them since I was a kid."

Josie concentrated on her sandwich, as if she could magically transform it into an everyday hamburger. Despite her intense gaze, it didn't change.

"I can see the furrows in that brain," she said. "I can practically hear it thinking."

"You have an incredible imagination," Ted said. "It's one reason why I love you. Trust me. That is a good sandwich. I was right about the pig ear sandwich. You liked it, didn't you?" He used the coaxing tone that parents reserve for children who won't eat their peas.

"Yes," Josie said. The pig ear sandwich had been good.

But her stomach shouldn't have to jump hurdles for her job. Now it leaped like a startled trout when she contemplated the brain on bread.

"You'll like this sandwich, too," Ted said.

Josie wished she had his certainty. She wanted to believe him.

"Brains are a rare delicacy," he said.

"This doesn't look like one," Josie said.

"It is," Ted insisted. "Done right, brains are light and fluffy. They're a dying art."

"I can see why." The sandwich seemed to be getting bigger and greasier on her plate.

"Then quit staring and start eating," Ted said. "You don't want a cold brain. They're much better warm."

Josie thought she might gag.

Ted continued his relentless cheerleading. "You're a professional, Josie. This is an important test. You aren't eating that brain for personal enjoyment."

"That's for sure," Josie said.

"Don't interrupt," Ted said. "You're doing this for St. Louis. Only a few places in the country still serve brain sandwiches. Thanks to you, gourmets will make pilgrimages to our city for the chance to eat one of these. If you like it, of course."

The sandwich seemed to pulse on the plate. "I can't get past the idea of eating a cow brain," Josie said.

"Then don't think about it," he said. "Take a sip of beer for courage."

Josie obeyed. The beer was cold, clean, and reassuring.

"And pick up your sandwich."

She did. It felt warm and ordinary. That was good. She saw a dill pickle peeking out shyly from under the slice of bread. A friendly, familiar pickle.

"Close your eyes," Ted said.

Josie shut her eyes and thought of a hamburger. An ordinary gray burger on a pillow bun. One she could eat and forget.

"Take a bite—now!" Ted said.

Josie bit down, then chewed tentatively. Not bad. She kept chewing. Good breading. Not too heavy. Now she could taste the sandwich's full flavor. It was a pleasant surprise.

"It's a little like very good liver, but not so heavy. It's not squishy like I expected," she said. "It's sort of like a deep-fried cloud."

Ted smiled encouragement. "That's right."

Josie took another bite. "I like it."

Ted smiled. "What did I say? There's nothing quite like it. You don't often get food this quality in bars. Brain sandwiches are the saloon soufflé. A French chef would envy their texture." He took another bite of his own sandwich.

"Ferguson's is definitely an old city saloon," Josie said. She liked the sound of that old-fashioned word, saloon.

"A great old South St. Louis saloon," Ted said. "Like brain sandwiches, old-school city bars are disappearing. At Ferguson's, you can get a beer and talk with your friends. It wasn't designed by some decorator to look old. This is the real thing. No ferns or fake old-timey touches."

Two more bites and Josie had finished the sandwich and turned to munching her crisp brown fries. Ted had talked her through this career crisis. The brain sandwich turned out to be tasty, even enjoyable.

"I spent more time dreading that sandwich than eating it," she said. "I can give it high marks in my report."

"I didn't want to tell you before you ate your brain—" Ted said.

Josie interrupted him. "There's no way to talk about this without sounding like a horror movie, is there?"

"Nope. It's hopeless. Might as well savor the jokes. Anyway, I waited until you finished your sandwich to give you the gory details. You're lucky you got a good brain sandwich. If you ever eat a bad one, you'll never forget it. Brains are difficult to prepare. First, you have to remove the outer membrane and soak the brains in salt water to get out the blood, or they'll taste bitter."

Josie put her hands over her ears. "Stop! Too much information. I don't want that in my brain. I mean, my mind."

"I was trying to explain the secret to good brains," Ted said. "It's the preparation. Brains are time-consuming and difficult. That's why so many of the city's great brain sandwich restaurants are gone."

"I thought the fear of mad cow disease did them in," Josie said.

"Nope, they started disappearing before that," Ted said. "Also, fried brains are not health food. They're loaded with cholesterol. I read somewhere that there are three thousand milligrams of cholesterol in one sandwich. That's practically a year's supply on a plate, not counting the fries and beer."

Ted finished the last of his sandwich and said, "Want anything else? Maybe some fried chicken? Ferguson's has good chicken."

"No, thanks," Josie said. "I'll sit here and sip my beer before I pick up Amelia at school."

Ted signaled the waitress and ordered another draft. "How is your mom? I didn't get a chance to ask about her since I saw on TV that her friend Tillie was arrested for first-degree murder. I couldn't believe they had two big cops escorting her. That poor little lady. I imagine your mother is upset about her friend's arrest."

"Upset?" Josie said. "She's a wreck. I was upstairs in her kitchen when Tillie's story came on the news. She had to watch her lifelong friend do the perp walk in a powder blue pantsuit. I thought Mom would pass out. I brought her toast and tea and she slept for the rest of the day. Thank goodness she has Stuart Little. She hugged that dog like a teddy bear.

"This morning, Mom seemed better. She walked the dog, then stopped by on her way upstairs and made me promise again that I'd help find Clay's real killer."

"How are you going to do that?" Ted asked.

"I've already started. I talked to Tillie in jail last night. Tillie gave me the names of three suspects—Desmond the developer, Henrietta, and Gemma Lynn."

"Gemma's the girlfriend, right? Why would she kill Clay?"

"Tillie says they argued at the bar because Ted wouldn't marry Gemma. She heard the fights. I have my own suspect—Tillie's daughter. Lorena wants out of that restaurant bad."

"Bad enough to kill?" Ted asked.

"I think she's desperate to get away from there. Lorena has deluded herself that Desmond will marry her. She's an attractive woman, but guys like Desmond are interested in young honeys.

"Mom made the arrangements through the lawyer so I could see Tillie last night. She really wanted to go with me. She thought her old friend would feel more comfortable if she was there."

"Did you think Jane could have helped?"

"I don't know," Josie said. "Maybe. No, not really. I could have never asked about Lorena if Mom was there. She kind of butts in and takes over."

Josie had left her mother wide-open for Ted to bash, but he ignored the opportunity. Instead he took her slightly greasy hand and squeezed it. His eyes were amber brown. He locked his gaze on hers.

"Whatever you need, you tell me and I'll give it to you: You want a bodyguard, I'll go with you as your muscle. You want support, I'm there. You want to talk, I'll listen. You want money, I'll take out a loan. Just tell me what you need."

"Thanks, Ted. Money doesn't seem to be the problem right now."

"You don't have to be alone anymore," Ted said. "You have me and I love you."

Ted said everything she wanted to hear in that dark old saloon under the watchful eyes of the beer-drinking neighborhood women.

"I'd kiss you," Josie said. "But I don't want a man with brains on his lips."

Chapter 17

"Alyce, want to go mystery-shopping with me today?" Josie asked. It was 9:15 the next morning. She had calculated the timing of this call, waiting until after Alyce's husband had left for his office and Justin's nanny had arrived at the house.

"Uh," Alyce said.

Her friend was stalling, looking for a polite way to refuse. "I wouldn't blame you if you said no. Not after what happened at Tillie's," Josie said.

"It's not me; it's Jake," Alyce said.

"He was worried about you?"

"My husband wasn't happy that his dinner was late," Alyce said.

Typical, Josie thought. Jake was spoiled. Alyce catered to her husband—literally. He provided Alyce with the life she wanted, but he expected a gourmet dinner waiting when he came home. Her committees and dinner parties had to advance his career.

"I feel bad about our misbegotten lunch at Tillie's," Josie said.

"That wasn't your fault," Alyce said. "It was more interesting than my other alternative, the subdivision landscaping committee meeting. But Jake wasn't happy with a salad and reheated lasagna."

Did Jake ever hear of pizza delivery? Josie thought. "I promise no dead bodies today," she said. "I need to mystery-shop chocolate for TAG Tours."

"What kind of chocolate?"

Ah. Alyce couldn't resist chocolate. "The good kind," Josie said. "Kakao has a store in Maplewood. We're supposed to try the sea-salt caramels made with cream, amber honey, and Tahitian vanilla beans. They're dipped in semisweet chocolate and then—"

Alyce interrupted. "Josie, you wouldn't know a Tahitian vanilla bean from a common Madagascar bean. What are you reading?"

"The description TAG sent me, which was probably ripped off Kakao's Web site. It says the caramels are 'finished with a few grains of sea salt' and 'also available with toasted Missouri pecans.' "

"Guess we'll have to try both kinds," Alyce said. "I'm partial to pecans, but I can be persuaded to change my mind."

"You'll have to eat a marshmallow pie, too," Josie said.

"I'll make the sacrifice," Alyce said. "Is Kakao on Manchester Road?"

"Right in our little shopping district," Josie said.

"Near Vom Fass?"

"The store that sells the fancy oil? It's a couple doors away."

"Good," Alyce said. "I want to get some pistachio oil. My special dinner for Jake tonight is pan-seared wild salmon with pistachio oil and tarragon. I wanted to make up for tossing something together when I came home from Tillie's. I'll pick you up in forty minutes."

Josie threw in a load of laundry and vacuumed the

living room while she thought about her conversation with Alyce. Was her friend really making Jake a special dinner?

Josie knew better than to criticize her friend's husband. She didn't have to live with Jake—Alyce did and she loved him. She loved her life as a full-time homemaker and happily devoted her considerable talents to advancing her husband's career. She seemed content.

Jake wasn't concerned that his wife might have been frightened or tired after the police questioned her. He wasn't worried that she'd seen a man clutch his throat and collapse. Jake was concerned about himself.

Was marriage worth it if a woman was a housekeeper with benefits? Josie attacked a clump of cat hair on the carpet, running the roaring machine over the area long after the cat hair disappeared. She turned off the vacuum, afraid she might suck the life out of her tired carpet, and put the machine away. She decided to use that excess energy on her bathroom.

Josie scrubbed her claw-foot tub. The tub was her refuge. She loved to fill it with bubble bath and light scented candles for a half-hour vacation. She rubbed at a persistent ring with cleanser and a sponge.

How could Jake expect a home-cooked meal when he came home that evening, like some midcentury adman? Josie knew she'd rather be a single mother than married to a man like that.

Not my husband, not my life, not my business, she reminded herself. In the past, that's how she'd shrugged off Jake's imperfections. Now that Josie was seriously in love with Ted, Alyce's stories made her uneasy. What if Ted asked her to marry him? Would walking down the aisle turn her considerate lover into a demanding spouse?

He's hardly going to marry you for your cooking skills, Josie thought. He's a better cook than you are.

Better wait till Ted pops the question before you borrow trouble. She gave the bathtub another vigorous scrub and then a rinse. Clean at last.

She changed into fresh jeans and a button-down blue shirt, then checked her hair and makeup in the bathroom mirror. Good to go.

She heard Alyce tap the horn. Josie grabbed her jacket and ran out into the pale golden sun. The warm day felt so good she nearly danced down the sidewalk to Alyce's shining black Escalade.

"You look like a teenager running to my SUV," Alyce said.

"I feel like one. I have to enjoy the sunshine before winter hits," Josie said, as she climbed inside.

"Let's walk to the shopping district," Alyce said. "We shouldn't waste a day this perfect."

The two women strolled through a shower of red and gold leaves. Many of the trees were more than a century old. Maplewood houses had wide porches and big windows. They were generous homes, built when the city's expectations were just as expansive.

After three blocks of crunching through leafy confetti, they were on Manchester. One side was lined with two-story buildings brightened by huge plate-glass windows. The red-brick shops were time-mellowed and their glass sparkled.

"You're lucky to have a real shopping district instead of a boring mall," Alyce said. "Each store is different." She studied an outfit in the window of Femme, a clothing shop with giant pink polka dots on the glass. "How do you think that blue sweater would look on me?"

"Blue is your color," Josie said.

"Maybe I'll buy it when I lose twenty pounds."

Josie knew that day would never come. Alyce would never have a fashionable stick figure. She also knew there was no point in giving her friend a body-image lecture. Instead, she pointed to the shop next door. "We're here. This is Kakao."

They stood in the doorway and inhaled. "Chocolate, my favorite perfume," Alyce said.

The shop was tall, long, and filled with light. A brightly-painted red tree hung with dark cocoa pods spread across the walls. But the chocolates, displayed in little baskets like works of art, captured their attention.

"Dragées!" Alyce said. She noticed Josie's blank look and said, "Almonds toasted in sugar and dredged in chocolate. I have to get those. Almonds are good for you."

"A source of protein," Josie deadpanned. "And chocolate is good for your heart."

"Definitely a health food. And a vegetable."

"The only vegetable I truly like," Josie said. "I'll get some of those for Mom and Amelia, too. What about this chili pepper chocolate?"

"Don't even say the words 'chili pepper,' " Alyce said. "Not after that lunch at Tillie's."

"Sorry," Josie said. "I've been snorting too much chocolate."

"I want that coffee bark covered with locally roasted coffee," Alyce said. "Locavores are good for the environment."

"What's a locavore?" Josie asked.

"People who eat locally grown food," Alyce said.

"Not only are we eating locally, we'll walk off the calories locally."

"I could walk all the way back to Wood Winds and I wouldn't be a pound thinner," Alyce said. "But I'll be happier if I eat chocolate."

"That's the spirit," Josie said. "Don't forget the sea salt caramels and the marshmallow pies."

"With Missouri pecans," Alyce said. "Dr. Oz says nuts are good. I love wicked virtue."

After their chocolate binge, they stopped at Vom Fass for Alyce's pistachio oil. She treated herself to date oil, orange oil, and two olive oils from Greece.

"Now we should go back," Alyce said. "These packages are heavy."

"Better lighten the load by eating the caramels and the marshmallow pies," Josie said.

They set their packages down at a bus bench, unwrapped the sea salt caramels, and popped them into their mouths.

Josie craned her neck to examine the clear blue sky.

"What are you doing?" Alyce asked.

"Checking for clouds," Josie said. "I don't want to get hit by a lightning bolt when I say this caramel is a religious experience. Marshmallow pies next and then my work is done."

"These sure don't taste like the ones I had as kid," Alyce said. "The marshmallow is sandwiched between dark chocolate."

"I may collapse in a chocolate swoon," Josie said.

"I assume Kakao passed the TAG Tour test," Alyce said. She and Josie divided the packages and continued their trek back.

"The walk home seems faster," Josie said. "Must be the sugar high."

"We made it to my car before the chocolate melted," Alyce said.

"Or we ate it all," Josie said. "Now I need a favor. Will you go with me to Gemma's Junktique? She runs a sort of antique and junk shop not too far from Tillie's."

"She's Clay's girlfriend, right? The wide-bottomed brunette? Not that I should talk."

"That's her," Josie said. "Tillie thinks Gemma could have killed Clay."

Alyce checked her watch. "We have time, but I'm not parking on another deserted street. It was too creepy last time."

"We'll park in front of the store. I promise, if you don't feel safe, we'll turn around and go back. I'll take my car and you can follow, so you can leave straight for home. I'll put your chocolate in a cooler so it won't melt."

"Your mother really wants you to save her friend Tillie, doesn't she?" Alyce said.

"Mom blackmailed me into it," Josie said. "There's a price for that free babysitting. I want to see Gemma in her natural habitat and find out if she's really grieving over her loss.

"At the bar, she was all lovey-dovey with Clay. I wonder if she loved him to death."

Chapter 18

Gemma's Junktique was aptly named. The dusty display window showcased lackluster cut glass, stained quilts, and unloved children's toys.

Gemma Lynn Rae perched like a crow behind the counter. She wore full modern mourning: black T-shirt and jeans and a veil of lank dark hair. A box of tissues waited like a faithful pet to comfort her. The counter's shelves were cluttered with brassy costume jewelry, some of it missing stones.

"May I help you?" Gemma Lynn asked, her voice as flat and dull as the display window.

"I want to look at your tin advertising signs," Josie said.

"I want to see your china," Alyce said.

"The china is over there," Gemma Lynn said, waving her hand to the left. Her arm dropped as if the movement exhausted her.

"The tin signs are propped against that wall," she told Josie, waving in the other direction. Gemma Lynn picked up a fat paperback, exhausted by her labors.

Alyce seemed to float toward the shelves like the dust motes in the air. Josie moved carefully through the clutter, banging her hip on a wooden plant stand decorated with water rings. She nearly upset a lumpy glass vase, the kind that florists gave away. Gemma had priced it at ten dollars.

Josie edged her way past a brass bed draped in faded pink chenille and a rusty velvet Victorian settee. The settee, all knobs and brass nails, looked too uncomfortable for a tryst. Josie pitied the long-gone bottoms condemned to pass time on that torture device. The brass bed looked fairly comfortable. She tried not to imagine Clay and Gemma Lynn bouncing on it.

The stack of tin signs leaned against the wall behind the bed. They were either genuinely weathered or artfully reproduced. Josie was captivated by the bright red sign screaming for King Edward Cigars. She also liked the delicately drawn 1920s Clown Cigarettes ad, but thought the name had too many possibilities for parody. She could almost hear detractors saying: "Smoke like a Clown" or "Only Clowns smoke our tobacco."

The King Edward Cigars sign was big enough for a barn. It would never fit in her flat. The Clown sign cost sixty dollars. Both out of my price range, Josie thought. Now that I've used my excuse to be in here, I should talk to Gemma.

She picked her way back to the counter without breaking any merchandise.

"Find anything?" Gemma Lynn asked from behind her paperback, and turned the page. Josie thought the woman had raised indifference to an art form, and she'd encountered masters as a mystery shopper.

"Your prices for those signs are a little higher than I can pay," Josie said.

"Hm." Gemma Lynn yawned. She didn't bother hiding it. She didn't stop reading, either.

"I was at Tillie's the day your friend Clay took sick," Josie said.

Now Gemma Lynn looked stricken. "He wasn't sick," she said. "He was murdered. And he wasn't my friend. He was my fiancé. We were going to be married." Her grief changed to anger and that gave her energy. She brushed her limp hair out of her face and sat up straighter.

Before Josie asked the next question, she looked for Alyce. There she was, a sunny spot of blond hair near a crooked red ginger jar lamp. Alyce was examining the bottom of a teacup. Josie caught her friend's eye and nodded slightly. Gemma was already angry. If she turned threatening, Josie could grab Alyce and bolt for the door.

Josie unleashed her question: "Did his wife know you wanted to marry Clay?"

"She didn't love him," Gemma Lynn said.

That's not an answer, Josie thought.

"She's playing the grieving widow now," Gemma said, "but Henrietta was cheating on him and Clay knew it."

"Who was the guy?" Josie asked.

"Clay never found out, but he saw the signs. Henrietta stopped complaining that he wasn't looking for a job—and she used to nag him about that constantly. She even called Clay a mooch."

"No!" Josie said. Alyce coughed delicately. Oops, Josie thought. I should be careful not to overact.

"Clay wanted to work," Gemma said, "but he couldn't find a company that appreciated his talents."

"I'm sure," Josie said, hoping she sounded sympathetic.

"Henrietta started going into work early and leaving late," Gemma Lynn said, "but there was never any overtime on her paycheck. Clay found matches from a hotel by the airport. That made him more curious. He searched her purse while she was asleep. He found her cell phone, but he didn't see any numbers that weren't family or business. Clay thought she had another cell phone hidden somewhere, but he never found it.

"Henrietta didn't love him, but she wouldn't let him go. It wasn't fair. No one loved Clay like I did, and now he's gone." She erupted in a gusher of tears.

"I'm sorry," Josie said. "I didn't mean to upset you."

That was exactly what Josie had wanted. She still couldn't tell if Gemma Lynn was a good actress or a grieving lover.

"I can't go to the funeral," Gemma Lynn wailed. She grabbed a fistful of tissues and dabbed at her tear-reddened eyes. "His wife had the nerve to call me."

And you had the nerve to sleep with her husband, Josie thought.

"Henrietta said she'll have me escorted out if I show up at Dell-Merriam tonight."

"That's the funeral home on Manchester?" Josie asked.

"Yes." More crying; then her voice was drowned in tears. "The funeral mass is at St. Christopher's tomorrow. I can't even tell my Clay good-bye."

"Oh, Gemma, that's so sad," Josie said. "Do you think his wife killed him?"

Gemma's eyes were hard, flat granite gravestones. "I hate that bitch, but she didn't kill Clay. Tillie did. I heard her say so. The whole restaurant heard her. She wanted him gone for good and now he is. I'm going to say that at her trial, too."

"You're testifying against Tillie?" Josie asked.

"The prosecuting attorney said the jury will love me," Gemma said. "Henrietta can't stop me, either." Gemma spoke like a woman with a mission. "I'm going to tell everyone that Clay loved me. It will be part of the court record. Then I'm going to get Tillie. I owe my Clay Baby."

Clay Baby? The dead tomcat didn't deserve that indignity, Josie thought.

"When I finish testifying, they're going to lock up that old lady and throw away the key. She doesn't have many years left. She'll die in jail. She deserves it. She killed the only man I ever loved."

Gemma put her head on the counter, as if her grief were too heavy to bear. Great gasping sobs were torn from her chest. Josie looked around helplessly for Alyce. She wanted to escape Gemma's raw grief—or histrionics. Fortunately, Alyce glided toward them holding a white teapot.

"Pretty teapot," Josie said.

"It's a coffeepot," Alyce said. "Rose Point pattern by Pope Gosser. See the raised white roses around the rim?"

Gemma sat up and mopped her eyes, her sorrow soothed by the prospect of a sale. "If you like flowered coffeepots, I have a Royal Worcester on the same shelf. It's the white pot with the blue roses."

"I saw that," Alyce said. "It's nice, but this one matches my china pattern."

Alyce had so many sets of china, Josie couldn't keep track of them. Alyce's table settings were thoughtful compositions, from the flowers to the forks. Josie turned away from the two women to poke through a bin of framed prints near the counter so she could watch them in a splotched mirror.

"Guess you want the less expensive coffeepot," Gemma said.

Nice move, Gemma, Josie thought. You've insulted a paying customer. People aren't trampling one another to buy your junktique.

"I'm looking for the gravy boat in the same pattern," Alyce said. "Do you have it, by any chance?"

"I might," Gemma said. "I still have to unpack another crate of china. That coffeepot will be ten dollars."

"I have a twenty," Alyce said.

Gemma opened her cash register. "I don't have change," she said. "And I don't take credit cards."

"Wait a minute." Alyce began counting out ones. "That's four dollars. And here's a five."

Josie threw a dollar on top of the pile. "That should do it."

"Thanks," Alyce said.

Gemma wrapped up the coffeepot, while Josie thumbed through the framed art. One painting looked like it had been rescued from the rubbish. Another was covered with diseased globs of orange and yellow oil. Josie thought it might be a paint-by-numbers autumn woods. Most of the artwork were faded prints of masterpieces.

One gold frame looked less shabby than the others. Josie pulled a cross-stitch sampler out of the bin. The white linen had aged to a gentle brown. The thread colors had faded to warm gold, soft blues, and pale pinks. The impossibly tiny stitches spelled out the motto FRIENDSHIP, LOVE & TRUTH surrounded by roses. Thornless roses.

"This is lovely," Josie said.

Gemma was wrapping Alyce's coffeepot in white paper. "That's fifty bucks," she said.

Josie put it back in the bin. She appreciated all three of those values, but she didn't have the money.

"I can buy it for you," Alyce said, "if Gemma will take a check."

"Thanks, Alyce, but I'll come back when I get paid."

"You sure you want to wait? It won't be here forever," Gemma said.

The thick layer of dust on the frame said that wasn't true.

"Here's my name and phone number if you decide to lower the price." Josie scribbled the information on a piece of notepaper.

"I won't change," Gemma Lynn said. "My prices are the result of careful research."

"Josie, I need to get home," Alyce said. "We'd better go." She practically dragged Josie out the door to her Escalade.

When they were away from the store Josie asked, "What's wrong?"

"Carefully researched prices, my eye," Alyce said. "That Rose Point coffeepot retails for more than a hundred dollars. Gemma gave it away. She marked that Royal Worcester coffeepot fifty bucks. I could buy it online for less than thirty."

"She was trying to sell a free florist's vase for ten dollars," Josie said. "I have a dozen of those stashed under my sink."

"Everyone does," Alyce said.

"No wonder Gemma's shop is failing. She hasn't a clue what she's selling," Josie said.

"It's one o'clock, Josie. We've had a good day's shopping, but now I need to go home."

"I'll swing by my house, then pick up Amelia," Josie said. "Thanks for coming with me."

"Sorry the visit was such a waste for you," Alyce said. She patted her prize coffeepot.

"It wasn't," Josie said. "I got something valuable from Gemma."

"What's that?"

"Why would Henrietta hang on to a husband she didn't want or love? If I can find the answer, I can solve Clay's murder."

Chapter 19

Something was wrong with Jane. Josie knew it. She remembered how her mother had behaved in the grip of her shopping addiction: angry, evasive, secretive. The signs had been there, but Josie hadn't recognized them. She hadn't noticed that Jane was neglecting her home. Her house-proud mother hadn't replaced a torn lampshade. Her living room was draped in cobwebs and the end tables were dull with dust.

As her addiction consumed her, Jane had quit seeing her friends. She'd holed up in front of her television, mindlessly ordering more things she didn't need. One day Josie had opened Jane's linen closet and been buried in an avalanche of boxes. Steak knives, Snuggies, and other "as seen on TV" temptations poured out. Jane had bought them all and needed none of them.

Josie had to know if her mother's problem had returned. *I can't help Tillie if I'm worried about my mother,* she told herself. She was manufacturing an excuse to invade her mother's privacy—a lame excuse, as Amelia would say.

Jane had an emergency appointment with her hairdresser at one o'clock to repair her fractured hairdo. It was a good sign that Jane still cared about her appearance. Josie had an hour before she had to pick up Amelia. Enough time to search Jane's flat.

I'm doing this to help my mother, she told herself. She repeated that sentence out loud. She still wasn't convinced, but she was going to do it anyway.

She parked her car in front of the Phelan Street flat, careful that the Honda's bumper did not hang over into Mrs. Mueller's territory. Maplewoodians did not own the parking spaces in front of their houses, but Mrs. Mueller lived by her own rules. She chased off cars that tried to park at her curb. Heaven help anyone whose tires touched her lawn.

Last winter, Jane had had a falling out with their prickly next-door neighbor. The two women had made up. Sort of. Now their friendship limped along. Josie was proud of her mother for standing up to the bossy old snoop. She thought Jane had been under Mrs. M's thumb for too long.

Josie locked her car and hurried up the front walk. She was relieved to find the porch empty. When her mother's addiction was at its worst, towers of boxes had turned their porch into a cardboard maze.

She climbed the front stairs to her mother's flat and knocked loudly. "Mom!" she called. "Are you home?"

"Woof!" Stuart Little answered through the door. She could hear his nails scrabbling on the kitchen floor as he ran to the front room.

Josie knocked again, just to be sure. Then she unlocked the door. The lively shih tzu was in the living room, wiggling and wagging in a frenzy of delight. She took time to scratch his ears. He leaned against her, asking for more scratches.

"Sorry, little guy," she said. "I have to work."

She started in the most obvious spot—the closets.

Josie slid open her mother's bedroom closet and was greeted with a cloud of Estée Lauder and the comforting sight of her mother's clothes in plastic. Even her shoes were in plastic boxes. The linen closet was piled with neatly stacked towels and freshly laundered sheets. First test passed. Josie felt better.

The kitchen was so clean it gleamed. Then she noticed Jane's deep blue oven mitts hung on a hook by the stove. They were burnt and losing their protective covering. Troubling. Her mother was careful about her kitchen.

Jane's fridge usually overflowed with food. Now it was almost bare. Josie saw half a carton of eggs, a small chunk of margarine, two slices of wheat bread, and an open can of dog food. That was it.

Now Josie was worried. Jane's fridge should be bursting with meat, cheese, and produce.

The Formica kitchen counter shone. *CSI* wouldn't find a fingerprint on the four cobalt blue canisters. Josie lifted the lid on the sugar canister and saw less than a cup of white sugar. The largest canister held a dusting of flour. The third had a handful of egg noodles. Barely a quarter cup of brown sugar was in the fourth.

Jane wasn't restocking her staples.

Stuart yapped, dropped a yellow squeaky toy at Josie's feet, and wagged his tail. She tossed it into the living room. The shih tzu trotted after it. Josie tried to follow and nearly tripped over the throw rug Jane used to protect the carpeting at the kitchen threshold. She lifted the rug. It had lost its rubber backing. More bad news.

Like many older women, Jane feared falls. So why did she have a dangerously worn rug?

Oh, Mom, Josie thought. Is it worth breaking your hip to save a little wear on your wall-to-wall carpet? She knew the answer: Jane's generation protected their precious carpet at all costs.

Jane's pale green living-room was model-home neat. The *TV Guide* was set precisely on the polished end table, with the clicker laid on top. She could see the vacuum cleaner tracks on that precious carpet.

Josie checked her watch. Forty minutes before she had to get Amelia. She patted Stuart good-bye, closed and locked Jane's door, and ran down the front stairs.

Josie picked her mail out of the box by her door; then she saw her mother's mailbox was stuffed with envelopes. She could see an electric bill, a phone bill, and two letters from charities: Our Lady of the Sheets and the Sisters of Divine Poverty.

Josie had never heard of either, but she wasn't devout like her mother. She was almost inside her flat when one of the names hit her: Our Lady of the Sheets? What kind of religious group was that? Was it a charity? An order of sisters?

Josie went back out and filched the two religious letters from her mother's mailbox. She checked their return addresses. Both were post office boxes in Kansas City. She put on the kettle and found her sharpest knife. When the water was boiling, Josie held the letter from Our Lady of the Sheets over the steam, careful not to burn her fingertips. The flap started puckering and she used the knife to slowly ease the envelope open.

Damn! She'd ripped the flap. That didn't happen in the movies. Now there was no way Josie could hide that she'd steamed open her mother's mail. She tore open the letter.

Our Lady of the Sheets used thick, expensive stationary. The message was typed over a color picture of the Virgin Mary listening to an angelic choir, her blue eyes aimed toward her son in heaven.

"Thank you for your monthly donation of $250 to Our Lady of the Sheets," the letter began. "Without your generosity, we could not continue to provide sheet music to poor Catholic churches in Africa.

"Thanks to you, native people are able to lift their voices in praise to Our Savior and His Mother. God will continue to bestow his riches on those who have shown generosity to the least of our brothers and sisters.

"Enclosed please find the envelope for next month's donation."

Sheet music for poor Africans? Could they even read music? That didn't sound right. And which part of Africa?

Josie didn't bother steaming open the second letter from the Sisters of Divine Poverty. She ripped the envelope. These good sisters did not waste money on four-color stationary. Their simple black letterhead showed a cross lassoed by a rosary. The sisters were equally grateful for Mrs. Jane Marcus's donation of $250 a month. They also thoughtfully included next month's donation envelope.

Jane was sending five hundred dollars a month to charities, when she lived on a small bank pension and Social Security? No wonder she was scrounging for spare change in the sofa cushions.

It is Jane's money, Josie told herself. If Mom wants to spend it on church charities, that's her business.

But were they bogus charities? Our Lady of the Sheets sounded like a joke. Josie carried the letters into her home. As she fired up her computer, she heard her cell phone ring. Josie ran back to the living room and searched in her purse for her phone. It was Ted.

"Josie," he said. "I've had a heckuva day. I need to see you."

"What happened, Ted? Did you have to put down a pet?" Ted knew this could be the kindest way to care for a suffering animal who could not recover, but it left him feeling low.

"Not today. I was wounded at work. I wrestled a kitten this afternoon. The furball nearly won."

Josie giggled.

"You won't think it's funny when you see me," he said. "I look like I was attacked by a barbed-wire fence. Can we go out to dinner tonight or do you have other plans?"

"I have other plans," Josie said. "I'm seeing another man."

There was a long pause. "So you don't want to see me?"

She shouldn't have teased Ted, not after he'd had a rough day. "He's a dead man, Ted. I'm going to Clay Oreck's visitation this evening. Maybe I can learn something that will help Tillie."

"I'll go with you," Ted said.

"No, you turn too many heads," Josie said. "I need to slip in, be invisible, listen, and leave."

"You? Invisible?" Ted said. "You're too beautiful. Anyone with a pulse will see you. How about after the visitation? A client brought me a gooey butter cake from Gooey Louie. Isn't that on your TAG Tour list?"

"You have a terrific memory," Josie said.

"I don't forget gooey butter cake. My place or yours?"

Yours, Josie thought. I want to eat gooey butter cake naked in bed. I want to have mad, passionate sex. I want—

Amelia's cat bumped Josie with his forehead and brought her back to responsible motherhood. "My place. We'll invite Mom and Amelia. I'll make the coffee and you bring the cake. Eight thirty work for you?"

Gooey butter cake with two chaperones, Josie

thought. That should be safe. She checked her watch. She'd have to leave shortly for Amelia's school, but she had time to Google those two charities. She tried Our Lady of the Sheets and got this message: "Are you sure you don't mean Our Lady of the Streets?"

Josie thought the name was another joke until she saw the statues and paintings devoted to that aspect of the Virgin Mary.

She searched for Our Lady of the Sheets several different ways without success. She found no results for the Sisters of Divine Poverty. She couldn't find either charity. Josie tore up the letters and buried them in her trash.

Maybe I should pray to Saint Jude, the patron saint of lost causes, Josie thought. Or maybe Mom is being scammed.

Chapter 20

Clay Oreck died young, at thirty-two. That guaranteed a big turnout at his wake. Clay was no child, but the death of one of their own was still a novelty for most people his age. His sensational exit meant his funeral would include curiosity seekers as well as close friends.

Josie felt lucky to find a parking spot in the acres of blacktop at the Dell-Merriam funeral home.

She watched the mourners enter in clots of three and four. She attached herself to a trio of women in dark pantsuits. They didn't notice her as they gossiped about the victim. Josie assumed they were related. They had the same well-shaped noses and full lips, nut-brown hair, and tanned skin. They looked like stair steps. Josie nicknamed them the Step Sisters.

"I hear he was poisoned," said the tallest sister, Step One, lowering her voice to a confidential whisper.

"I'm not surprised," said Step Two.

"He had it coming," said Step Three. "I'm surprised Henrietta put up with him as long as she did. Clay had a good job when they were first married, but his wandering eye got him in trouble. You know why Clay was fired from his last job, don't you?"

"No," Step One said.

"He had a fling with the boss's wife. He caught them in the act." Step Three was breathless with this information.

"How do you know?" asked Step Two. Josie caught a whiff of sibling rivalry.

"I heard it from Miriam, who heard it from Clay's cousin Janis," Step Three said. "Clay was supposed to be working on those roofs in that new subdivision out in St. Peter's."

"The one near I-70?" Step One asked.

"I can't believe how much that area is growing," Step Two said.

"Am I going to get a chance to tell my story before he's buried?" Step Three said. The other two Step Sisters shut up.

"Clay had a thing for the builder's wife. The builder was a tub of lard. She was a hot little thing, twenty years younger than her husband. She was supposed to be decorating the display house. The builder found the two of them going at it on the display house bed."

"Do they use real mattresses on those beds?" Step Two asked.

Step Three blasted her with a glare. "If I can continue, the builder found them in the bedroom. Clay had dropped his nail gun and his pants on the marble threshold. The builder picked up the nail gun and nearly nailed Clay's thingie to the bed."

The three Step Sisters shared a delicious shocked silence as Josie trailed them into the funeral home's foyer. The Step Sisters bobbed through a sea of somber clothes while they deep-sixed the dead man's reputation.

"You don't think Henrietta killed him, do you?" Step One asked.

"Wouldn't blame her if she did," Step Three said. "*Sh!* There's Father Murchison."

"He looks like a giant water bird," Step One said.

Step Two giggled.

"Show some respect," Step Three said. "He's here to lead the rosary. Heaven knows Clay needs all the prayers he can get." She checked her watch. "It was supposed to start at seven and it's seven ten now. These things never run on time."

"Good evening, Father." The three women bowed their heads in meek innocence. Josie thought Step One was right: the stilt-legged priest did look like a heron in a Roman collar. She left the trio and gently elbowed her way through the crowded entrance.

A small, solemn sign said Clay was in Parlor A. That was the largest room, nearly the size of a high school gymnasium. Parlor A reeked of hothouse flowers and dry-cleaned clothes. Almost every seat was taken. Clay's receiving line snaked from the back of the room to his flower-covered bronze casket.

Josie spotted an empty chair in the second row near the casket. It was far enough away from Clay's family that she could sit there and blend in with the other mourners. Josie slid between a big-bellied man in a dark gray suit and two well-powdered women in dark dresses. She'd just reached the coveted seat when there was a commotion near the casket.

A woman with dead-black hair was weeping and wringing her plump pink hands. "I can't find my rosary," she repeated for the third time.

"Use mine, Mother Oreck," Henrietta said.

The distraught woman must be Clay's mother, Olivia Oreck. Clay's wife hovered around the poor woman as if she were afraid her mother-in-law would escape. Josie was startled by how much Henrietta looked like her mother-in-law. Both were big-busted, wide-hipped, and maternal. Both had the same dark hair curled behind their left ear. Both wore plain black pumps and black suits with pale gray blouses.

Clay's mother had Henrietta's same sharp temper. "I don't want yours," Olivia snapped. A few seconds later, she seemed to regret her flare-up. "I'm sorry, dear." She patted Henrietta's hand. "Of course I'll use your rosary. I don't know what's wrong with me. I only meant that lost rosary was special. It was a gift from Clay. He bought it for me when you went to Cancun, remember?"

"Of course I remember our honeymoon," Henrietta said. She put her arm around her mother-in-law's shoulders. "We've checked your purse, my purse, and both our cars. Before we left your home, we searched your dresser and chest of drawers. Maybe it will turn up later when we're both not so upset."

She pressed a worn black velvet bag as big as a business card into Olivia's hand. "This rosary belonged to my grandmother. It's made of crystal." The two women had pretty hands with nails like tiny seashells.

"Thank you, dear. I promise not to lose it. It's such a shame I can't find Clay's rosary. It had such beautiful brown beads."

"They were just brown beans," Henrietta said. "They weren't precious stones."

"Well, they were precious to me."

"Of course they were," Henrietta said.

Josie wondered if Clay's mother carried on about that missing rosary as a way to mourn her lost son. The fruitless search had stopped the receiving line, which was now three-quarters of the way around the room. Older women were fanning themselves. Younger people looked pointedly at their watches.

"Oh, dear, I've been neglecting Clay's friends," Olivia said. Clay's mother took the hand of a slim woman in a navy suit. "I know you're sorry, Carol dear. It's so sweet of you to come here when you have the children. Would you like to see him?" She took Carol's arm. Together they made the solemn pilgrimage to the casket.

"What are you doing here?" Henrietta hissed at the next mourner. Her angry voice carried above the subdued crowd sounds.

"I—I wanted to pay my respects." It was Lorena, neatly dressed in black.

"You got nerve coming here," Henrietta said.

Tillie's daughter backed away as if Henrietta might strike her.

Desmond Twinings stepped protectively in front of Lorena. His dark eyebrows looked like they might take wing.

"Easy now," Desmond said. "She meant no harm." Was the developer's scout escorting Lorena or protecting his investment? He wore a conventional gray suit and dark tie, but his hands seemed to have disappeared. No, wait. He was wearing thin black gloves. On a warm September night. What was that all about?

"Meant no harm?" Henrietta asked, her voice rising to a screech. "Meant no harm?" Her voice went up another octave.

Clay's mother had been kneeling at the casket with Carol. She looked up. All conversation died.

Henrietta's matronly body waded through the pool of silence. She moved closer to Lorena and said, "My husband is lying there dead." She pointed at the carnation-covered casket. "Your mother put him in that coffin. She wanted him that way."

"No!" Lorena said. "Mom didn't have anything to do with Clay's death."

"He was murdered," Henrietta screamed. "Your mother left me a widow and you've come here to gloat. I want you out of here! Out! Now, before I have you thrown out."

An anxious undertaker materialized alongside the casket, but his shooing services weren't required. The thin old priest stood next to Henrietta and Clay's mother, fluttering and gulping like a giant wading bird.

"Shall we begin the rosary?" he asked.

Mrs. Oreck managed a nod.

Desmond guided Lorena toward the door. The crowd parted for them, backing away from the couple as if Lorena's touch was poison.

Chapter 21

Ted showed up on Josie's doorstep at eight thirty that night with a flat yellow box and a face full of scratches.

"Ouch," Josie said. "You look like you wrestled a thornbush."

"Aw, shucks, ma'am, it's just a scratch." Ted gave her a cowboy grin.

Josie kissed him carefully on his right cheek, avoiding the long scarlet seam. He had a zigzag slash down his neck, tiny stab marks on his forehead, and deep gashes on his right hand.

Ted got a careful hug and a smile from Jane. Amelia shook his hand gravely and said, "Hi, Ted. It's Mel."

She is still going by Mel, Josie thought.

Ted said, "Good to see you again, Mel," as if people changed their names every day.

"You survived death by a thousand cuts," Josie said. "I see seven slashes and I'm still counting. Let me take the Gooey Louie cake box." She inhaled the buttered sugar scent.

"Who cut you?" Amelia asked.

"Kinsey," Ted said.

Jane looked mildly shocked. "Like the report?"

What report? Josie wondered. Then she remembered three sophomore girls sniggering in her high school bathroom over a dog-eared paperback about a sex survey.

"I don't think the cat was named for the Kinsey Institute for sex research," Ted said. "Probably the detective Kinsey Millhone."

"Oh, Sue Grafton's Kinsey." Jane looked relieved. She didn't like any mention of sex in front of her granddaughter.

"That's my guess," Ted said. "Every time Dina Willner brings in one of her cats, I see her reading a different mystery. Dina just adopted this stray kitten. Kinsey is only eight weeks old, a furball with a long tail. I tried to examine the cute little kitty and she exploded into razor-sharp teeth and claws."

"What did this feisty cat look like?" Amelia asked.

"Like your Harry with long hair."

"Harry would never act like that," Amelia said. "He didn't attack you when you took care of him."

"He wasn't feeling well enough to attack," Ted said.

He saw Amelia's frown and said, "And I'm sure he's naturally calmer than Kinsey."

Jane was indignant. "I blame that Dina woman. She couldn't control her cat," she said. "She let that creature claw your face. She should have stopped it."

"Dina was laughing too hard to help," Ted said. "Kinsey ran right up my face. You can see her path. I had to pry her off my scalp."

"You shouldn't be treating that wild animal," Jane said. "You could be scarred for life."

"It's my fault," Ted said. "This was Kinsey's first visit and she was a stray. I should have known she'd be scared. Dina felt so bad she brought me this gooey butter cake from Gooey Louie."

"Sweet," Amelia said.

"Almost worth getting attacked by a ferocious kitten," Ted said.

"Let's quit discussing the cake and eat it," Josie said. "I have coffee in the kitchen."

She opened the box on the kitchen counter. All four admired the golden square coffee cake covered with drifts of powdered sugar. *"Mm,"* they hummed, united by their love of the St. Louis specialty.

"Your table looks nice," Ted said.

Josie flushed at his praise. She'd put yellow plates on a cornflower blue tablecloth and filled a vase with branches of gold and scarlet leaves.

"I like the maple leaf centerpiece," Jane said.

"I had to travel really far to get those leaves," Josie said. "They're from our trees."

"Too bad you couldn't use poison ivy," Ted said. "It's so colorful this time of year."

"Leaves of three, leave them be," Jane chanted as Josie poured coffee into the grown-ups' yellow cups.

Amelia fixed herself a glass of milk and said, "I want an end piece, Mom."

Josie raised an eyebrow.

"Please?" Amelia said.

Josie cut her a fat corner with two buttery-crusted sides.

They took their first few bites in respectful silence, broken when Harry trotted into the kitchen. "Hi, big guy," Ted said, and held out his hand. Harry sniffed it, then jumped into Ted's lap. Ted scratched the cat's ears with one hand and ate his cake with the other.

"I read somewhere that gooey butter cake started as a mistake," he said.

"Wish my mistakes turned out this well," Josie said.

"That's the story my mother told me," Jane said. "She said gooey butter cakes were invented in South St. Louis.

Those old German neighborhoods had great bakers. Still do. Mother said this baker tried to make a plain yellow cake, but he put in too much butter or sugar or maybe both. Anyway, he overdid it and ended up with a gooey mess. This was during the Great Depression when people didn't waste things. They also weren't obsessed with calories."

"Ah, the good old days," Josie said.

Jane glared at her and Josie stuffed in another bite.

"As I was saying," Jane continued, "the baker covered his mistake with powdered sugar and sold it as gooey butter cake. Soon he was making more mistakes and getting paid for them."

"And gooey butter cakes spread like cellulite on fat thighs," Josie said.

"I prefer to think of them as happy accidents that were repeated," Jane said. "I hope Gooey Louie qualifies for your TAG Tour, Josie. Gooey butter cakes don't sell well outside of St. Louis."

"Not sure that's true anymore, Mom," Josie said. "Gooey Louie has been on the Food Channel and some big-time foodies wrote about it."

Amelia finished one crust and was working on the other. "This gooey butter cake tastes different than yours, Grandma."

Not only different, Josie thought, it tastes better. She banished that traitorous thought. She'd never hurt her mother by saying it. She stuffed more cake in her mouth in case she was tempted to talk.

Jane slowly chewed her next bite, as if breaking down the ingredients. "More vanilla."

Amelia took a thoughtful bite. "Maybe more butter," she said, "but it's not heavy."

Josie decided this discussion was too technical. Eating seemed her safest response.

"Well, that was good to the last bite." Jane delicately blotted her lips with her napkin. "Now it's time for me to go upstairs. Thank you, Ted, for a lovely treat." She kissed him lightly on his unscratched cheek and left.

They heard Jane's footsteps on the back stairs.

"What are you studying in school now, Mel?" Ted asked.

"The parts of the brain," Amelia said.

"We ate brains for the TAG Tour," Josie said.

"Gross, Mom." Amelia sounded impatient. "I'm learning about the limbic system, Ted." She closed her eyes and counted on her fingers. "There's the thalamus, the hypothalamus, the amygdala, and the hippocampus."

"Very good," Ted said.

"The hippocampus is where they keep the hippos at the zoo," Josie said.

Ted and Amelia groaned.

"That was awful, Mom," Amelia said. She turned to Ted as if he were the only adult in the room. "I'm starting my own business and I wanted to ask your opinion."

New business? Amelia didn't say a word about this during the ride home from school this afternoon, Josie thought. Her crafty kid must be setting some sort of trap. She watched Ted's response.

"What's that?" he asked.

"Dog walking," Amelia said. "What do you think, Ted?"

Hm. The little slick didn't ask, "What do you think, Mom?" She was using Ted as a buffer to debut her idea.

"Do you like walking dogs?" he asked.

"I'm good at it. I've had practice walking Stuart Little."

"Winter's coming, so you could make some money," Ted said. "How does your mother feel about this business?"

Good move, Ted, Josie thought. He'd skillfully maneuvered his way around Amelia's first landmine.

"Mom?" Amelia asked.

"This is the first I've heard of your plan," Josie said. "Are you going to walk the dogs before school or after?" Amelia was no morning person.

"I'd like to do it right after school," Amelia said, "while it's still light."

"Smart," Ted said. "But winter dog walking is cold work. You know you'll have to scoop."

"I do that for Stuart Little for free," Amelia said. "I could get paid."

"Will you handle big dogs or little ones?" Ted said.

"Mostly little dogs," Amelia said. "I've scouted all the dogs for three blocks. I've counted two Chihuahuas, a Yorkie, and two old golden retrievers. They're big, but too fat to cause any trouble."

"What do you know about their owners?" Ted asked.

"The Chihuahua belongs to a business lady who gets home late. So does the Yorkie. They might hire me. One of the retrievers belongs to an old, old lady. She doesn't leave the house much, so she might hire me. I just thought of one more. There's a brick house with a white Scottie dog."

"I think that's a Westie," Ted said. "A West Highland terrier. The owners like it when you know the breed's real name. Westies are good dogs. One of my patients, Teddy, ate a pinecone. The pinecone got stuck in its intestine and I had to operate to remove it. Teddy recovered, then went out and ate another pinecone. Those two meals cost his owner more than two thousand dollars."

"Dumb dog," Amelia said. "I'd find one who didn't like pinecones."

"Would you really?" Ted asked. "Did you abandon Harry when he needed a vet?"

"No," Amelia said.

"I didn't think so. Teddy's owner felt the same way."

"You think my business is a good one, right?" Amelia said.

"I think the idea is good, but it needs a little work. You should put together a business plan. Think about how many dogs you want to walk and what you want to charge, and then make a flyer to get your customers."

"I can do the flyer on my computer," Amelia said.

"Good," Ted said. "I'll be happy to read it when you're ready to unleash it."

"That was an awful pun," Josie said.

"It will require dogged persistence for you to succeed, Mel," Ted said.

"It's time to paws," Josie said. "You have school in the morning."

Amelia didn't protest. "Good night," she said. "Stay away from savage felines, Ted."

"I'll try not to let any more kittens beat me up," he said.

Harry jumped off Ted's lap to follow Amelia to her room. She waved good night and shut her door.

"Thanks for talking to Amelia about her business," Josie said.

"I hope I didn't discourage her," Ted said.

"You gave her some good ideas and things to think about. She'll listen to you," Josie said. "I'm just a mom."

They could hear Amelia giggling with her cat.

"Harry is her faithful friend," Josie said. "He's like a puppy dog."

"I'd like to be your faithful friend," Ted said, his arm around her. He kissed her lightly, then more forcefully. "I want to be more than a friend, if you'll let me. You know I love you."

Josie felt frightened. Was he going to propose? Right

in her kitchen over a demolished gooey butter cake? She felt trapped, panicky.

"You already are," Josie said. "My friend, I mean. Tillie's Off the Hill is reopening. Will you go with me?"

"I'd follow you into hell," Ted said.

"Tillie's restaurant will be enough," Josie said.

Chapter 22

Six fifty-two in the morning. Josie had had a sleepless night, but she couldn't wait a minute longer to call Alyce. Her friend answered on the first ring.

"What's wrong?" Alyce asked. She knew Josie wouldn't call this early without a good reason.

"I need help," Josie said. "I thought Ted was going to propose last night, but I headed him off. Now we're going out again tonight. I'm afraid."

"Afraid of what?" Alyce said.

"Marriage. I need to talk to someone neutral. I can't discuss this with Mom. She's pushing me to marry Ted. She's already measured him for a son-in-law suit. Mom has always wanted me to marry, even though her marriage wasn't a success."

"Your father deserted you, didn't he?" Alyce asked.

"He left Mom and me in St. Louis, gave her this house, and started another family in Chicago. We haven't heard from him since I was nine."

"I'd say that's an unsuccessful marriage," Alyce said.

"You know my history. I haven't had much luck with men. I need to talk to someone who's happily married."

"Honey, if you think this old married lady can give

you romantic advice, I'll be happy to talk to you. Stop by after you drop off Amelia at school. I'll make breakfast and we can dish."

Josie felt better as soon as she hung up the phone. Alyce would tell her the truth and help Josie decide her future. Despite the sleepless night, she was energized. Josie hurried Amelia through breakfast, then made sure she fed the cat and cleaned his litter box. She had Amelia in the car ten minutes early. Amelia wasn't happy about being rushed through her morning routine.

"So what do you think of my idea to make money, Mom?"

"It's a good one," Josie said, trying to make the light before it turned yellow. A rusty orange Datsun cut her off and she hit the brakes. Josie automatically put out her arm to protect her daughter.

"Mom, I'm wearing a seat belt. I'm not a baby," Amelia said. "I asked you about dog walking."

The light changed to green, but the traffic crawled forward. They'd moved only two car lengths by the time it turned red again.

Something is slowing those cars down, Josie thought. A rush-hour fender bender? I'd better find a side road or we'll sit here all morning.

"So talk to me," Josie said. If she could get to the corner, a right turn would take her through a subdivision and get her back out on Lindbergh.

"I think walking dogs on Washington Avenue after midnight would bring in major money," Amelia said. "I could thumb my way downtown. I know some kids who'd buy me beer, too. That would make the job go faster."

"Um-hm," Josie said. She eased the car around the corner and narrowly avoided a clueless pedestrian talking on his Bluetooth.

"Mom!" Amelia made the word a four-syllable complaint. "You didn't hear a word I said."

"Of course I did," Josie said. "You were talking about walking dogs."

"At midnight on Washington Avenue while drinking beer."

"I'm sorry," Josie said. "I'm distracted by the traffic. It must be a full moon. People seem to have a death wish today, Amelia."

"My name's Mel." Her voice was loaded with preteen pout.

She's still on the Mel kick, too, Josie thought. "Go ahead, tell me about walking dogs."

"Never mind," Amelia said, dragging the word out to show her disgust. She sulked the rest of the way to school. Josie was grateful for the silence. It helped her concentrate. She wasn't really distracted by the traffic. Ted was driving her crazy.

Josie got to Barrington with time to spare and threaded through the semicircular drive. "There's your friend Emma." Josie smiled and waved. Emma waved back.

Amelia slammed the car door without saying goodbye and flounced toward her friend. Josie sighed with relief and aimed her car for the highway.

Fall was a favorite season. She should have savored the drive to Alyce's subdivision. The fiery fall colors blazed against the white limestone hills. Today, Josie hardly noticed. She pulled up at the gate to the Estates at Wood Winds, waved to the guard, and headed to Alyce's house like a homing pigeon in a Honda.

When she knocked on Alyce's side door, she was greeted with the rich aroma of hot coffee, baking apples, and warm caramel.

"Morning!" Alyce hugged her friend. Her eyes were

the same blue as the September sky. She wore a soft blue caftan. Her natural blond hair was pale as a child's.

"What smells so good?" Josie asked.

"I'm trying out my new *ebelskiver*," Alyce said.

"Gesundheit!" Josie said.

"*Ebelskiver* is a Danish pan." Alyce proudly pointed to an aluminum skillet with tennis-ball-sized holes, each filled with a puffy golden-brown confection. "Those are filled pancakes."

"You've been hitting Williams-Sonoma again," Josie said.

"Caught. I'm a kitchen junkie." Her kitchen was crammed with arcane culinary equipment.

"Admitting it is the first step," Josie said, "but I hope there's no cure."

Alyce's kitchen was paneled in linen-fold oak. Even the cabinets and the fridge were hidden by the golden oak. It was Alyce's refuge and her place of inspiration.

"I'm practicing on you this morning," Alyce said. "I want to make tarte tatin filled pancakes for Jake this Saturday. We're eating the inaugural batch."

She did a Vanna White wave at two white plates piled with golden puffs. "The pancakes are stuffed with caramelized apples. The extra caramel sauce is almost ready. And look at this. I have a new apple divider."

She was as excited by the spidery device as a teenager with a new iPad.

"I assume it slices apples," Josie said.

"It cores and cuts apples into the thin slices I need for the pancakes. Or I can adjust it to make thicker apple wedges. Justin likes to eat those."

"Where is the little guy?" Josie asked.

"He and Gracie are walking Bruiser. Let me drizzle some caramel sauce on those pancakes, take the new batch out of the pan, and we're ready."

"What can I do?" Josie asked.

"Pour us some coffee. I put out the Rose Point china in the breakfast nook."

Josie admired the old-fashioned white china with the raised roses twining along the edges. Real white roses with pink centers filled a Rose Point vase. A pink tablecloth and napkins provided the backdrop.

"The roses are gorgeous," Josie said. "They smell good, too."

"Jake gave me those for our anniversary." A rosy blush painted her fair skin. "This, too." Her wrist sparkled in the breakfast room sunlight.

"A diamond tennis bracelet," Josie said. "You're the best-dressed chef in Wood Winds."

"Better try those pancakes before they get cold," Alyce said.

Josie took a forkful without hesitation. Sampling this unfamiliar dish wasn't as risky as trying pig ears and brains.

"Those caramelized apples are amazing," Josie said.

"Do you want vanilla ice cream?"

"No, thanks. They're perfect," Josie said.

"So, what's your problem with Ted, who's also perfect?"

"That's the problem," Josie said. "He's too perfect."

"There's no such thing," Alyce said. "He's a good man."

"Of course he is. But I've never been married. I have some serious mistakes in my past."

"Then you're smart enough to know a good choice now," Alyce said.

"How do I know we'll be happy?"

"You won't be, not all the time. Jake and I have had our problems—you know that. But we still like each other and we love each other. We have a beautiful son.

I'm happy with my career and he's happy with his. We have a good marriage. You will, too, with the right man."

"But how do I know if he is?" Josie asked.

"My mother used to say you had to answer three questions: Do you love him, do you like him, and can you tolerate his faults?"

"He doesn't have any faults, except he likes snakes."

"He won't keep them in the bedroom, will he?" Alyce asked.

"No, he quit keeping snakes at home after his last one died."

"So what's the problem, Josie? You've known Ted more than a year. Your mother likes him. Your daughter adores him. Even your cat is crazy about him."

"I don't know," Josie said.

"I think you're afraid," Alyce said.

"What does that mean?"

"You're afraid you'll pick the wrong man again," Alyce said.

"Nate was my first and biggest mistake," Josie said.

"Nate wasn't such a bad choice," Alyce said. "You had a sizzling romance. You made a beautiful daughter."

"I was going to tell him I was pregnant so we could marry, when I discovered he was a drug dealer."

"You were blinded by love," Alyce said. "When you saw who Nate really was, you left him. You've brought Amelia up right."

"I've tried. I didn't love anyone for ten years after Nate. Then I fell for a barista named Josh. He turned out to be selling something more addictive than caffeine. When I accidentally discovered that bag of coke in his closet, I refused to see him again. After that, I didn't really didn't trust men. I never intended to date Mike the plumber, but he coaxed me into loving him. I nearly had his engagement ring on my finger when I realized Mike had a psycho daughter and he would always side with her. I couldn't give Amelia a mean, drunken half sister."

"And you didn't," Alyce said. "Josh and Mike didn't work out, but you were smart enough to walk away as soon as you realized that."

"Ted is gentle and patient," Josie said, then sighed. "I make him sound like an old man. He's so sizzling, I want to tear off his clothes when we're together. But I don't. I can't marry him. Not with my history of bad choices."

"Josie, you've chosen well this time," Alyce said. "Ted wouldn't work for me. I don't like big galumphing dogs or their hair. He couldn't support me as a stay-at-home mom. But he's right for you. Are you going to keep punishing yourself for what you see as your mistakes? Or are you going to forget the past and marry the man you love?"

"Where would we live?" Josie asked.

"He has a house," Alyce said.

"Ted rents," Josie said.

"Then buy a home of your own."

"But what about my mother?"

"You're thirty-one, Josie. It's time you left home. Your mom could rent out your flat for what it's actually worth. Jane could use the income. Maplewood has become a hot place to live. She'd have real money coming in every month. She'll never raise your rent and you know it. Marry Ted and you'll have a new life."

"And a place of my own," Josie said.

Possibilities were opening for Josie like the fragrant bouquet on the table. She and Ted could have a home that didn't have garage sale furniture. Or a glowering Mrs. Mueller next door, watching every move.

Josie would live happily ever after with Ted. They would have a yard with a deck. And patio furniture. Maybe a table with a striped sun umbrella. They would barbecue after work. Ted's dog and cat and Amelia's cat would play together.

Josie and Ted would help Amelia grow into a young woman. Her daughter needed a father's guidance. Ted had shown good judgment last night when Amelia asked him about her dog walking business.

Through the sweet sugar haze of pancakes and white roses, Josie could see Amelia, dressed for her prom. She would take pictures when her daughter's date showed up, awkward in his first tux.

And Josie would have pictures of her own. Wedding pictures. She would no longer be an unmarried single mother, handling all the problems alone.

Josie saw herself happy and fulfilled, spending the rest of her life with Ted, Amelia, and a house full of hairy pets.

For a moment, her mind flashed back to another flower-filled scene, one that wasn't so happy. Last night, a black-clad Lorena had been shamed and shunned at Clay's wake. Desmond had escorted her out of the funeral home, but Josie didn't think the developer's scout would be by her side for life. He didn't love her. Josie could see that by the way Desmond held her arm. He didn't keep her close, the way Ted would. Poor Lorena.

Josie understood how Lorena felt, shut up in that dingy restaurant, unloved and unwanted, growing older and lonelier. A woman might kill to escape that fate.

Chapter 23

"I can't believe our luck," Ted said. "I've never been seated at Tillie's without at least a twenty-minute wait. Today we walked right in at noon and got a booth in the bar."

"Good luck for us," Josie said, "bad luck for Tillie."

The life had gone out of Tillie's Off the Hill. Tillie needed to be bustling behind the bar, laughing, joking, calling hello to her customers, threatening to eighty-six Clay.

Without its usual noonday hustle, the restaurant seemed old and dingy. Josie noticed the chips in the paint and the scuffs on the floor. Sounds echoed uncomfortably, constant reminders that the restaurant was nearly empty. Conversations shriveled in the silence.

Poor Tillie. She'd gotten her wish. Clay was gone for good. It looked like her business might be, too.

Clay's regular seat at the bar was empty. No, it was filled, Josie thought. The dead man's rage seemed to linger like black smoke, covering all the empty bar stools like a seething fog.

Only two other tables had lunchtime diners. A pair of gray-suited men sat near the door. One twirled spaghetti around his fork. The other had a napkin tucked under his chin to protect his white shirt and tie. Desmond Twinings sat at his usual table in the corner with a half-empty glass of soda in front of him.

Two plates of spaghetti and a soda couldn't support the rambling restaurant. How long could Tillie's stay open with this trickle of business? How would Tillie survive the scandal—and the looming court cases?

Josie and Ted studied their great slabs of red, white, and green menus. "I wore a tomato-colored shirt," he said. "I plan to do some serious eating."

"That red plaid should hide anything from Alfredo sauce to baked ziti," Josie said.

"Matches my eyes, too," Ted said, and waggled his eyebrows at her. "What are you getting?"

"Not toasted ravioli, that's for sure," Josie said. "The lasagna looks good."

"Chicken parmigiana for me," Ted said.

A shadow crossed their menus. Lorena appeared at their table, armed with an order pad and pen.

"Josie, how nice of you to be here," Tillie's daughter said. "And you brought a guest. I appreciate your support. Business is light today."

The last time Josie had seen Lorena at the restaurant, she'd been so overworked, Josie had wanted her to sit down and rest. Her server's uniform of a white blouse and black pants had showed signs of battle fatigue. She'd had a tired droop to her shoulders. Even her hair had seemed exhausted.

Today Lorena looked worried. The tiny frown lines in her pretty face seemed slightly deeper, but her blouse was fresh and white. She was wearing a new addition to her uniform: white cotton gloves.

"This is my friend Ted," Josie said. "He's been here

before. You've changed your uniform. Now we're getting white-glove service."

Lorena lowered her voice to a near whisper. "Josie, your mom is a family friend, so I'll tell you the real reason. I've got this weird rash on my hands. I have to keep it covered. The doctor gave me some cream, but I still hide it with white gloves. We can't afford to lose any customers because people think I have a skin disease."

Josie could see a red, blistered patch at Lorena's wrist. "What is it?"

"I'm allergic to our new kitchen soap," Lorena said. "Mom bought a case on sale. I spent every penny she saved on a dermatologist. He says it should go away shortly. It itches, but it's not catching."

"That's a relief," Josie said. "Why is your friend Desmond wearing gloves? Is he allergic, too?"

"No, he has eczema," Lorena said. "Brought on by stress. Desmond is still trying to put together that land purchase and it's taken a toll. Important people are pressuring him to close the deal. Mom is the last holdout. She won't sell—not even after Clay died. She expects to get out of jail and go right back to work here."

Josie felt a twinge of guilt. Desmond wasn't the only one under pressure. Jane was pushing her to help free Tillie. She decided to chance an ugly question. She had Ted here if Lorena turned nasty.

"The pressure must have just started getting to him," Josie said. "I saw him wearing gloves at Clay's wake."

"You were there?" Lorena gave a shrill laugh. "Was that a circus or what?"

"I admire the way you handled Henrietta," Josie said. "You kept your dignity when she lost hers. You did the right thing, trying to pay your respects to his widow."

"I'm lucky I had Desmond there to protect me," Lorena said. "I'll put your order in, hon. You must be starving and I'm standing here yakking." She sprinted for the kitchen as if demons were chasing her.

Josie glanced over at Desmond, a glowering shadow brooding over his drink. One black-gloved pinkie sparkled in the dim light. He was wearing his gambler's diamond. How much of a gambler was he? Was he still betting he could get Tillie's property and close the casino land deal? Had he and Lorena helped turn the odds in his favor?

Desmond shifted in his seat. Josie, concerned that he might see her staring at him, turned her gaze to the window by their booth. The fall wind whipped through the vacant lot next door, and the weeds rustled and rapped against the window.

"What are you staring at, Josie?" Ted asked.

"Weeds," Josie said. "I was thinking about what you said last night—that poison ivy was pretty. It's taking over the lot next door."

"Where?" Ted asked, watching the wind-whipped weeds. "I see yellow ragweed, white Queen Ann's lace, and black-eyed Susans."

"Back there." Josie pointed with her fork. "By the kitchen door. There's a fiery red patch of poison ivy surrounding the castor bean plants with the purple-black leaves. The castor beans are maybe five or six feet tall with leaves as big as dinner plates."

"They're pretty poison," Ted asked. "Not all those plants are weeds anymore. I read that florists are using Queen Ann's lace in fancy bouquets. Around here, the highway department mows them down with all the other weeds."

"Landscape artists still use castor beans in their designs," Josie said. "I can see why, but they're too dangerous. What if kids get hold of them?"

"Not just kids," Ted said. "They poison dogs, cats, even horses and cattle. They grow wild everywhere around here. I somehow doubt that poison ivy will brighten a bouquet, no matter how attractive it looks."

"Who wants to smell a bouquet and wind up with a nose full of poison ivy?" Josie said. "That's not how to say it with flowers."

Ted looked around to make sure there was no sign of Lorena. "Do you have another toasted ravioli restaurant for your TAG Tour?" he asked.

"Yep, they want me to try Zia's."

"That's on the Hill, right?"

"Since 1984," Josie said. "The restaurant is almost as old as I am. Guess TAG wants a more traditional venue this time. It's a shame about Tillie's. I would have—"

Ted lightly kicked Josie's shoe and she shut up. They were wrapped in a warm cloud of spicy tomato sauce.

"Lunch has arrived," Lorena said. She set a steaming blue china platter in front of Josie. "Your lasagna," she said.

"And your chicken parm," she said to Ted. "Here's more bread and extra butter."

Lorena refilled their water glasses, then asked, "Anything else I can get you—another beer? Some coffee? Grated cheese?"

"I'm fine, thanks," Josie said.

"Me, too," Ted said.

"Then *mangia*!" she said, giving the traditional Italian command.

Eat they did, feasting on the steaming Italian specialties.

"That was good," Ted said. "Would you like dessert?"

"No, thanks," Josie said. "I'm glad you're driving. I'm about to go into a comfort-food coma."

"Maybe a short stroll would wake us up," Ted said. "We have time."

Josie hesitated, then said, "I know you've offered to help, but I need to ask you a big favor. Something most men won't do."

"Go to a spa?" Ted asked. "Manscape my chest?"

"Your chest is fine. Better than fine. I want you to go shopping with me."

"No problem. Where?"

"Gemma's Junktique. It's about two blocks away. It's owned by Clay's girlfriend. She was barred from Clay's visitation and funeral. I wanted to check on her."

"That's really nice," Ted said.

"I'm not being nice," Josie said. "I'm trying to learn things. I want to get Mom off my back and Tillie out of jail."

"Noble goals," Ted said, and grinned. "Let's get the check and go."

Josie was shivering by the time they got to Gemma's Junktique. The day was turning cold and the shop looked dumpier than when she'd been there with Alyce. The remnants of cast-off lives seemed to weigh down the old beds and furniture, coating them with dead hopes and lost dreams.

Today, Gemma Lynn looked like a Victorian widow. Her drapey black top was a styleless shroud. Black baggy pants and lace half gloves completed her ensemble. Her eyes were still red. She had a new box of tissues at her side.

"I remember you," Gemma said to Josie. "You were in the other day with a blond lady, the one who bought the coffeepot."

"That's Alyce. I'm Josie."

"Nice to see you again. I wasn't going to open up today. I live right upstairs and I was so exhausted I could hardly make it down those steps there." Gemma nodded toward some grimy brown-painted stairs in the corner.

"I'm sorry for your loss," Josie said. "I went to Clay's visitation last night."

Gemma bowed her head. "Thank you," she said. "It's nice to be with someone who understands my situation. I should have been at that visitation. He was going to leave Henrietta for me. He even gave me a ring."

She held out a lace-covered hand. A gold ring with a tiny chip of a diamond gleamed on her left hand. She still had those talons, but the rhinestone-tipped manicure had been replaced with clear polish. "It's a promise ring," Gemma said. "Now I'll die an old maid." She started sniffling and reached for another tissue.

Under the lace half gloves, Josie saw the blistered rash on her hands.

"You weren't wearing the ring when I was in yesterday," Josie said.

"I was shy about wearing it in public," she said. "Until we were official. Now it makes me feel closer to him. It's all I've got. I couldn't go to Clay's visitation. I didn't want to make a scene. I took the high road for his sake.

"But I was at the burial. She saw me. She stood by his casket, glaring right at me, the witch. She couldn't say a word. I had a right. My mother's grave is two rows away from where Clay is buried. I brought flowers and stayed on Mother's plot the whole time. I was a nervous wreck. Look at my hands. My doctor says I have atopic dermatitis."

She said the words proudly, as if the condition was an achievement, and held out her gloved hands.

Josie was no dermatologist, but the rash looked like plain old poison ivy to her. Gemma spent enough time at Tillie's that she could have gotten her hands on those castor beans—and the poison ivy that surrounded it.

"Señoritas!" Ted called. He was wearing a black sombrero embroidered with silver and tiny mirrors. He danced over to Josie, shaking a pair of yellow maracas painted with red flowers. "Is it me?"

"No," Josie said. "But I like it."

"The hat's from Mexico," Gemma said. "It's hand-embroidered. The maracas are hand-painted. I have a real Stetson hat on the same rack. It's got a snakeskin band."

"No, thanks," Ted said.

"Those maracas have been selling," Gemma said. "I sold two sets last week. That's my last pair."

I bet, Josie thought. Why would there be a run on maracas in this white-bread neighborhood?

"That Royal Crown Cola sign is cool," Ted said. He held it up.

"I like it," Josie said.

"Me, too. I don't have room for it in my place," Ted said, "but if I had a bigger house it would look good in my den."

A bigger house. Once again, Josie had that dreamlike vision of the green backyard, the deck, and the barbecue. And maybe a real office for herself, instead of a computer in a corner of her bedroom. That sampler would look perfect in there. She could have a room of her own.

"Here's what I like," Josie said. She showed him the softly mellowed sampler embroidered with FRIENDSHIP, LOVE & TRUTH.

"That sounds like you," Ted said.

She looked wistfully at the sampler before putting it back. "If you come down on that sampler price, let me know, Gemma."

"I may have a buyer," Gemma said. "I can let you know in a day or two if she doesn't want it. I could reduce the price ten dollars."

Josie smiled. She could afford that. "Would you let me know one way or the other?"

"I have your number," she said. "I'll call you."

Gemma sounded as if she might die of boredom first.

Chapter 24

Josie wanted to flee Gemma's dusty bargains and widow's weeds. She needed to escape the burden of those lost, sad lives.

"I have to pick up Amelia at school," she said, and dragged Ted out of the stuffy store. She felt better outside on the cracked sidewalk. Josie took deep breaths of the brisk September air.

They walked quickly to Ted's orange Mustang.

"Why did you want to leave so suddenly?" he asked. "We have plenty of time to drive to Amelia's school."

"I felt like the shop walls were closing in on me," Josie said. "I enjoy antiques and looking for bargains, but Gemma seems to suck the air out of that store. I had to get away. Thanks for leaving with me."

Ted shrugged. "No big deal. Like I said, I'm here for you. I wish you'd believe that."

He kissed her, slowly, tenderly, and the sad old street disappeared. Josie felt young again, with fresh new choices waiting for her.

Ted unlocked her door and she slid into the Mustang's white leather seat. "How does Gemma stand it day after day, shut up in that shop?" she asked.

"Not very well, judging by the look of things," Ted said. "Maybe her affair with Clay was the only excitement in her life."

"That's even sadder," Josie said. "I'm glad I'm out of that depressing place."

"Did you learn anything?" Ted asked.

"I think so," Josie said. "Those castor beans grow next door to Clay's murder scene, but the only way to reach them is through a thicket of poison ivy. Three people who may have wanted Clay dead—Gemma Lynn, Desmond, and Lorena—and all have rashes with exotic names.

"Desmond keeps his hands hidden with black gloves. Gemma Lynn called the creeping crud on her hands 'atopic dermatitis.' I swear it's poison ivy and I've seen enough of it to know."

"Do you get poison ivy?" Ted asked.

"I've had it a few times," Josie said. "Amelia breaks out if she even walks by a poison ivy leaf."

"I seem to be immune and hope I stay that way," Ted said. "I could tear out that patch of poison ivy with my bare hands and never get a rash. One of my clients got a wicked case of poison ivy just by petting her dog. She broke out from the poison ivy oil on the dog's fur."

"Do dogs get poison ivy?"

"No," Ted said. "Cats don't, either. Goats can eat it and it doesn't bother them. But it's misery for humans. If I remember right, Gemma's atopic dermatitis is just a fancy name for a rash. It really can be brought on by stress. She sure acts brokenhearted over Clay's death. Being barred from his funeral might make it worse."

"I'm not sure how grief stricken she is," Josie said. "Tillie told me Gemma was furious at Clay because he wouldn't marry her."

"Gemma was wearing a promise ring," Ted said.

"She's sitting behind a whole case of secondhand

jewelry," Josie said. "She could have given herself that ring."

"Tillie's not exactly unbiased," Ted said.

"I know," Josie said. "I'm trying to put some pieces together."

"Sorry," Ted said. "I thought I was helping by pointing out the flaw in your theory."

"I appreciate it," Josie said, but she didn't. She didn't want Ted to challenge her ideas. She wanted him to tell her she was right.

"What's the matter?" Ted asked. "You're so quiet."

"I'm starting to realize this is hopeless," Josie said. "So what if I've found three people who have poison ivy? All they have to do is shut up. Their rashes will go away and Tillie will be convicted. Mom will be shattered."

"I should have kept my mouth shut," Ted said.

"No, no," Josie said. "Agreeing with me won't find the real killer. Tillie is in jail. The case is closed, as far as the police are concerned. They won't be happy when I come up with another murder suspect—they'll look like fools. I need to build an airtight case. Keep showing me where the holes are."

"Keep talking and I'll try to spot them," Ted said.

"Desmond has no quarrel with Clay that I know of," Josie said. "But he has a first-rate reason to ruin Tillie's business. If her restaurant failed, he could buy her land cheaper. Lorena is dating him and she's restless with her life. Those two could have killed Clay together. If that's what they were after, their plan succeeded. Tillie's was deserted at lunchtime."

"Didn't you say Clay's wife wanted him dead, too?" Ted asked.

"Not dead, but definitely gone. Tillie said Henrietta was sick of being married to a mooch."

"Did Henrietta have a rash when you saw her last night at the funeral home?" Ted asked.

"No," Josie said. "I remember thinking how pretty her hands were. Tillie, who's accused of killing Clay, is locked away in jail. She didn't have any rash when I saw her. If Tillie grabbed the castor beans from the plant next door, she'd have been itching herself crazy in the lockup."

"Maybe she's immune, too," Ted said.

Josie sighed. "This is so frustrating," she said. "I need proof that someone else killed Clay, but I don't know where to start. I could follow Lorena and Desmond, but that takes time. I'm a single mom with a job. I can't do surveillance."

"Maybe you need to look at the problem from a different angle," Ted said. "That weedy lot next to Tillie's can't be the only source of castor beans. Where else can people find them? Look for other sources.

"If that approach doesn't work, I'll take some vacation time and help you investigate your three suspects in depth. I'll need to give my clinic partner a little notice so she can rearrange the schedule."

"You're brilliant," Josie said, and kissed him. "I'm sorry I grumped at you. You were right. My theory needed testing. We make a good team."

"Yes, we do," Ted said, and Josie felt her heart leap like a rabbit. Ted started the car. "Should we go pick up Amelia at school together?"

"She'd like that," Josie said.

"What about you?" Ted asked.

"I'd like that very much," Josie said. "Do you want to stay for dinner tonight?"

"It's my turn for evening hours at the clinic." Ted took Josie in his arms. She cursed the car's four-on-the-floor gearshift for making the embrace so awkward. "I'll have to take a rain check. But I want to see you more often. In fact, Josie—"

He's going to ask me, Josie thought. He's going to propose to me on this glorious fall afternoon. This time I'm ready. I'll tell him yes. I'll—

An unearthly cry split the air.

"What's that?" Josie asked. "It sounds like a baby crying."

Ted jumped out of the Mustang and prowled the street. His brief search sent a paprika-colored tabby streaking around the corner of an abandoned brick building.

Ted climbed back into the Mustang. "I think it was that cat," he said. "They can make some spooky sounds. We'd better go if we're going to pick up Amelia."

I hate you, cat, Josie thought. He was going to pop the question if you hadn't opened your big mouth. Now I'm playing my own cat-and-mouse game to catch him.

The traffic was with them, and they were at the Barrington School with time to spare. As Ted's vintage orange car eased through the driveway traffic at the school, he asked, "Should I call your daughter Amelia or Mel?"

"Call her Mel and let's hope that phase passes soon," Josie said. "The more we fight it, the more she'll resist."

"You're learning to be a teenager's mom," he said.

"She's not even a teenager and she's acting like one," Josie said. "So far, her rebellions have been fairly harmless. I hope they stay that way."

"They will. She's a good kid and her mother brought her up right."

"Amelia Marcus!" the speaker blared. Josie's daughter came flying out, a blur of dark brown hair and coltish legs.

"Is she getting taller?" Ted asked.

"Daily," Josie said, and climbed out of the two-door sports car.

"Hi, Ted! Hi, Mom," Amelia said. "I've got the coolest ride at school." She nimbly crawled into the narrow backseat with her backpack.

"Certainly the oldest ride, Mel," Ted said.

Josie watched her daughter's face blush with pleasure at that "Mel."

"Your 'stang isn't old," Amelia said. "It's vintage. It has more style than that stupid yellow Hummer. That thing looks like a box on wheels."

"I agree," Ted said. "But I'm prejudiced."

"Any more cat attacks?" Amelia asked.

"They kept their claws off me," Ted said. "I wasn't in the office today. But yesterday, I had an apricot poodle named Mikey who ate a bar of chocolate. Mikey's a toy poodle, so that much chocolate could have killed him. Good thing his owner, Becky Hutchison, noticed he was acting strange. She came home and found him weaving around the living room like he was drunk. She picked him up and he started acting hyper, jumping on and off her lap and refusing to lie down."

"Aren't poodles hyper anyway?" Amelia asked.

"Mikey is fourteen, so he's settled down some," Ted said. "Becky went upstairs and found out Mikey had gotten in the hidden stash of chocolate she keeps in her bedroom drawer. Becky saw the torn-up chocolate wrapper all over the floor and brought him straight in. We had quite a fight, but it looks like we'll save the little guy. Mikey spent the night at the clinic. If he's still there, I'll see him tonight."

"If chocolate is poison for dogs, why do they eat it?" Amelia asked.

"Animals are like people," Ted said. "Dogs can develop a taste for things that aren't good for them. Cats can, too."

"I know," Amelia said. "Mom wouldn't let Harry have chocolate ice cream."

"Your mom was right. We don't want your cat to learn to like it. Becky's dog is such a chocoholic that she jokes Mikey needs a twelve-step program. This was his second serious chocolate binge, so Mikey obviously didn't learn he should avoid it. Becky will have to keep her stash on a top shelf or in a locked closet.

"She felt bad about Mikey and called herself a terrible pet owner. She's not. We've had people abandon their animals at the clinic because they didn't want to pay the bills."

"That's how Grandma got Stuart Little," Amelia said. "Some man wouldn't pay for him."

"That's right," Ted said. "He was too dumb to know he lost a good dog. Becky will pay Mikey's bills. She blames herself, but it wasn't her fault. She had the chocolate hidden. Mikey found it. He couldn't resist what was bad for him."

Gemma Lynn wanted another woman's husband, Josie thought. Desmond wants another woman's restaurant. And Lorena wants a life. Did any of them kill to get what they craved?

Chapter 25

Ted walked Josie to the door and gave her a chaste kiss on the cheek. "Until next time," he whispered. "I love you."

"I love you, too," she said. She watched Ted jog to his car, his lean, muscled body moving in long, easy strides.

If we were married, you'd come home to me tonight when you finished work, she thought. She remembered how good it felt to have a man in her bed. Not just for sex, but the small pleasures of sleeping like spoons, of having someone warm to hold on a cold night. She could feel the fall chill in the air. Winter would be here soon, and Josie would be shivering alone.

Josie looked up and saw her nosy neighbor, Mrs. Mueller, was also watching Ted. She stared out her bedroom window through the miniblind slat. Josie waved at her and the blind dropped. If we were married, I'd be free of that old bat, Josie thought, as she picked her mail out of the box.

Josie saw another letter from a religious organization peeking out of her mother's mailbox. The letter seemed to call her name.

Won't hurt to look, she told herself. Let's see if more

leeches are feeding off my poor mother. This letter was from the St. Thalamus Society for Indigent Children. Josie stuffed it into her purse, away from Mrs. M's prying eyes.

St. Thalamus. The name sounded familiar. Josie tried to remember the stories of the saints Jane had taught her. Was St. Thalamus a Roman martyr? An early Christian virgin? Maybe the letter would give her a clue. Josie opened it in her living room.

The letterhead showed a photo of a smiling dark-skinned child with her hair in braids, supposedly a student at the St. Thalamus Orphanage. The letter thanked "Dear Mrs. Marcus" for her generous donation of one hundred dollars.

"Your money will help educate a poor African orphan for an entire school year. The children are depending on you, Mrs. Marcus. We've enclosed an envelope for next month's donation. Please help."

A hundred dollars a month? On top of five hundred a month to Our Lady of the Sheets and the Sisters of Divine Poverty? Nearly all of Jane's Social Security check was going to those charities. Were they helping the poor—or helping themselves to her mother's money?

The Lord helps those who help themselves, Josie told herself. She checked on Amelia. Her daughter was sitting at her bedroom computer with Harry curled next to her on the desk. Josie went into her own bedroom and flipped on her computer, ready for a thorough Internet search.

She checked the name St. Thalamus online and couldn't find a trace, except for a colorful Web site dedicated to the St. Thalamus Society for Indigent Children. Josie scrolled through two pages of adorable dark-skinned children reading, sleeping in sparsely furnished dormitories, sitting respectfully in a whitewashed church, playing soccer in a dirt field. Photos that could be easily Photoshopped. A donations page offered to take credit cards, PayPal accounts, or checks. The checks could be sent to a post office box in Kansas City.

Josie's search was interrupted by squeals, giggles, and pounding feet. She swung around on her chair and saw Amelia chasing Harry down the hall.

"Keep it down, will you?" Josie said. "I'm trying to work. You two sound like a herd of buffalo."

The thumps and giggles turned into surly silence. Josie went back to her computer search. The name sounded familiar. Was St. Thalamus a medieval bishop who'd helped care for plague orphans? Josie knew she'd heard the name somewhere. Recently, too. And not from Jane.

Come on, she told herself. Use your brain.

Brain. Of course. Amelia had told her and Ted about the parts of the brain she was studying in school the night they ate the gooey butter cake. The thalamus was one of those parts.

St. Thalamus, indeed.

Josie did another search and confirmed her hunch. The thalamus was part of the brain. Next she searched Guidestar and the Better Business Bureau, then checked the state attorney general's Web site. There were warnings against all of Jane's charities. They were three frauds, preying on the generosity of the devoutly gullible.

Josie checked the clock. Her mother should be leaving shortly to see Tillie. Let's get this over with, Josie thought. I'm not going to spend all night fretting about these bogus charities. Jane won't like hearing this news, but she has to know. She could give her money to real charities that would actually help poor children.

Josie prayed for courage as she dragged herself up

her mother's front stairs. Her body seemed to be resisting her command to move forward. She had to fight gravity and her own reluctance.

Woman up, she told herself. *What's the worst a seventy-six-year-old can do to you?*

I'm about to find out.

Josie tapped on her mother's door.

"Come in," Jane said. Her voice sounded weak. She was on the couch, watching *The Young and the Restless* with Stuart Little. Jane had on her best pink pantsuit, and Stuart rested his head in her lap. A few months ago, Jane had banned the dog from the living room. Now he was sprawled on the couch, shedding on Jane's good suit. Josie caught the sweet scent of Estée Lauder and hair spray. Jane must have added more Final Net to prevent another follicle malfunction. Despite the fresh powder and pink lipstick, Jane looked gray with fatigue.

She brightened when she saw Josie. "Stuart and I are watching our favorite show."

"What's happening with Victor?" Josie asked. That was always a safe question. Josie could never remember the plots. It would allow her to stall a little longer.

"That Victor! If he doesn't straighten up, I'm going to start watching the Oprah channel instead," Jane said. "Now he's taken up with Diane, who is no good, and he's done it just to spite his son, Nick, who was having an affair with her."

Stuart growled.

"Even Stuart knows he's bad," Jane said. "Not only that, he is making some kind of devil's pact with Adam."

"Nick is?" Josie asked.

"No," Jane said. "Victor. Adam is also Victor Junior—his child by Hope."

"Right," Josie said.

"And you remember that Adam stole Sharon's baby

and gave it to Ashley, but now Sharon has her baby back and is living with Adam and all is forgiven, I guess, but gee whiz, would you live with a friend like that?"

"Absolutely not," Josie said. "They sure do a lot of bed-hopping."

"That's life, Josie," said Jane, church woman and serious celibate. Josie was pretty sure her mother had lived like a nun since her father had left more than twenty years ago. Time to talk about their own soap opera.

"How are you, Mom? How's Tillie doing? Have you heard anything else?"

"I'm tired," Jane said. "And worried. Josie, I don't know how Tillie's going to survive. This arrest is hard on her."

"I'm sure it is, Mom. Her friends know she's innocent. You'll tell her that, won't you?"

"It won't help, Josie. The shame is killing her. I talked to her daughter today and Lorena said business is way down. Why didn't you tell me you and Ted went there for lunch?"

"I didn't want to worry you, Mom."

"I found out anyway, didn't I?" Jane said. "You can't fool me, Josie Marcus. I can read you like a book. Now you want to ask me something but you're afraid. Out with it! I'm seeing Tillie as soon as my show is over."

Here goes, Josie thought. "Uh, Mom, you've been sending money to the St. Thalamus Society for Indigent Children, Our Lady of the Sheets, and the Sisters of Divine Poverty."

"So? Why is that your business?" Jane's glare should have burned a hole in Josie's forehead. "And how did you find out?"

"I, uh, saw the envelopes in the mailbox," Josie said. "Mom, they're not real charities. They're crooked. I checked them out on the Internet."

Frail Jane rose up out of her chair like an avenging

fury. Any trace of weakness was gone. Her eyes burned with anger. Stuart jumped off the couch and stood next to his mistress, alert and on guard.

"I refuse to believe that, Josie Marcus," Jane said. "Mrs. Mueller donates to all three of those charities. So does Mrs. Gruenloh at our church. Are you telling me we're all wrong?"

"Yes, Mom," Josie said. She hated the trembling in her voice.

Jane reached for her purse and car keys. "You can't believe everything you read on the Internet, Josie. I'll thank you to keep your nose out of my business. If you must investigate something, then help my friend. I'm going to see Tillie now. I'll call Mrs. Mueller and find out what happened on my show tomorrow. You may leave."

Jane brushed past her and marched down the front steps. Josie felt twelve years old as she slunk down the stairs. Jane waited at the bottom. She watched Josie open her own door. Once Josie was inside her own flat, Jane slammed her front door and locked it.

Chapter 26

Everyone seemed to be giving Josie the same message.

Ted had told her, "That weedy lot next to Tillie's can't be the only source of castor beans. Maybe you should find out where else people can get them."

Jane had said, "If you must investigate something, then help my friend."

Maybe I should try listening and start searching the Internet, Josie decided.

She'd almost made it to her room when Amelia said, "Mom, I'm hungry. Can we order pizza?"

A good mother would make sure her child had a well-balanced diet, Josie thought. A good daughter would listen to her mother and investigate Tillie's case. I can't be a good mother until I get Jane off my back.

"Let me make sure I have enough cash to buy pizza," Josie said. She rooted a twenty-dollar bill out of her purse, pulled a pizza coupon off the fridge, and told her daughter, "Make the call and take care of Big Dave the pizza guy, will you?"

"Yay!" Amelia said, bolting for the phone. Harry charged behind her, a striped furry streak.

Josie sat down at her desk and started Googling castor beans. She was amazed by their deadly power, even after she'd seen what they'd done to Clay. One site warned, "As few as four ingested seeds can cause death in an adult human, and lesser amounts may result in symptoms of poisoning." The long list of symptoms, all violent and unpleasant, was almost enough to put Josie off her pizza.

Castor beans were "among the most lethal naturally occurring toxins known today," said eMedicine, another site.

Josie thought of the beautiful big-leaved plant outside Tillie's kitchen door. Six feet of death, prettily packaged and bearing brown speckled beans. The castor beans looked like hand-painted art in the online photos.

"The beans are most commonly used for ornamental purposes," the site continued, "such as prayer or rosary beads, or in musical shakers (maracas)."

Maracas? Gemma Lynn told Josie that her shop had a sudden run on Mexican maracas. Someone had bought two pairs of the musical instruments. Josie had dismissed that story as a salesperson's exaggeration, but maybe Gemma was telling the truth. It made sense. Clay's killer could crack open a couple of cheap maracas for a lethal dose and avoid a nasty rash and a bug-infested lot.

Gemma Lynn would know who bought those maracas. If Josie went there tomorrow, she could talk Gemma into giving her the buyer's name. That would be easier than trying to follow Lorena or Desmond, hoping they'd slip up.

She'd take Alyce. Her friend was looking for more pieces of that Rose Point china. Even a shopkeeper as lazy as Gemma would dig out the china once Alyce flashed her cash.

Josie would even tighten her own belt and buy that

sampler at full price. Gemma wouldn't be able to resist that much business. Josie would have to watch the grocery budget and cut unnecessary car trips to save gas money, but it would be worth the expense to end this investigation. Then she could—

"Mom," Amelia called, "pizza's here. I'm starved."

"Me, too," Josie said. She opened the boxes on the kitchen table and inhaled. "Mmm. That smells good."

Harry jumped up on the table and stuck a paw on a mushroom. "Hey!" Josie said. "Amelia, get that cat out of here."

"Aw, Mom, he's so cute."

"Not on my pizza, he isn't. He dug around in his litter box with that foot and now it's on my dinner."

"Mom, you're disgusting," Amelia said.

"Not as disgusting as Mr. Litter Box Foot."

"He took a bath. I watched him."

"Terrific. Now his foot is covered in cat spit instead of cat—" Josie's tirade was interrupted by a knock on the front door.

"I'll get it," Amelia said, eager to get away from her angry mother.

"Check who's on the porch first before you open the door, Amelia," Josie said.

"It's Grandma!" Amelia said. She greeted Jane with delight—and probably relief. Harry disappeared under the couch.

"We're having pizza," Amelia said. "Do you want to join us, Grandma?"

"Thanks, honey, but I'm not hungry. I need to see your mother right away." Jane's face crumpled and she collapsed, weeping, into the living room chair.

Josie ran in and kneeled beside her. "Mom! What's the matter? Were you in an accident? Are you hurt? Are you sick?"

She was shocked by her mother's appearance. Jane's lipstick was bitten off and her sprayed hair stuck out in sticky wings. Her skin looked grayer than her hair.

"It's not me. It's Tillie," Jane said. "That lawyer you like so much—Renzo Fischer—wants a hundred thousand dollars for her trial. He says he can't work for toasted ravioli now that she's facing the death penalty. He has to hire expert witnesses, get lab tests and exhibits, and if it goes to trial he'll need more. He has the nerve to claim he's giving her a special discount rate because she's a friend."

Jane gave a most unladylike snort. "Some friend."

"Mom, I can ask Alyce to talk to her husband and see if Jake can find a better lawyer for her, but I think that may be a low price for a capital murder trial. I've heard they can cost a quarter million or more."

"Where's she going to get the money for that terrific discount?" Jane's voice trembled and her head wobbled a little. "She'll have to sell her restaurant to that Desmond buzzard. And he's withdrawn his offer for a million dollars. He says her business isn't worth that anymore. Now he wants to give Tillie one hundred ten thousand dollars for her business and building.

"After she pays the lawyer, she'll have almost nothing for a lifetime of work," Jane said. "Tillie can't live on ten thousand dollars. And that leaves nothing for Lorena. She'll be out of a job. Lorena was duped by that Desmond with his flashy diamond ring. *Ha!* He chased after that girl, pretending to be such a Romeo. Ruined her life, that's what he did. And her mother's. If Tillie needs more money for that trial, she's out of luck. You've got to do something, Josie."

Jane seemed exhausted after recounting Tillie's tribulations. She sat back in the chair and shut her eyes. "My friend is going to be in jail forever. She could wind up on death row. Can't you help her? Haven't you found anything yet?"

"I have one small lead," Josie said. "Gemma Lynn may be able to help. Alyce and I can see her in the morning."

"This can't wait until morning, Josie. Desmond's given Tillie forty-eight hours to accept his offer. You have to go now."

"I'll call Gemma Lynn and see if she's still at her shop." Josie dialed the number. It rang and rang, but no one picked up.

"She's not at work, Mom, but I expect her store is closed at this hour."

"Then call her at home." Jane didn't bother hiding her impatience. "Do you know where she lives?"

"She has an apartment above the shop," Josie said.

Josie found Gemma's home number through directory assistance and called. Her phone rang four times, then went into voice mail. She left a message. "Hi, Gemma. It's Josie. I was in the other day with my friend who bought the white coffeepot. I need to talk with you as soon as possible." She left her cell phone number and hung up.

"You heard, Mom," Josie said. "She's not home."

"Then go see her."

"Now?" Josie said. "It's seven thirty. It will be eight o'clock by the time I get there. Gemma's street is deserted during the day. I shouldn't go alone at night."

"Then I'll go with you," Jane said. Her color was improving.

"No, I need you to stay with Amelia, Mom."

Amelia, who'd been lurking by the kitchen door, said, "I can take care of myself, Mom."

"The last time you said that, I found out you'd hitchhiked to Clayton with a backpack full of wine coolers,"

Josie said. "We had three people searching for you at midnight."

"I was trying to help you, Mom. Besides, I'm a different person now. I'm almost a teenager."

"That's what worries me," Josie said. "You are not staying home by yourself."

"Could Alyce go with you?" Jane asked.

"Not at night. That's her family time."

"What about Ted?" Jane's eyes were bright and she was standing taller.

"He's working at the clinic tonight," Josie said.

"Can't he get his partner to take over for an hour or so?" Jane looked a decade younger. The defeated old woman was growing stronger now that she had some hope.

"I can call him and find out," Josie said.

"Call him from your car," Jane said and pushed her toward the front door. Now Jane seemed as strong as a quarterback.

"Thanks for doing this," she said briskly. She handed Josie her purse and keys and shoved her out her own door.

"But, Mom," Josie said.

"Don't dillydally," Jane said, and slammed the door in her daughter's face.

"I didn't get any pizza," Josie said to the closed door.

Chapter 27

Ted's clinic was less then ten minutes from Josie's home. She drove straight there to pick him up. She was relieved to see his tangerine Mustang in the lot and no other cars. Maybe he could get free.

The clinic door was unlocked. Josie ran inside and saw the powder blue waiting room was empty. Magazines were neatly stacked on a side table. Josie caught the light scent of dog hair under the thick odor of disinfectant. The receptionist's computer was off and her desk was neat. Ted must be here alone.

Josie ran down the narrow hall to his office. All the examination rooms were empty. Good. In Ted's office, his black Lab was sleeping under the desk. Festus barked a greeting and ran over to Josie, tail thumping.

"Where's Ted?" Josie asked the dog.

Festus nosed open the swinging door to the back rooms and led her to the surgery. Ted was in green scrubs, standing by a long table, setting sharp, scary-looking instruments on a tray, including what looked like a saw. Josie's stomach turned. Ted was so engrossed in his work that he didn't see her.

"Arf!" Festus said. That got Ted's attention.

"Josie, what's wrong?" he asked. "Why are you here? Is Harry sick? Is Amelia all right?"

"Everyone is fine," Josie said. "I need you, Ted. I may have a lead on who killed Clay."

She paced the room, wringing her hands.

"Calm down, Josie," Ted said. He found a blue plastic chair and pushed her gently into it. "Here. Sit down. Let me get you some coffee."

"That will only make me more jittery," Josie said.

"How about some tea?"

"Please, Ted, I don't need anything except for you to listen."

"Then I'm all ears."

Josie took a deep breath and said, "I took your advice. I did an Internet search and found another source for castor beans."

She told him what she'd read online about castor beans and maracas. "Remember when Gemma said someone bought up all but one pair of her Mexican maracas? I thought she was trying to pressure you into buying that last set. Now I don't. I think the person who bought those maracas wanted them for their castor beans. The buyer could be Clay's killer. Gemma knows the name. I have to go see her tonight. I need you to go with me."

"Josie, I can't. I'm getting ready for emergency surgery. Can't this wait till morning?"

"No," Josie said. "Tillie needs a hundred thousand dollars right away."

She told him about the lawyer's need for more money and Desmond's demand for an immediate sale. "Mom says this can't wait until morning. She wants me to see Gemma Lynn tonight. She's at my house taking care of Amelia. I need you.

"If Gemma Lynn tells me who bought those maracas,

we could find Clay's killer. I tried to call Gemma at the store. Then I called her home. No one answered, so I'm driving there now."

"You can't go alone, Josie. That street is too dangerous at night."

"I was hoping you'd come with me," Josie said.

Ted made a whimpering sound, almost like Festus. "I can't, Josie. I just got off the phone with Hans's owner. He's a sweet old Great Dane who likes to chase cars. This time, a Buick caught him. He got hit in the leg. His owner is bringing him in. From what he said, it sounds like Hans has a compound fracture of his right front leg. He said the bone is sticking through the skin."

Josie hissed in sympathy.

"He's five—that's old for a Dane. If the break is as bad as he's telling me, I'm going to have to operate on the old boy. At his age, he may not make it."

"What about your partner, Christine?" Josie asked. "Couldn't she do it?"

"She's at her son's basketball game. She told me she was going to turn off her cell tonight. Let me see if I can reach her."

Ted picked up the receiver on the wall phone and dialed. He waited, then said, "Hi, it's Ted. I'm at the clinic. I'm sorry to bother you on your night off. Any chance you could call me? Thanks."

He hung up and shook his head. "Her phone is definitely off, Josie."

Josie gathered up her purse and found her keys. "It was selfish of me to bother you. I still have that canister of pepper spray you gave me to ward off wild dogs. I'll be fine. I'd better go."

Ted grabbed her arm. "No, you won't. I promised I'd be there for you. Now the first time you need me, I'm stuck at work."

"This is ridiculous," Josie said. "I can take care of myself."

"Yes, you can," Ted said. "But what about your daughter? You're looking for a killer, Josie. Someone who poisoned a man in front of a restaurant full of witnesses. That's cold-blooded. He won't hesitate to hurt you. Do you want your mother raising Amelia if anything happens to you?"

"No, but—"

"Then turn on your phone. I'll stay with you while you find her."

"But I'm only twenty minutes away from River Bluff," Josie said.

"I don't care," Ted said. "You can't go there alone. Do you want me to abandon that poor dog?"

"No, that would be cruel," Josie said.

"Then turn on your cell phone and call me."

"What if Hans's owner needs to contact you again?" Josie said.

"Call my cell. That will keep the clinic line open. I'm not going to run out of minutes. Are you?"

"No," Josie said. "My plan is unlimited."

"Then do it, Josie. Please."

Josie dug out her cell and called Ted. His pocket rang and he took out his cell phone and pressed a button. "Okay, it's on. Don't hang up. Keep your phone within reach on the car seat. I'll hang on, but I won't talk unless you need me. I'll be right here, Josie. And if that line goes dead, I'll leave poor Hans and come after you. His future depends on you."

Josie didn't like the choices facing her. To help her mother's friend, she had to risk her daughter's future and that poor dog's life.

"I can do this," Josie said. "I'll be fine. Amelia is safe

with my mother and I'll find Clay's killer. I'm safe as long as I have backup."

She kissed Ted good-bye, rushed into the chilly fall night, and turned her Honda toward Gemma's neighborhood. Traffic was light at that hour. Seventeen minutes later, she parked in front of Gemma's Junktique and picked up her cell phone.

"I'm here," Josie told Ted. "The lights are off in the shop and upstairs in her apartment."

"Give me the address, just in case," Ted said.

"It's thirty-eight sixty-seven Gluckman Avenue," Josie said. "That's in River Bluff. I'm getting out of my car now."

"Wait!" Ted said. "Any other cars on the street? Do you see any people?"

"It's completely deserted," Josie said. "I don't even see that cat you flushed out last time."

"I don't like this, Josie," Ted said.

"You worry too much." Josie slammed her car door, locked it, and walked carefully toward Gemma's shop, scanning the empty street and boarded buildings. "We saw Gemma yesterday. It's only eight o'clock. She's probably at dinner or grocery shopping. I have no reason to be frightened. The streetlights make Gluckman Avenue bright as day. You're talking to me on the phone. I'm approaching the shop now. I'm on the sidewalk right in front of the store."

Josie stopped. "That's funny," she said.

"What's funny?" Ted asked. "Josie, are you there?" She heard the fear in his voice.

"Of course I'm here, Ted. The shop door is wide-open. I'm going inside to check."

"NO!" Ted's voice blasted out of the tinny speaker. "Josie, do not go in there. Go back to your car and lock the doors. I'm calling nine-one-one."

"I can call the police myself," Josie said.

"Get in your car, Josie, please. Don't hang up. I need to stay in touch with you. Otherwise I'll have to abandon Hans and drive straight there. I'm calling the cops now. Hang on."

Josie didn't run to her car. She stayed on the sidewalk calling, "Gemma! Gemma Lynn. Are you there?"

No answer. But she heard a hollow *tappety-clip, tappety-clip* sound. Josie jumped, then saw an empty fast-food cup blowing down the street. Her heart was banging against her ribs like it was trying to escape. Josie didn't feel quite so secure now.

She ran back to her car, climbed in, locked the doors, and felt in her purse for the canister of pepper spray. She didn't think she needed it, but maybe if Ted knew she was holding it, he'd feel better.

"I've got the nine-one-one operator on the clinic phone, Josie," he said. "A police officer is on the way. The operator wants to know if you're safe."

"I'm in my car with the doors locked, parked under a streetlight," Josie said. "I have that pepper spray in my hand."

"Good. Keep it there. The operator estimates the police will be there in less than two minutes."

"I can hear the sirens now," Josie said.

"Thank God," Ted said.

Chapter 28

Was this cop old enough to carry a gun? Josie wondered. His skin was as pink as a baby's. His pale blond mustache looked like a lost caterpillar. It made him seem younger. His name tag said JARDEN.

Blue and red flashes from his car's light bar disco danced on the dirty brick front of Gemma's Junktique. Josie opened her door and slid out. The cop didn't tell her to get back inside.

"We got a call there's a problem here, ma'am," Officer Jarden said. His eyes darted nervously around the deserted street.

Ma'am? Josie thought. I'm a ma'am and he doesn't look much older than Amelia. He may even be younger than Officer Zellman. Where is River Bluff doing its recruiting—at a preschool? I must be getting old when the cops start looking young. Next it will be doctors and baseball players. Soon I'll be older than the President of the United States.

"Ma'am?" the officer said. "I asked why you were concerned. Do you believe a person is in danger?"

"The front door of Gemma's shop is open," Josie said. "Gemma's Junktique. I called Gemma Lynn Rae, the owner, but she didn't answer her shop phone or her home phone."

"And you are a relative? A friend?"

"I'm Josie Marcus," she said. "I'm a customer. And you're Officer Jarden?"

"Officer Dale Jarden, River Bluff police. That's right. You must be a good customer to come here at night when the shop's closed."

"It's not like that," Josie said. "I couldn't reach her and I was worried."

"How long has this Gemma Lynn been missing?"

"Well, she's not missing, not officially," Josie said.

"When was the last time you saw her?"

"Yesterday afternoon."

"Is she an old person?" Officer Jarden asked.

"No," Josie said. "She's about thirty or thirty-five."

"And she was in good health?"

"Yes. Well, fairly good. She was upset because her boyfriend had died and she cried a lot, but she seemed okay otherwise."

"Do you think she might harm herself?" Officer Jarden asked.

"Huh?" Josie said.

"Are you concerned that she might commit suicide?"

"No. I don't think so. But I don't know her very well."

"So you couldn't reach her by phone and you drove all the way here from—"

"Maplewood," Josie said.

"That's a good half hour away," the cop said.

"Twenty minutes," Josie said. "But I made it in seventeen. Going the speed limit," she added.

"I'm not a traffic officer, ma'am. I'm not concerned about how fast you were traveling. I'm trying to understand your story. You say you drove all the way from Maplewood to see a person you hardly know."

"That's right," Josie said. She sounded stupider with every syllable. Why had she let Ted call 911?

"What did you do when you got here, prior to calling nine-one-one?"

"I didn't call nine-one-one," Josie said. "Someone else did. I got here and parked my car. I was going to knock on the shop door, but it was wide-open. I called her name several times, but Gemma didn't answer. That open door didn't look right. I was talking on the phone with my boyfriend. He's a vet. When I told him the shop door was open, he called nine-one-one from his office phone. I stayed on his cell phone. He couldn't be here, but he didn't want me to go into the shop alone."

"Yes, ma'am. Did you enter the shop after that?"

"No," Josie said. "But this isn't the sort of neighborhood where you leave shop doors hanging open at night. I didn't see any lights and I didn't want to enter the building by myself. So Dr. Ted Scottsmeyer—he's my boyfriend—called you. I mean, called nine-one-one. Ted said if anything was wrong, I should have the police check it."

"He's right, ma'am. That's not a job for a civilian. Do you see the lady's car parked nearby?"

"I don't know if Gemma has a car," Josie said. "That's my Honda in front of the shop, and it's the only car on the street. A driveway runs alongside the building. Gemma's car could be around in the back. I didn't look for it. I just saw the door open. A woman alone wouldn't do that. Not on purpose."

How many times did she have to mention that door before the patrol cop checked it? Josie wondered.

"Well, I'll take a look around, since the door's open."

Finally, Josie thought.

"That is irregular. You stay by your car, ma'am. Good thing I've got my flashlight in my car." Officer Jarden pulled a Maglite about the size of a baseball bat out of his patrol car, then squared his shoulders and unsnapped his holster.

The cop switched on the flashlight and approached the building calling, "Gemma Lynn? Ms. Rae? Are you there? Hello?"

The door was open wide enough that Officer Jarden didn't have to touch it to enter the building. He walked through the doorway and said, "Hello? Anybody here? Hello?"

Suddenly, his voice was lower and faster. "Omigod. Omigod. Lady, are you okay? Speak to me."

The young cop flipped on the light.

Josie ran forward and saw Officer Jarden on his knees next to Gemma Lynn. She was lying behind the Victorian settee. Her head was covered with something black. A scarf? A hat?

Josie tiptoed past the counter. The shelves had been cleaned out. She glanced at a pile of receipts, clippings, and printouts next to the cash register but didn't see the paper with her phone number. On top was a piece of notebook paper with one word written on it: "Hartford."

As she got closer, Josie saw Gemma wasn't wearing a black hat. That was dark blood. Gemma's blood. Her head had been bashed in.

Chapter 29

"Is Gemma dead?" Josie's voice echoed in the woman's high-ceilinged shop. The three-word question seemed lost in the cavelike store. It bounced off the dull mirrors and thudded into the Victorian settee.

Officer Jarden, crouched over Gemma's body, didn't seem to notice Josie.

How could a shop so crammed with junk seem empty? Josie wondered. The dusty vases and chipped china seemed to be huddling together. Josie shivered. The shop was cold and the shadows were creepy: A spindly table looked like a crouching spider. A fat ginger jar lamp with no shade was a disembodied head.

Josie moved away from them, closer to the cop. The glaring overhead light drained the color from his pale skin. His small brown eyes were buried deep in his round face. A dust smudge on his nose made him seem even younger, like a boy playing in the dirt.

Officer Jarden was talking to himself, his voice trembling and a shade too high. Josie could see sweat rings on his uniform, even though the store was cool inside. "She's dead," he said. "Real dead. Must have interrupted a burglary. That case is cleaned out. No point in getting an ambulance. I better call dispatch. Shit! I shouldn't have turned on the light. Mullanphy will have my scalp."

Josie felt sorry for the flustered cop. She took a step closer to the dark pool near Gemma's head. "I won't tell him," she said softly. "We can pretend the light was on all the time."

He looked up, first startled, then angry. "What are you doing in here?" he shouted at Josie. "I told you to remain outside in your car."

"I'm sorry," Josie said.

"Sorry? I should arrest you for interfering with a police investigation. I can't have you compromising this crime scene."

"That empty case was full of jewelry," Josie said. "Mostly junk jewelry, I think."

The officer didn't answer her. Josie stood unmoving in the desolate store. Finally Jarden said, "Get out and go wait in your car."

Josie retreated, relieved to be ordered out of Gemma's shop. She couldn't walk as fast as she wanted. Her legs felt heavy as tree stumps. She had to command each foot to move: left foot. Right foot. Left. Right.

It seemed hours before she reached her car. She'd left her door hanging open, and her cell phone was abandoned on the passenger seat. She could hear Ted shouting through the tinny speaker. "Hello? Josie? Are you okay? Are you there? Please, Josie, tell me you're all right."

She picked up her phone and tried to reassure Ted. "I'm right here. I'm okay."

"No, you're not," he said. "I can tell by your voice. What's wrong?"

"She's dead," Josie said. "Gemma's dead."

"How? Did she have an accident?"

"She was murdered," Josie said. "Somebody killed her."

Even though she'd seen Gemma's bloody head, this was the first time Josie connected the woman's terrible injuries with a brutal death.

She'd failed to reassure Ted. Josie could hear him shouting. "Murdered! How? Was she shot? Strangled? Robbed?"

"I couldn't get close to her body, but I think she was beaten to death. Her head's all bloody. It was horrible." Josie gulped back tears. "I'm sorry," she said. "I don't mean to cry."

"Why are you sorry?" Ted asked. "You saw something horrible. You should be upset. Are you by yourself? Are you safe? Where are you?"

"I'm in my car, but there's a police officer within shouting distance. He's staying with Gemma. With her body, I mean."

"What are you doing outside?" Ted asked.

"The cop chased me out," Josie said. "He said I would contaminate the crime scene. I saw Gemma Lynn's body and he made me leave. He says it's a murder scene. I'm glad to be out of there. That shop is spooky at night and she smells funny. I shouldn't say that about a dead person, should I?" She gave a high-pitched giggle.

"Josie, you're in shock. And yes, people—and animals—don't smell so good when they die. Do you feel safe sitting alone in your car?"

"There's nobody around, Ted."

"Are the crime scene techs there yet?" Ted asked. "What about the homicide detectives?"

"I don't think River Bluff has a homicide department," Josie said. "It's too small. From what Officer Jarden said, they'll send in the same detective who investigated Clay's collapse at the restaurant—Brian Mullanphy. He gave me his card when he interviewed me at Tillie's. He investigates 'crimes against persons.' Gemma's murder definitely fits that."

"I'm glad you're not in that shop, Josie. If Gemma was beaten, it's probably a bloody scene. That detective will be looking for blood spatter, bloody shoe prints or handprints. If there's no blood on you, you can't be connected with her murder."

"But, Ted, there's already a connection," Josie said. "I called her this evening and said I needed to talk to her. They're going to find my message on her answering machine."

"That may not be a bad thing. If the call is time- and date-stamped, it could be your alibi," Ted said. "Do you know when she was killed?"

"No idea," Josie said. "I only caught a glimpse of her body."

"This is going to sound gross, but did you see any flies?"

"Why would I see flies?" Josie asked.

"Um, if she's been dead awhile, she'll attract flies."

"Not that I noticed," Josie said.

"Oh, you'd notice them," Ted said. "They'd look like—" He stopped suddenly.

"Like what?" Josie asked.

"I don't want to get too graphic. Let's just say there would be a swarm of them."

Josie shivered, even though her car was warmer than the chilly store. "My phone number will probably be in Gemma's files," she said. "The detective will find that."

"So? You wanted that sampler and you gave Gemma your number if she lowered the price. Be sure to mention that. He'll know you didn't kill her for a fifty-dollar sampler."

"People kill for less than that," Josie said.

"Teenage hotheads, maybe. Not responsible moms," Ted said. "I remember a big stack of paper on her counter. Did you see your phone number in that?"

"I wasn't in there long enough to see much of anything," Josie said. "No, wait! I did see one thing. There were papers scattered all over the counter—receipts, printouts, a newspaper or two. I saw a piece of paper by her phone. Gemma had written one word—at least I think it was her writing. It looked like the same scrolly letters she'd used for Alyce's receipt. The word was Hartford."

"Like Hartford, Connecticut?" Ted asked. "Or the insurance company?"

"I don't know," Josie said. "Isn't there a Hartford Street in St. Louis?"

"There is. Near Tower Grove Park on the South Side. Hartford is near Connecticut, but the two streets don't cross, which I always thought was weird. Hartford has a lot of big old brick homes. I think there's a Hartford Coffee Company on Hartford Street. Nice little coffee shop."

"I can't imagine what a coffee shop would have to do with anything," Josie said. "Clay drank beer. A lot of beer."

"There's Hartford, Illinois, too," Ted said "Right across the Mississippi, about fifteen miles north of downtown St. Louis."

"The word can't have anything to do with this," Josie said. "It just caught my eye."

Headlights stabbed the night. "Ted, there's a car coming."

"Stay on the phone, Josie. Don't hang up. I want to make sure you're safe."

The car was large and square, an old Crown Victoria.

Josie relaxed a bit. Only cops and old people drove Crown Vics. The car parked behind hers. Josie heard its door creak open. A tall man unfolded himself. She recognized the profile in the streetlight: That lump of a nose stuck on a square-cut face.

"Detective Brian Mullanphy is here," Josie said. "He's going into Gemma's shop now. I'm sure he'll want to talk to me. I'll go straight home afterward."

"Josie, promise me you'll treat Detective Mullanphy like a three-hundred-pound gorilla," Ted said.

"What's that mean?" Josie asked.

"Be very careful. Don't lie to him. Tell him the truth, no matter what. I'll be right there," Ted said. "I'll leave for River Bluff as soon as Christine arrives."

"You're leaving the clinic?" Josie asked. "What about Hans, your Great Dane with the bad break?"

"His people brought him in while you were inside the building. Hans is sedated and prepped for surgery. My partner should be here any moment. She answered my message while you were in the building with the police. Christine said she'd handle Hans."

"Ted, you can't abandon your patient."

"I can't abandon you," Ted said. "I couldn't operate. I'm too worried about you. Chris will do a better job. She'll fix up Hans, I'll check on you, and then I'll come back and spend the night with Hans. Christine will take good care of him until I get back here."

"Ted, I can't ask you to do that," Josie began.

"You didn't ask it," Ted said. "I volunteered. Chris owes me. I've covered for her plenty of times when her son was sick or she had some activity at his school. I hear a car in the parking lot. I'm pretty sure it's her. Yep, that's Chris coming down the hall. Josie, I have to tell her about Hans and then I'll be right there."

He hung up before Josie could protest. She called her

mother. Jane answered on the first ring. "Josie, did you get the information? Did—"

"Mom, I'm at Gemma's. There's been a problem. She was murdered and I saw her body. The police are here. I may be a while."

Jane gave a squawk, then peppered her daughter with a dozen questions: "Murdered! How? Why? Where are you? Are you safe?"

"Mom," Josie began.

A man's voice shouted, "Drop that phone. Drop it right now!"

The young cop startled Josie. The phone spurted out of her hand like a slippery bar of soap and slid across the passenger seat. She could hear her mother shouting, "Josie? What's going on? Answer me!"

She grabbed the phone again and said, "I think the police want me to hang up."

"Don't you dare hang up on me, Josie Marcus. I'm your mother."

She couldn't see her mother, who was still shooting questions at her. But she knew Jane's face would be a furious pink. She could definitely see the young cop at her window. Officer Jarden was bristling with anger and his gun was still unholstered.

"Sorry, Mom, you're outranked," Josie said and hit the END button.

If only I could really end this by pressing a button, she thought, as the cop ordered her to get out of the car.

Chapter 30

"You've developed an intense interest in River Bluff, Ms. Marcus," Detective Brian Mullanphy said. "You drove here all the way from—Maplewood, is that right?"

"Yes," said Josie in small voice.

"What time did you arrive at the victim's shop?" he asked.

"About eight o'clock," Josie said.

"Did you know the store had been closed for two hours?"

"Yes," Josie said.

She remembered Ted's advice to treat this man like a three-hundred-pound gorilla. The detective's high forehead and shrewd eyes reminded her that Ted was right. But Mullanphy's potato nose threw her. How could she take the knob-nosed detective seriously?

The more time she spent talking to the detective, the more she agreed with Ted's advice. Mullanphy was smart. She'd have to be careful.

"So what made you drive all the way across St. Louis County tonight?" Mullanphy asked. "Aren't you a single mother with a preteen daughter?"

"Yes," Josie said. She was impressed. Had Mullanphy

reread her statement from Tillie's before he came here, or did he remember those details?

"And yet you abandoned her to make this long, gas-guzzling trip."

"My mother is watching her," Josie said, relieved that she'd been able to tell the truth three questions in a row.

"Why drive here tonight, Ms. Marcus? What was so important it couldn't wait until tomorrow morning? Was Ms. Rae holding a special late-night sale?"

"No!" Josie yipped like a stepped-on puppy. He was closing in.

"I didn't think so." Mullanphy's voice was smooth as honey and just as sticky. "Judging by the dust on this merchandise, I don't think you have to worry about someone dashing in and snapping up a fantastic bargain before tomorrow. Unless that's a Ming vase on that table."

He pointed to an ugly blue pottery jar. "That poor lady surprised a burglar, Ms. Marcus, and got her head bashed in. Doubt if he got enough for a bottle of cheap wine. You're just lucky he cleared out by the time you arrived. So why did you come here?"

"I—"

She was saved by the arrival of the medical examiner and two techs from the crime scene unit. Mullanphy talked to them while Josie tried to gather her scattered thoughts.

The techs set up harsh white lights to illuminate the murder scene. Josie caught grisly glimpses of Gemma's battered head. She saw thick gobs of dark blood on the floor. Black splashes on the settee looked like clots of tar.

She tried to drag her eyes away from the murder scene and concentrate. The relentless Mullanphy would return shortly to lob hard questions at her. She had steeled herself for the next onslaught when another squad car arrived. Josie recognized Officer Zellman. Mullanphy gave him orders to check the Dumpster behind the shop.

That was the last interruption. Now she was facing that chiseled profile with the clown's nose. "Why were you here tonight, Ms. Marcus?" Mullanphy asked.

Tell the truth, Josie reminded herself. "I tried to call Gemma and talk to her, but she didn't answer her phone. I decided to see her in person. I knew it was a long shot that I'd catch her working late at the store, but I thought she might be upstairs in her apartment and she'd come down and talk to me."

"Why? Were you good friends?"

"No," Josie said.

"How long did you know the victim?"

"The first time I saw Gemma Lynn was at Tillie's," Josie said.

"And that was?"

"The day—" She paused, then said, "The day before Clay died. But I didn't talk with her until a couple of days later. I brought my friend Alyce here. She bought a china coffeepot—a Rose Point pattern. I saw an old-fashioned sampler I liked and asked Gemma the price. I didn't buy it. It was too expensive."

A tech interrupted. "Detective, I think we have the murder weapon." He held up a winged statue that looked like it had black paint on its base.

"More evidence she surprised a burglar," Mullanphy said to the tech. "The smart ones don't carry guns. They don't want to get sent up for armed robbery. Must have been some young punk who panicked. This one reached for the first weapon he could find and bashed her with it."

Josie stared at the statue. The tech carried it using both gloved hands, as if it were heavy. It was definitely ugly. Made of some dull metal, the statue had wide wings attached to a woman's body.

Was it a clumsy copy of the Winged Victory? Josie wondered. Then she caught the statue's syrupy smile. That was an angel. A guardian angel, caught off guard. Gemma was touched by an angel, Josie thought giddily, and fought a crazy urge to laugh.

Mullanphy caught her wrestling her face back into a solemn expression. "What's so funny, Ms. Marcus?"

"Nothing," Josie said, and gulped.

She was pretty sure Mullanphy didn't consider her a suspect. When she'd entered the shop, he'd shone his flashlight on her pant legs and shoes, looking for blood. "Slip off your loafers," he'd said, then examined the soles in the strong light.

I need new heels, Josie had thought, looking at her worn right sole.

Mullanphy had checked her hands and prodded her fingernails. She had no blood on her hands—or anywhere else. Only after he'd been satisfied that there was no blood spatter or transfer on her clothes, shoes, or hands did he let her put her shoes back on and start questioning her. Despite the reassuring lack of damning physical evidence, he still seemed skeptical.

Josie wished she'd worn a warm jacket. Even on a warm fall night, the shop had a cold spot, like a haunted house. Had it felt that cold when she'd been there with Alyce? Or when Ted had admired the sampler she'd found? She couldn't remember.

"Ms. Marcus, if I could have your attention," Detective Mullanphy said. "What were you doing alone in River Bluff tonight? Did you have a knickknack emergency?"

"I wanted to check on a sampler," Josie said. "I really liked it and hoped Gemma would lower the price."

“Is this sampler in the shop window?” he asked.

“No,” Josie said. “It’s in that bin of pictures.” She pointed toward it. “Most are bad prints of old masters, but this sampler was a fine piece of needlework. It says FRIENDSHIP, LOVE & TRUTH and it’s surrounded by roses.”

“I’ll see if it’s there,” he said.

Mullanphy put on latex gloves and carefully moved each framed picture in the bin. When he came to the oil of the overly orange autumn scene, he winced. That painting must be bad if it makes a homicide cop cringe, she thought.

He went through the bin a second time, then held up the sampler. “Is this it?” he asked.

Josie nodded.

“Maybe you should concentrate on that message,” he said. “Especially the part about ‘truth.’ Now, tell me the truth, Ms. Marcus: Why did you rush over here tonight? You can tell me the real reason, then write your statement and go home. Or you can stay in the River Bluff lockup while I find out the truth. What’s it going to be?”

I might as well tell him, Josie thought. Once she made up her mind to talk, the words tumbled out.

“I don’t think Tillie did it. Killed Clay Oreck. She’s my mother’s friend. Mom’s known her since she was a little girl and she says Tillie wouldn’t kill anyone. Mom wanted me to find Clay’s real killer.”

Detective Mullanphy gave a snort.

“I know it sounds stupid. I know there’s no way I can outsmart the police,” Josie said. “But you’ve never met my mother. I went through the motions to make Mom happy. She’s my on-call babysitter, and she’s free. Not many single mothers have that luxury.

“I looked up castor beans on the Internet and saw they were used in maracas. Gemma told me that she’d sold two pair right before Clay’s murder. I thought that was an important clue. All I had to do was ask Gemma who bought the maracas and I'd know the name of Clay's killer."

"And then what?" Mullanphy glared at her.

"Then I'd tell you and you could arrest the right person."

"I already know who bought them," the detective said.

"You do?" Josie looked stunned.

"I've heard of the Internet, too, Ms. Marcus, and I read that same article. I asked Ms. Rae who bought those maracas. She showed me the receipt. Molly and Alan Portman purchased two pairs of maracas for a Mexican dinner party they're giving. I went to this shop and Ms. Rae gave me the last pair from here. Alan and Molly are public-spirited citizens. They let me break open their maracas. They all contained the same thing—small sea shells. No castor beans. So much for your theory."

Josie felt smaller than the dusty china miniatures on the wall.

"Oh," she said.

"You did notice the castor beans growing in the vacant lot right next to Tillie's restaurant?" he asked.

"Yes," Josie said.

"So did we."

Chapter 31

Josie finished writing out her statement, signed it, and handed it to Detective Brian Mullanphy. He pulled out a pair of reading glasses and frowned at her writing like a disapproving teacher.

"This is the truth?" he asked.

"Yes," Josie said. She sneaked a glance at her watch. Eleven thirty. She stifled a yawn.

"Am I boring you, Ms. Marcus?"

"No, it's been a long night and I'm tired," she said.

"I'm tired, too, Ms. Marcus, and I'll be here long after you're asleep. And you know what makes my job harder? People who lie."

"I wrote the truth," Josie said and looked him in the eye. Would he believe her? Or did accomplished liars look people in the eye?

"I'm going to believe you," Mullanphy said. "But you're on probation. If I find one fact wrong, you're going to be a permanent guest of River Bluff. Got that?"

"Yes," Josie said. She sounded like a mouse. "Yes," she repeated, this time louder.

"Get out of here. Your boyfriend is waiting outside for you."

Josie grabbed her purse and ran to the door. Ted was pacing up and down on the sidewalk like a sentry. He'd walk to the driveway, stop, turn around, and walk past Gemma's shop to the driveway on the other side, then repeat the process. She watched him make one circuit, then ran outside. Josie threw her arms around Ted. His broad chest felt warm, solid, and safe. He smelled of antiseptic and dog hair.

"Ted, you're here." She kissed him.

"I said I would be." Ted sounded slightly offended. "It's heading on toward midnight. I talked with your mother."

"Oh, thank you," Josie said. "I'm too woozy to deal with Jane."

"Your mom took the news well," Ted said.

"She would, since it came from you," Josie said. "Besides, she's the one who insisted I drive here tonight."

"I reminded her of that," Ted said.

"Thank you," Josie said. "But I should get some guts. I'm a grown woman."

"I don't care how old you get—there's no way to handle your own mother," Ted said. "I act like a frightened bunny rabbit around my mother. I'll expect you to take over my mom-wrangling duties when the time comes."

When the time comes. Josie thought she'd never heard four sweeter words. Ted was telling her they had a future—maybe a permanent future.

"Let's leave your car parked here overnight and I'll drive you home," he said.

"I can't, Ted. I have to take Amelia to school in the morning. And you're spending the night with Hans. How's he doing?"

"Not sure," Ted said. "Chris said she'd call me when she got out of surgery. The old Dane must still be alive, or she'd let me know. Let's go to Uncle Bill's Pancake

House for a late dinner or early breakfast or whatever it is."

"The one on Manchester?" Josie asked.

"That's the one. I'll meet you there, then follow you back to Phelan Street to make sure you get home safe."

"Deal," Josie said.

Twenty minutes later, Josie parked under the Uncle Bill's sign. Ted's orange Mustang pulled in right beside her. They walked into the restaurant bathed in the rosy glow of the sign's pink neon, and were greeted by the perfume of sugary grease. Josie and Ted settled in a booth. The menu had everything from burgers to bagels, but they ordered breakfast.

Uncle Bill's had all the virtues of a Midwest grease spot. It was fast, cheap, and cheerful. The booths were big enough so they could sit side by side. The waitress kept them well coffeed. Josie felt herself reviving after her first cup. By the time the waitress brought their food—a steaming stack of pancakes for Josie and steak and eggs for Ted—Josie was talking faster than the cook was slamming out food.

"Thanks for telling me to be careful talking to that detective," Josie said. "I told him the truth and nothing but the truth. Otherwise, I'd be sitting in jail right now."

The dignified woman in the booth alongside them was clearly eavesdropping, but she didn't raise an eyebrow when Josie mentioned jail or detectives. Hangovers, breakups, and breakdowns were standard topics after midnight.

"I was surprised the detective let you go so soon," Ted said.

"Soon? I thought that Mullanphy and I were going to grow old together," Josie said.

Ted took her hand. "Seriously, Josie, how are you? That had to be horrible, finding Gemma dead."

"It was," Josie said. "I don't think it's quite hit me yet. Thank you for being there."

"You don't have to be alone anymore, Josie. I'm here to help you. I love you." Ted took her hand in his. "I want to ask you something."

He's going to propose, Josie thought. At long last. She was sure Uncle Bill's had seen its share of late-night engagements, too.

"Yes?" she said softly. Her voice was barely audible over the canned music.

"I want to go to Tower Grove Park for a walk while the weather's still good. Before it gets too cold."

"Oh, sure," Josie said. "That would be nice." She took back her hand and hid her disappointment with another forkful of pancakes.

"Is something wrong?" Ted asked, cutting his steak into more pieces.

Of course something's wrong, Josie thought. Why do men ask that question when they know darn well something is wrong?

She followed the time-honored path of millions of women and avoided telling him the real reason. "I'm worried about my mother," Josie said. "She's been donating some six hundred dollars a month to charities. Mom is so hard up for money she's hunting for change in the couch cushions to buy dinner. Most of her pension goes to these bogus organizations. I wouldn't mind if they were real charities, Ted, but they're fakes. I did some research and found out all three are frauds."

"Did you tell her that?" he asked.

"I did and she got mad at me. She said that Mrs. Mueller and Mrs. Gruenloh, a church lady, both sent money to these charities and they wouldn't make mistakes. She said I was wrong."

"Nothing you can do about that," Ted said. He recaptured her hand and kissed it.

"Well, I did something," Josie said. "Winter's coming and Mom won't be able to pay the heating bill. She refuses to raise my rent. She'll spend all winter freezing and living on eggs if I don't stop this."

"So how did you convince her?"

"I sent her a letter asking her not to donate to those charities. It's not from me. It's from someone I know she'll obey."

"Who?" Ted said. "I can't imagine Jane acknowledging any higher power. It's not her parish priest, is it?"

"No," Josie said, and whispered her solution in his ear.

Ted laughed, and said, "Clever. She can't say no to her uncle, can she? Did your plan work?"

"I don't know yet," Josie said. "Depending on the post office, she should have the letter in a day or so. I'll keep you posted."

"I can't wait to find out," Ted said. "What are you going to do about your other Jane problem—finding Clay's killer? You can't rile up that detective by poking around in his case."

"I won't do anything obvious," Josie said. "My theory that the fatal castor beans came from the maracas in Gemma's store was stupid."

"No, it was a reasonable deduction," Ted said.

"I was wrong," Josie said. "Detective Mullanphy sneered at me and said he'd tracked down the maracas from Gemma's store and they had seashells inside. I felt like a fool."

Ted put his arm around her and kissed her. "Any good detective would have reached the same conclusion."

"Any professional detective would have done what Mullanphy did—checked the maracas. I'm back to my original theory that the killer got the beans out of the poison ivy patch next to the restaurant."

"So what's the next step?" Ted asked. "And what can I do?"

"I thought I'd make one more trip back to Tillie's, where the trouble started. If I don't see anything useful, I'm going to pack it in. Mom will just have to live with that decision, unless she wants to see me in jail."

Ted's cell phone beeped and he checked the display. "It's Chris," he said. "I'll take the call outside."

"Take it right here in the booth," Josie said. She signaled the waitress for the check.

Ted pressed the CALL button on his phone. "Hi, partner," he said. "How's the patient? Good. I'll be there in half an hour."

He pressed END and told Josie, "Hans is resting comfortably. Chris thinks the surgery will be a success. I'll stay with him tonight after I follow you home."

They finished their last gulps of coffee, left enough for the check and a generous tip, and strolled outside to their cars under the Uncle Bill's sign. Ted held her again, and Josie wished they were going home together.

"Josie," he said, "when you go to Tillie's restaurant tomorrow, promise you'll call me if you see anything even slightly off. I've already proved I'll be there if you need me."

He kissed her good night in the pink neon glow.

Chapter 32

Who killed Gemma Lynn Rae?

It was going on one o'clock when Josie fell into bed. She woke up three hours later. It wasn't the heavy pancake supper. Or Ted's proposal that remained tantalizingly out of reach. Josie had to listen to a one-woman debate in her head. She tried desperately to sort through Clay and Gemma's murders.

She was mortified that Detective Brian Mullanphy already knew about the maracas. She'd burned with shame when he'd mocked her amateur investigation. Worse, the man was right. So was Ted. Josie had underestimated Mullanphy.

But she was convinced that Tillie did not murder Clay Oreck.

Josie had only her mystery-shopper instincts, honed at the suburban malls. Those were good. She made a living as a mystery shopper—not much of one, but she could pay her bills—if she lived in her mom-subsidized apartment with her free maternal babysitter upstairs. That's why she had to solve those murders, no matter what the odds. For her mother, who held the Marcus family together. For Tillie, Jane's childhood friend, who would die in jail if Josie didn't save her.

Josie gave up on sleep. She slipped out to the kitchen, made herself a pot of strong coffee, and padded back to bed. Then she arranged her pillows into a comfortable nest, settled back, and tried to reason through the problem.

Detective Mullanphy thought Gemma had surprised a burglar.

Josie didn't. Anyone in the neighborhood would know Gemma's junk shop wasn't worth burglarizing. Anyone from outside River Bluff would have a hard time finding the place. Josie had heard that meth heads and psychos would kill for a handful of change. Gemma's street was deserted. But it wasn't infested with criminal crazies and wacked-out wanderers.

Josie believed Gemma Lynn's murder was connected to Clay's death. It was more proof of Tillie's innocence. Josie had seen Gemma's body. Her head had been bashed in with real rage. Gemma didn't die because a surprised intruder had hit her on the head. Gemma's killer had tried to obliterate her.

Why? Gemma had frightened someone—or angered him—and he'd tried to wipe her out.

Gemma had sat next to Clay while he ate his last meal. She'd watched him collapse and claw his throat. What if Gemma saw something during that mind-searing moment? Something she didn't realize was important until recently?

Gemma sat in her dreary store and brooded on her lover's murder. What if she realized who'd killed Clay? Josie thought. She died with that knowledge. How am I going to discover it?

Follow the money, Josie thought. That's what investigators—real investigators, not amateurs like me—say. Where was the money and who needed it?

Lorena. Tillie's daughter wanted her mother to sell the restaurant for a million dollars, so the two women could retire. What if Lorena had killed Clay to force her mother to sell?

Then Lorena's plan had failed. Now Desmond was blackmailing Tillie to sell at a bargain, while Lorena had to single-handedly fight to keep the hated restaurant open. Why would she do that? In the hopes that Tillie's Off the Hill would recover and Desmond would once more buy the place for a million dollars?

Lorena couldn't be so deluded that she believed Desmond still loved her. She wasn't that crazy, was she? Or had she helped her lover kill Clay? Were they in it together?

It was worth a trip to the restaurant to find out, Josie thought.

Desmond. He was the only other source of money. Everything came back to him. Desmond was at Tillie's the day Clay died. He could have poisoned Clay. Desmond hung around with the casino crowd, so he'd know about sleight of hand. He worked for ruthless men who were pressuring him to put together a major land deal. Desmond was desperate to buy Tillie's property.

So desperate he killed a barfly and romanced the restaurant owner's aging daughter. Did Gemma see him slip the poison into Clay's food? Where was Desmond when Clay was served that platter of ravioli with the hyperheated sauce? Josie couldn't remember.

But Gemma might.

She'd spent a lot of time thinking about his death and her lost chance to marry. Did Gemma finally understand what she'd seen that afternoon? Did she try to blackmail Desmond?

Killing Gemma wouldn't be much of a risk, Josie decided. She lived alone on a deserted street. She didn't have a weapon. She'd be easy to overpower in a one-on-one fight.

And that's exactly what had happened.

Josie took another sip of her coffee. It was cold. She'd reached the dregs. Time for a fresh pot. As she stood up and stretched, her alarm went off.

Seven o'clock. The restaurant opened at eleven o'clock. Josie was determined to go back to where the trouble started, to Tillie's Off the Hill.

Josie hustled her grumpy daughter off to school. She was relieved when a sullen Amelia slammed the car door again and stalked into the Barrington School.

On the ride back to Phelan Street, she worried about her sulky daughter. I can't just dismiss her behavior as teenage rudeness, she thought. I need to pay more attention to Amelia. I need to either solve this case or give it up.

Today is my last day. I'm making that clear to Mom. It's time I stood up to her. I'll see her as soon as I get home. I'm not going to wimp out. I'll march right upstairs and tell her. I'm her daughter, not a doormat.

Josie didn't have to gather the courage to face her mother.

Jane was waiting on the front porch when she came home. Stuart Little wagged his tail in a friendly greeting. He wanted to play. Jane frowned and stuck out her chin like a bulldog, a sign she was ready to bite. Josie straightened her shoulders and prepared for battle.

"Josie, I want to talk to you," Jane said. "Tillie's deadline is closing in. What are you doing about it?"

"That's exactly what I want to talk to you about," Josie said. "Come on in."

She threw open her front door and walked in first. I can handle this better on my own territory, she told herself.

Jane followed, unhooking the dog's leash. Harry was sitting on the couch back. He pounced on Stuart like a lion leaping off a ledge. The dog gave a yip and the two of them went tearing through the house.

"Stuart, come back here!" Jane called.

Josie captured Harry and corralled him in Amelia's bathroom. Jane caught Stuart by the collar and dragged him into the kitchen, lecturing him all the way. "Bad dog!" Jane said.

Stuart whimpered and slid under the kitchen table.

"Coffee, Mom?" Josie said.

"No, thank you," Jane said primly. She sat at the table and folded her hands.

"Water for Stuart?"

"Josie, are you going to talk or not?"

Josie poured herself the tarry sludge left over from her breakfast coffee and gulped it. The bitter brew tasted worse than it looked, but she wanted that concentrated caffeine. She sat across from her mother, looked her in the eye, and said slowly, "I am doing everything I can to help Tillie. I spent last evening with the River Bluff police. A homicide detective nearly threw me in jail for interfering with a police investigation. What more do you want?"

"I have faith in you, Josie. I know you can find that man's killer."

"How, Mom? I'm not a professional investigator. I'm not even a private eye. I'm blundering around where I don't belong."

"But you've done it before," Jane said.

"And nearly got myself killed," Josie said. "I have my child to worry about, even if you don't care about *your* daughter."

Jane's face crumpled. Her stubborn look dissolved in tears. "I do love you, Josie," Jane said, sniffling. "And I admire everything you've done. Maybe I expect too much from you, but I thought you could do this."

Josie felt her steely resolve bend like a worn paper clip. Stay strong, she told herself, unless you want Amelia to be an orphan.

"Mom, I have one more idea. I'll go to Tillie's about one thirty today, when the rush hour is over, and check it out. If that doesn't work, I quit. I can't do this anymore. In fact, I shouldn't be going to Tillie's on my own for this. Do you want to go with me?"

"I can't, Josie," Jane said. "I have a sodality meeting."

"And that's more important than your friend's future and your daughter's life?" Josie asked.

"Call me if you see anything scary, Josie, and I'll get there as quick as I can." Jane's voice trembled.

"I will, Mom. Let's hope it won't be the last thing I do."

Chapter 33

At one thirty, the lunch rush was over at Tillie's Off the Hill—if it had ever begun. Josie was blinking in the doorway, waiting for her eyes to adjust from the brilliant sunshine to the bar's dim light.

She could make out a hulking figure in the back corner. Desmond was hunched over his usual table, as far away from the door as he could get without sitting in the vacant lot.

That man had nerve, Josie thought, perching there like a vulture. He was watching the restaurant die, waiting to pick its carcass.

Won't be long now, Josie thought. Desmond was the only customer.

Why did Lorena let him sit there? Did she need somebody—anybody—to fill an empty table? Or was she still in league with the casino's devil?

"Josie?" a woman called tentatively from behind the bar.

Josie could see better now. Tillie's daughter was tending bar. Lorena seemed older, even in the poor light of the back bar. Her skin sagged along the jawline and she had pouches under her eyes. Her hair looked flat and greasy.

Josie moved a step closer. Lorena still had that rash on her hands, hidden by cotton gloves. The white gauze bandage on her arm glowed in the faint bar light. Judging by the size of the bandage, the rash had spread almost to her elbow. Josie could see a bit at its very edge. Lorena could call that raw, blistered skin any name she wanted. It still looked like poison ivy to Josie.

The light from the window by the booths helped Josie see Desmond more clearly. He was wearing those black gloves. Who wore gloves when it was eighty degrees? What was he hiding? Desmond was doing something with his hands. Wringing them?

No, he was rubbing them. Not rubbing like he was trying to get warm. Desmond was digging his gloved fingers into the dark fabric. He was scratching. He seemed frantic to stop the itching, but he couldn't.

Josie wanted to see if he had the same kind of rash as Lorena, but she couldn't wander over to his table to check his hands. She had to be cautious with those two in the bar. If Lorena had worked with Desmond to kill Clay, she'd be threatened by Josie, too. If the couple had had a falling out, Lorena would have to protect her future. She could still go to jail.

Josie wondered if Lorena was desperate enough to force Desmond to marry her. She didn't want to think about that match. They were a deadly pair.

Lorena had a whole back bar full of ammunition to use on Josie, plus the tape-wrapped pipe Tillie kept under the cash register for protection. No one else was around. It would be too easy to bop Josie on the head. Then she and Desmond could hide Josie's body in a car trunk.

"May I get you something?" Lorena asked.

Josie jumped. "Oh, no. Sorry," she said. "I thought my mom was going to meet me here for lunch. I must have gotten my wires crossed."

"Haven't seen her," Lorena said. "Want to call her on the bar phone?"

"Uh, no, thanks. I have my own phone. I'll call her from my car." Josie reached into her purse and pulled out her cell phone. "See?" She held it up and hoped Lorena would see it as a threat.

I can punch in 911 before you can swing the first liquor bottle, lady, Josie thought.

"Suit yourself," Lorena said, and shrugged. "But if you find your mom, tell her Jeff made some dynamite mushroom tortellini. It's today's special."

"Will do." Josie hoped her voice didn't betray her fear. She forced herself to walk slowly out of the restaurant. Once she was past the windows, she ran for her car. She'd parked around the corner, out of sight. Josie scrambled inside, slammed and locked the door, and stuck the key in the ignition. She was ready to flee if she had to.

Then she speed-dialed Ted. Come on, she prayed as his cell rang. Be there for me again. I need you.

One ring. Two. Three. No one there.

Ted answered on the fourth ring.

"Josie," he said. She heard what sounded like a puppy yipping in the background. "Hold on a second, while I give Karen her pup. I'm in the van."

Ted and his partner took turns driving the clinic van to clients who didn't want to take their pets to the office. Josie waited for Ted to talk to her, watching the street carefully. Before Clay's murder, a parking spot around here was a prize. Now she saw only three cars besides her own. Two must belong to Lorena and Desmond. The third one was probably Chef Jeff's. He'd made the tortellini special.

Josie's stomach growled at the thought. Breakfast had been another pot of coffee. She hadn't had lunch.

She could hear Ted assuring Karen that the puppy was perfectly healthy. "He's not going to be happy about those shots," he said. "He may act a little subdued or off his feed. He could be cranky and tired. He might even have a low-grade fever. If it lasts more than a day, or if you have any worries—and I mean any—call the clinic. We'll be glad to talk to you."

Josie melted, despite her distractions. Shots were a routine part of puppy care, but Ted sounded so concerned. Karen paid with her Visa card and cooed over the whimpering pup. Josie heard the van door slam. A chair creaked.

"Okay, I'm back," Ted said. "What's wrong?"

Josie told him about Lorena and Desmond and her suspicions.

"You were smart to leave the restaurant," Ted said. "Stay out of the building. That's my last van patient. I can be there in half an hour. Can you wait that long?"

"Sure," Josie said.

"Promise me you won't go in there alone if either Desmond or Lorena is still in the building. It's too dangerous."

"Uh—" Josie said.

"Promise?" Ted asked.

"I promise," Josie said. "Wait! I see Desmond leaving the restaurant."

Desmond strolled out of the building, still scratching his hands. He tore off his gloves, stuffed them in his pocket, and dug at the rash on his hands. It made Josie itch watching him. At last, Desmond stopped tormenting his hands, unlocked a shiny black Lincoln, and drove off, tires screeching angrily.

"Only Lorena is left," Josie said.

"Still too dangerous," Ted said. "Wait till I get there."

A dented silver sedan rolled down the street and

parked in Desmond's spot. A woman with a generous figure and carefully styled dark hair got out. Henrietta. She wore a well-cut black business suit and a fresh white blouse. Her black high heels pattered on the sidewalk. She was in a hurry to get inside Tillie's.

"Josie, are you there?" Ted asked.

"I just saw Henrietta go into the restaurant. What's Clay's widow doing at Tillie's?"

Ted sounded impatient. "Josie, I don't know. I need to take the van back to the clinic and pick up my car. Just wait until I can get there. Josie? Are you listening? I'm worried."

"There's no reason to worry," Josie said. "Desmond is gone."

"Lorena isn't," Ted said.

"She's twenty years older than I am and out of shape," Josie said.

"Josie, I have to go," Ted said. "Promise you won't go alone into that restaurant while Lorena is there."

"Okay, I promise. I love you."

"I love you, too," Ted said, and hung up.

Josie's phone rang again. It was Jane. "I'm still in my sodality meeting," she whispered. "Stuart is here with me and he's being so good. The meeting will be over in a minute. I'll come there right after his walk."

"No!" Josie said. "It's too dangerous."

"Don't you treat me like an old woman. You asked if I was serious about helping you. Well, I am. I'm bringing Stuart. He's brave. We might need him."

Stuart was about as tough as a baby bunny.

"Please, Mom, don't. Ted—"

Too late. Jane had hung up. She was on her way with the ferocious shih tzu.

Chapter 34

Josie drummed her fingers on the dashboard and shifted restlessly in her seat. She'd talked to Ted half an hour ago. Where was he? She hoped Ted showed up before Jane arrived with Stuart Little. Even with Desmond gone, Josie still thought the situation could be dangerous.

As she scanned the street, she wondered why Henrietta ran into the restaurant. Clay's widow had sworn she would sue Tillie. She'd hauled a lawyer into the emergency room. Was Henrietta trying to work out a settlement with the restaurant? Didn't the lawyers do that?

Maybe Lorena and Henrietta were working together. Had the two women made a pact to kill Clay? No, that was ridiculous. None of it made sense.

Josie heard a high-pitched grinding, a prehistoric scream of metal, then a hollow thud like someone had dropped a monster metal drum. A trash truck was crawling down the alley one street over. The hooks on the front of the truck picked up the car-sized blue metal trash Dumpster, emptied it into the truck, then dropped it back into place and moved to the next.

The police had searched Gemma's trash last night. The fresh-faced Officer Zellman had been the designated Dumpster diver. He didn't find anything useful while Josie was there, but his neatly pressed uniform had been smeared with chocolate ice cream, ketchup, and worse. Much worse. He'd apparently struck cat litter at one point. That had set off a spurt of cussing.

He'd complained to Detective Mullanphy, who'd then made Officer Zellman search every Dumpster in Gemma's alley. "The killer's clothes and shoes will be covered in blood," Mullanphy told him. "He'll have to get rid of those clothes somewhere."

Gemma's killer could have thrown his blood-spattered clothes in the Dumpster behind Tillie's Off the Hill, Josie decided. It was the perfect solution. Desmond had hung around the restaurant long enough to know the trash pickup days. Lorena would know them, too.

Mullanphy believed Gemma's murder was an interrupted burglary. He didn't have the personnel to check every trash Dumpster in the neighborhood and didn't suspect anyone connected with the restaurant.

Josie watched the trash truck make its slow progress down the alley, grinding, screeching, and thumping. At that speed, it would pick up Tillie's restaurant trash in about twenty minutes. She had to check the restaurant Dumpster before vital evidence was lost.

She'd promised Ted that she wouldn't go into the restaurant if Lorena and Desmond were still there. Desmond had left. Lorena was still inside.

She tried to convince herself: If I don't go into the restaurant, it's okay to check the Dumpster, right?

I made a promise. Ted promised to be there for me, and I promised to obey him. Sort of a preview of our marriage vows, except the subject is trust and trash.

The grinding and squealing stopped. Josie saw the trash truck idling at the end of Gemma's alley. It made a left turn and started down the alley behind Tillie's restaurant. It was six stops from the crucial Dumpster.

Should I stay or should I go? Josie wondered.

I should go and please my mother.

I should stay and please my man.

Stay. Go. Stay. Go.

The trash truck crept forward while Josie debated with herself. She felt like her whole future hung in the balance. Would she stay with her mother forever or go forward to a new life with Ted?

The trash truck emptied another Dumpster and moved forward. Four more to go, and vital evidence would be lost forever. She heard a door slam. Lorena walked wearily to a matronly maroon Saturn, carrying a foil-wrapped package. Tonight's dinner? Lorena set the package on the car's roof, unlocked the doors, and set the package on the floor in the backseat.

Grind. Squeal. Shriek. Only three more trash Dumpsters left. Come on, Josie thought.

At last, Lorena drove away. Josie sighed in relief. Now she was free to search the Dumpster before the truck swallowed its trash. She dropped her cell phone into her pocket, pushed her purse under the front seat, and locked her car.

She was around the corner and rooting through Tillie's trash quicker than she could say "fat rat."

Frantically, she ripped open stinking bags with her car keys. She found smelly shrimp shells, putrid clams, and butcher paper reeking of blood from rotting meat. She rummaged through grease-stained cartons and decomposing lettuce. Nothing. Nothing. More nothing.

Rip. Slash. Tear. She slit the last bag and saw white

covered with bright red. Red smears and thumb prints, red streaks and crimson puddles. She'd found it. She'd found the clothes Gemma's killer had thrown away. Tillie would be free as soon as the police saw this.

Josie reached into the bag and pulled out a paper tablecloth, splashed with marinara sauce.

Chapter 35

Josie had a stinking shrimp shell stuck in her hair, red sauce on her blouse, and who knows what smeared on her pants. A rotting lettuce leaf clung to her right breast like a drunken frat boy's hand. Her cheek had a sticky streak. She felt a crawly creature inching along her neck.

She flicked the creature off her neck, then peeled off the lettuce and finger-combed the shrimp shell out of her hair.

She wanted to stay downwind of anyone until she could clean up. Tillie's restrooms were in the rear of the restaurant. If she sneaked in the back door, she could wash off the worst of the garbage and get rid of some of the reek.

Josie eased her way along the side of the brick building, duckwalked under the window by the booths, and slipped in the back door. She was in a narrow hall with two restrooms and what looked like an office door across from them.

She sprinted to the women's restroom and heard something in the hall. Josie ducked inside, cracked the door, and peered out.

Jeff the chef was in a full-body embrace with Henrietta, just inside the office doorway. Josie had never seen a kiss so passionate except on romance novel covers. Their eyes were shut and their lips were locked. They seemed to be sucking out each other's souls. Jeff shifted his round body. Now Henrietta's dark head was buried in his plump shoulder and Jeff was kissing her hair. One of Jeff's hands was unbuttoning Henrietta's white blouse. The other was working its way down the back of her slacks like a pink starfish.

Josie froze in shock and was glad she did. She could hear them now—hoarse whispers between hungry groans and whimpers.

"I don't know how much longer I can stand to be away from you, baby," Henrietta rasped.

"Just a little more time," he said. "Think of his life insurance money."

Life insurance? Josie nearly choked. That's why Gemma wrote down "Hartford." It wasn't a street or a city. Gemma had stumbled on the motive for Clay's murder.

"I wouldn't have that two million without you," Henrietta groaned.

"You don't have it yet," Jeff said. "But you will if we're careful."

"I can't believe Gemma tried to blackmail me for half his insurance," Henrietta said. "The way you got rid of her was perfect. It looked like a burglary."

"We did it together," Jeff said. "You marched into that shop and told her she wouldn't get a penny. You kept her distracted until I took her out."

"You were so strong." Henrietta sighed. "You solved our problem in a couple of swings." The memory of Gemma's murder seemed to excite Henrietta. She groped the front of his white chef's coat, fumbling with his buttons.

"Good thing that statue was strong," Jeff said. "Once

the old lady is locked up, it will be safe for us to come out and play. It will all be worth it. You'll see. Soon I'll have my new restaurant. Something cutting-edge downtown, maybe in the loft district. Or Clayton. Clayton would be good. Then I could have one of those celebrity chef shows."

Jeff left a trail of kisses from her neck to her breast while he kept popping buttons on her blouse.

"My mother-in-law is driving me nuts over that stupid rosary," Henrietta said. "She says it's all she has left of her boy. She wants me to help her find it. Olive thinks it's somewhere in her house. If I have to search her place one more time, I swear I'll make sure she joins her boy."

Jeff mashed his mouth against hers and she moaned quietly. When he came up for air, he said, "Humor her. Just a little longer." His pink paw scuttled up her back. He rubbed her shoulders and ground his hips into hers. "Two million dollars is one hell of an incentive to pretend you're looking for that rosary. Did you throw that thing out?"

"I hid it at my office," Henrietta said. She was panting. "I can't give it back to her. We used ten beads. Then you came back here and stuck them in his food. That was brilliant."

"I had to crawl to that old witch," Jeff said, "but it was worth it. She's gonna get hers."

"What am I going to do about his mother?" Henrietta whined.

"Get her another damn rosary," Jeff said.

"But it's a Mexican rosary," she said.

"Buy it on eBay. You can get anything on eBay. You've still got the old one, so you know what it looks like."

Gotcha! Josie thought. Motive and evidence. All I have to do is slip out of here, call 911 from my car, and the police will get a search warrant for that rosary.

The couple were twined around each other like jungle vines. Their bodies blocked Josie's way out the back door, but she could make a quiet break for the bar and run out the front of the restaurant. She started inching her way out the restroom door when it squeaked like a stepped-on mouse.

The surprised couple jumped apart. Josie sprinted for the restaurant, looking for somewhere to hide. She looked over her shoulder and saw Chef Jeff reach into a holster. Was he going to shoot her? Josie was moving too fast to get a good look, but she saw a knife fly by her ear.

She dodged it and raced for the restaurant. Jeff pulled a second knife from his holster and threw it. The knife stuck in the molding near her shoulder with a *thwang!* Josie paused to try to pull it out, but saw the two of them gaining on her. She abandoned the knife and kept running for the bar side. In the mirror, she saw Jeff had a third knife, about half as long as the first, with a sharp, pointy end. He handed another, shorter knife to Henrietta.

Josie shot straight toward the bar and the tape-wrapped pipe Tillie kept under the cash register. She ducked down behind the bar, dialed 911 on her cell phone, and shouted, "Help! I'm at Tillie's."

She didn't get a chance to say more. Jeff swung at her face with the knife. Josie swerved and Henrietta stabbed her shoulder with a paring knife.

Josie couldn't feel any pain, but the blood ran down her arm and she dropped her cell phone. She picked up the padded stool that Tillie kept behind the bar and held it like a shield while she hurled a vodka bottle at Jeff. It smashed at his feet, but slowed him down. Josie choked on the sharp fumes, but flung a fat bottle of Baileys Irish Cream at Henrietta. Baileys was stronger stuff. The bottle clattered and rolled but didn't break.

Henrietta and Jeff rushed her from the front end of the bar, blocking her way to the door. Josie dropped the stool in their path and ran out the other end, then realized she'd made a mistake. She'd left the tape-wrapped pipe under the bar. Henrietta pulled it out. Now she had the pipe in one hand and the paring knife in the other.

Josie was up against the back wall. Big mistake. She couldn't see any way out. She was backed up against the bowling machine as Chef Jeff swung the knife. It buried itself in the wood on the bowling machine. He'd missed.

Josie ducked and saw Henrietta right behind him, swinging that pipe.

Josie found the grapefruit-sized bowling ball in the machine's ball rack. She held on to it and delivered a knockout blow to Henrietta. She fell across the lane of the bowling machine. The knife skittered under a table away from Josie.

"Henrietta!" cried the chef and ran to her. She moaned in pain.

"You tried to kill her," he shouted at Josie. "Now I'm going to kill you."

He swung the knife in a wide arc as two River Bluff cops poured through the front door. Josie heard sharp barks coming from the back hall.

The chef saw the cops, dropped the knife, and sprinted for the back door. His exit was blocked by Jane and Stuart Little.

"Sic 'em," Jane cried. The shih tzu sank his teeth into the chef's ankle.

Chapter 36

It took hours to sort out what happened at Tillie's Off the Hill. The restaurant was chaos: Jeff tried to kick Stuart Little and Jane launched herself at the dog's attacker. She pulled the long-handled metal sharpening steel out of Jeff's holster and was beating him with it while she shouted abuse and Stuart barked and growled. A woozy Henrietta attempted to sit up. Josie tried to tell the police what had happened.

"Shut up, everyone!" Officer Zellman commanded.

There was silence, except for soft groans from Henrietta.

The police peeled an irate Jane off Chef Jeff's back and pried the sharpening steel out of her hand. They saw the blood on Josie's shoulder and called an ambulance and the crime scene van.

While they waited for criminal and medical help to arrive, they found Josie's cell phone and determined that she'd called 911.

That's when the crime scene van arrived, with the ambulance right behind it. The paramedics examined Josie's shoulder first. Josie was more worried about her lousy health insurance than the damage from the cut.

The paramedics were sympathetic. They asked if she had an updated tetanus shot, then said in their (non-medical) opinion that she didn't need stitches.

Detective Brian Mullanphy arrived while the paramedics were cleaning Josie's wound. The man looked gray with exhaustion. Josie almost felt sorry for him.

The crime scene techs took prints from Jane, Jeff, and Henrietta. The couple refused to talk without their lawyers present.

"I'll be happy to tell you what happened," Josie said. "Ouch. That stings." A paramedic slathered orange Betadine on her cut shoulder while his partner bandaged it with gauze.

"Let's wait till they finish," Mullanphy said.

The paramedics advised Josie to see her family doctor while they cleaned the garbage off her face and hands with alcohol wipes.

Chef Jeff limped over next, with Officer Zellman standing close by. Stuart had taken a substantial bite out of the chef's right ankle and it was bleeding heavily. Henrietta had a knot on her head as big as a baby's fist, thanks to the bowling ball. The paramedics said Henrietta might have a concussion and a doctor should see the bite on Jeff's ankle. They asked if anyone knew about the dog that bit him.

"Woof!" Stuart said. He still didn't look fierce, even with blood on his muzzle. Jane picked up her dog and said he had his rabies shots and the clinic would have the dates.

Detective Mullanphy read Jeff his rights and then Henrietta. The guilty lovers were handcuffed separately but taken in the same ambulance to the Holy Redeemer emergency room. Officer Zellman rode with them. Mullanphy said when the hospital released them they'd be taken into custody at the River Bluff jail.

A harried Lorena arrived as the ambulance was leaving in a burst of flashing lights. She pushed past the officer at the door and said, "Who's hurt?"

"Your chef got bit by a dog," Detective Mullanphy said. "The dog's fine. The chef needs to be looked at."

Lorena stared at the bedraggled Josie and sniffed. "You smell like a garbage dump."

"I know," Josie said. "Could I buy a T-shirt?"

"Have one on the house," Lorena said. "You want red or green?"

"Either one will smell better than this shirt," Josie said.

Mullanphy waited outside the women's restroom while she changed into a green GET TOASTED AT TILLIE'S shirt. Her slashed and smelly blouse was bagged as evidence. Josie figured it would be really ripe by the time Jeff and Henrietta went to trial.

She was stuck wearing the malodorous pants. Every time she moved her head she caught a whiff of decayed shrimp in her hair. The cat would love her new perfume.

When she came out of the restroom, she saw her mother on a chair in the kitchen, petting Stuart Little. "Who's a good dog?" Jane asked. "Who's a brave dog?"

"Woof!" Stuart said, and thumped his tail.

Once Josie had on a fresh shirt, Mullanphy made her sit in the restaurant office for their talk. She told the detective what had happened. The crime scene told its own story and backed up Josie's tale with hard evidence. The techs found a ten-inch kitchen knife stuck in the doorjamb, a boning knife jammed in the bowling machine, and a paring knife under a table. The techs reported that the knives all sported clear sets of fingerprints.

The uniformed officers had removed the black knife holster Jeff wore on his hip. It still held a short black-handled peeling knife, a meat thermometer, and tongs.

The crime scene techs discovered the teddy bear that was actually a nanny cam. It had caught Jeff and Henrietta's attack on Josie behind the bar and would confirm that part of her story.

Josie was telling Detective Mullanphy what had happened for the second time when Ted arrived. The uniformed officer refused to let him inside, but Josie could hear him on the sidewalk, demanding to know how she was.

"I'm fine, Ted," she shouted, and hoped he could hear her.

"Ms. Marcus, if I may have your attention, please," Mullanphy said.

"What time is it?" Josie asked.

"It's almost two o'clock," he said.

"My daughter! I have to pick her up at school."

"You can't leave now," Mullanphy said.

"What about my mother? Could she get her?"

"I still need to talk to her," Mullanphy said.

"Dr. Ted Scottsmeyer is right outside. He can pick up Amelia, but I'll have to write him a note. He hasn't been cleared in advance by the school."

"You write the note and I'll call the school," Mullanphy said.

The detective called to the uniform guarding the door, "Let Dr. Scottsmeyer in. Make sure he comes around the back."

The uniform made Ted stand outside the back door and cautioned him not to say a word.

Josie recited the school's office number and said, "The principal is Miss Apple." She scribbled a permission note while Mullanphy punched in the Barrington number. She heard the detective say, "That's my shield number. Here's the main number for the River Bluff dispatcher, Miss Apple. You can call it and confirm this information."

He listened a moment, then said, "Your policy is admirable, Miss Apple, and our children would be safer if all schools had one like it. Ms. Marcus would pick up her daughter if she could, but she and her mother, Jane, are witnesses in a murder investigation and I need to talk to them. No, Ms. Marcus hasn't done anything wrong. Quite the opposite. Would you like to talk to her? Your secretary has already confirmed my information? Good. Ms. Marcus's note is on lined paper torn out of a pocket-sized notebook. I'll witness and date it if you want and put my shield number on it. The note authorizes Dr. Ted Scottsmeyer to pick up Amelia Marcus. He's driving an orange 1968 Mustang. Do you want the license plate number? No, I guess you don't have any other vintage Mustangs in that color.

"Here's my cell phone number. Ms. Marcus will stop by the office and fill out the official paperwork first thing tomorrow. Dr. Scottsmeyer is leaving now."

He pressed END on his phone and said, "That's one tough woman."

"She has to be," Josie said. She could hear Stuart Little yapping and barking while Jane praised and petted him.

"Dr. Scottsmeyer, will you take that dog with you?" Mullanphy asked.

"Go with Dr. Ted," Jane said. "Go on. Good dog. Go see Amelia." Stuart barked and trotted out the back hall to Ted.

Josie told the detective what she'd heard Henrietta say about Clay's life insurance policy, Gemma's murder, and where Jeff and Henrietta got the castor beans that killed Clay.

"The rosary was made out of castor beans," Josie said. "For real."

"Let us prey," Mullanphy said.

He started the process for the search warrants. Josie hoped she'd heard right over the groaning and groping. After she'd repeated her story three more times, the detective let Josie write out a statement in the kitchen while he interviewed Jane.

"I left my sodality meeting to help Josie," Jane said. "I brought my dog with me because I had a bad feeling. Stuart is a hero. He deserves a medal."

Chapter 37

A weary Josie and Jane arrived home at seven thirty that evening. Jane was too tired to drive her car around back to the garage. She parked behind Ted's Mustang. Josie parked in front.

An outraged Mrs. Mueller glowered at them, furious that three cars had invaded her street. Josie waved at the old woman and smiled. Mrs. M fluffed herself up like an outraged cat and dropped the miniblinds.

"Don't start trouble with Mrs. Mueller, Josie. We're finally talking," Jane said.

"I was just waving to a neighbor," Josie said.

"That innocent expression doesn't fool me one bit," Jane said. "Your daughter uses it, too. I hope it irritates you as much as it does me."

"Now, Mom, don't get in a huff," Josie said. "We're both tired. GBH?" She held out her arms and her mother came into them for a hug.

Josie could see—and feel—that her mother was aging. Jane's hair was thinning and her hands were veined and liver-spotted. Oh, Mom, Josie thought. How many more years will I have you with me?

"Josie, you did a good job today," Jane said. "I should have told you that."

"You didn't have time," Josie said.

"Well, I'm taking time now. I'm sorry you were hurt. That was my fault."

"You didn't stab me with a paring knife," Josie said.

"No, but I pushed you into helping Tillie and you had to deal with that terrible man and his disgusting paramour. You were right. You don't have the skills of a professional. But you do listen to people. You see things other people don't. That's why you're good."

"Thanks, Mom." Jane was quick to criticize but rarely praised her daughter.

"I'm too rough on you sometimes, Josie, but I do love you."

"Stop it, Mom. You'll make me cry."

"Nothing wrong with that," Jane said. Her voice sharpened and she pulled away from Josie's embrace.

"Good. You're mad at me," Josie said. "That's the mother I know and love. I'm starved. Let's order in pizza."

"Let's," Jane said. "I'm too tired to cook."

Josie unlocked the door to her flat and called, "Ted, Amelia, we're home."

Ted stepped out of the kitchen, a dish towel slung over his shoulder. His smile lit his square-jawed face and his blue eyes softened. "Josie, how's your shoulder? How are you?"

He started to kiss her, but Josie ducked. "I'm fine, except I smell like a landfill."

"You are a little fragrant," Ted said, and grinned. "You can shower before dinner if you want. We made a casserole with chicken thighs, garlic, tomatoes, and garbanzo beans, and A baked snickerdoodles for dessert."

"A?" Josie said.

"That's my name," Amelia said.

"Just A?" Josie asked.

"Short, sweet, and the very best," Amelia said. "That's me."

Ted winked at Josie.

"Okay, A," Josie said.

"While you take a shower, Josie, A and I will set the table. Jane, do you want a drink before dinner?"

"I'd like a nice glass of white wine," Jane said. "Just a thimbleful."

"Pour me a glass, too," Josie said. "I'll drink it after my shower. I don't want to ruin everyone's dinner."

"Yeah, Mom," Amelia said. "You're gross."

"Crime fighting is a dirty job," Josie said.

In her bathroom, Josie peeled off her new GET TOASTED AT TILLIE'S T-shirt and tossed it and her stained clothes in the wash. Was that egg yolk on one knee? She looked like she'd rolled in marinara sauce.

She turned on the water and stepped into the steaming shower. Josie sang "New Year's Day," a sad-sounding song from U2. Her rendition was even sadder. At least I didn't miss a career as a rock star, she thought. She scrubbed her hair and skin, washing away the medicinal scent of the alcohol wipes and the rotten shrimp smell. It would be a while before she ate seafood.

After she toweled off, Josie slathered herself with apricot lotion and dried her hair. She felt revived. It was good to come home to a man, especially one who cooked dinner and dealt with her tween daughter. Sure, I can raise Amelia on my own, she thought. But it's better with backup.

Josie looked at herself in the mirror. Fresh white shirt, clean jeans, brown bob with a bit of bounce, light lipstick for a little color. She was ready to face her family.

"You look nice," Ted said when she reappeared. He hugged her and handed her a glass of white wine.

"Smell better, too," Amelia said.

"A definite improvement," Jane said. "How's your shoulder?"

Jane still felt guilty, Josie thought. Good. That will make my life easier for a while.

"Better," Josie said. "Everything is better." She smiled at Ted. He kissed her cheek, then said, "You've finished your wine, Jane. How about a refill?"

"No, thanks. I have to walk the dog after dinner."

"The hero has already been walked," Ted said. "Amelia took him out. She thought it would be good advertising for her new business. Stuart has had his dinner, too. He's resting on his laurels on Amelia's bathroom rug. His pal Harry is curled up beside him."

"Then I'll take a smidgen of wine." Jane held her fingertips an inch apart. "I'd like a drink while I check my mail."

"I'll get it," Amelia said. "It's still in your mailbox."

Josie was glad her mother was fortified with wine when she saw the mail Amelia carried to her grandmother. The top envelope had a return address with a giant eagle, a flag, and "United States Department of Security." Josie recognized that letter. She'd created the hyperpatriotic stationary and the fictitious federal department.

"I wonder why the government is writing me," Jane said, tearing open the envelope. "I hope they don't want more money."

Fierce-eyed eagles spread their wings over the letterhead. Jane's eyes widened as she read and she gave a little gasp. "Oh, no. Oh, dear. No, no, no," she said softly. "That's not what I meant to do at all."

"What's wrong, Mom?" Josie asked. She knew exactly what was wrong and hoped Jane was too distracted to recognize Josie's pretend-innocent expression.

"The government says I've been donating to charities that are"—Jane read from the letter—"'known to give aid and comfort to terrorist groups.' The government is asking me to 'cease and desist donating to these organizations.' How could this happen? I've always been a good citizen."

"May I see the letter, Mom?"

Jane passed it to her daughter with a shaking hand.

Josie skimmed it and said, "These are the charities I told you about. The fake ones."

"I know you did and I should have listened. I wonder if Mrs. Mueller and Mrs. Gruenloh know about this. I'd better call them tomorrow."

"Are you going to keep sending money to those charities?" Josie asked.

"Of course not!" Jane said. "I don't help terrorists. What kind of citizen do you think I am?"

"Dinner!" Ted said.

Josie was relieved to be saved by the bell—the dinner bell. Jane was not eager to revisit the subject. Ted talked through the awkward silence. "We should toast Josie and her detecting abilities," he said.

They raised their glasses. "To Josie!"

"I almost got toasted at Tillie's," Josie said. "For real."

Jane's smile dimmed and Josie thought she was being too rough on her mother.

"When do you think they'll set Tillie free?" Jane asked.

"It depends if that search warrant Detective Mullanphy wanted produces the rosary with the crushed beads."

"Why is that important?" Ted asked.

"The rosary is from Mexico," Josie said. "Clay bought it for his mother when he and Henrietta were on their honeymoon. Castor beans are beautiful and they're used for necklaces and prayer beads in Mexico, the Caribbean, and South America."

"You sure know a lot about castor beans," Ted said. She loved the admiration in his eyes.

"Read it on the Internet," Josie said. "I guess Henrietta saw the same article. She took the beans from her mother-in-law's rosary. Jeff used them to poison Clay."

"But I thought Tillie fired him," Jane said.

"She did," Josie said. "I'm guessing here, but I think Jeff planned to murder Clay that day. He went to the restaurant to ask for his old job back. Tillie turned him down, but that gave him the excuse to be in the restaurant. He knew his way around the kitchen because he used to work there. He brought the beans with him and took advantage of the drunken confusion Clay created and Tillie's anger and slipped a lethal dose into Clay's toasted ravioli and the sauce."

"Using a rosary for murder," Jane said. "That's just sinful."

"So is murder," Josie said. "Clay knew his wife was having an affair with someone, but he wasn't sure who it was. Henrietta was definitely hot for Jeff."

"How do you know?" Jane said.

"I saw them groping each other in the back hall. That's when Jeff told his honey to hang on for Clay's life insurance. The police will have to verify that Henrietta has the policy, but I'm sure she does. Jeff is single and Clay was obnoxious. Henrietta wanted rid of her husband, but she also wanted that two million dollars."

"If the police can prove she killed him, Henrietta won't get a penny," Ted said.

"Jeff had planned to spend it all on an upscale restaurant anyway," Josie said. "I wonder if she realizes how desperate Jeff was for her money.

"That pair killed Gemma Lynn," she said. "I heard

them talking about it. Poor Gemma found out about Clay's life insurance and tried to blackmail Henrietta. They made her death look like a burglary."

"Poor Tillie," Jane said. "Those two deserve to spend the rest of their lives in prison."

Josie and Jane praised the chicken casserole. The five of them polished it off down to the last garbanzo bean. Over cookies, Amelia said, "My dog-walking flyer is ready. I made it on my computer. I'm going to post it all over the neighborhood. Want to see it?"

"Bring it on," Ted said.

She returned with a colorful flyer that read:

Experienced Dog Walker
Hire the Best and Stay Home and Rest
Call at 555-0513

It featured a color picture of Stuart Little and Amelia's school photo. "People around here will know I walk him," Amelia said. "It's good advertising."

"Whoa," Ted said. "You're using your photo and your cell phone number, A?"

"I want people to know who they're hiring."

"They'll find that out when they interview you," Ted said. "It's not a good idea to post your picture and cell phone number where anyone could see them. You can attract some bad people. Why not get the names and addresses of potential clients and send letters? Use your mother's phone. Your letter can tell them to call between four and eight p.m. I'll give you a reference letter and so will your grandmother. Does that make sense?"

"Sure," Amelia said. "There are lots of perverts out there." Josie was touched by how grownup her daughter sounded.

"A strong woman knows how to protect herself," Ted said.

Amelia tried to hide a yawn.

"It's eleven o'clock," Josie said. "Tell Ted good night. We've all had a busy day."

"Aw, Mom."

"I think I'll turn in, too," Jane said. "Where's Stuart?"

"The hero looks ready to go home," Ted said. "He's right here yawning."

Stuart managed one tired tail wag.

"What happened to the blood on his muzzle?" Josie asked.

"I wiped away the red badge of courage," Ted said.

Jane kissed all three of them good night. She looked like she could hardly drag herself up the stairs. The chef chomper followed, nails pattering on the tile.

When Ted and Josie were alone she said, "Thanks for picking up A at school, for cooking dinner, and for helping with her dog-walking business."

"My pleasure," Ted said. "I mean that. She's smart, funny, a darn good cook—and almost as clever as her mother. Your plan to save Jane from those crooks worked."

"I don't think I'll have to worry about Mom sending them money again," Josie said.

"What are you doing tomorrow?" Ted asked.

"Sleeping in," Josie said. "I've turned in my last TAG Tour report. My work is done."

"I have the day off, too," Ted said. He kissed her good night. The long, dreamy kiss made Josie feel lonelier when it ended.

"I have to leave, don't I?" he said.

"Yes," Josie said. "I don't want A surprising us on the couch. I'll walk you to your car."

Hand in hand they strolled outside. The moon was a gold disc in a black velvet sky.

"Look at that gorgeous harvest moon," Josie said, and sighed.

"Can I ask you something?" Ted said.

"Yes." Josie's voice trembled with hope. This was the perfect setting for a proposal, a golden moon with the promise of a bright future.

"Want to go for that walk tomorrow?" Ted asked.

Chapter 38

Josie sat straight up in bed, her heart slamming in her chest. She saw the time glowing on her clock: 3:12. She'd seen them in her dreams. The killers, Jeff and Henrietta, were twined together like snakes. Jeff was in his chef's whites. Henrietta wore her widow's weeds. Her eyes shone with blood and lust.

She'd killed her husband with a gift to his mother. The woman was incredibly cruel. But why am I afraid? Josie wondered. She's in jail and so is her lover.

Because I want to marry Ted. Did Henrietta ever love her husband?

If things go bad with Ted, would I divorce him or kill him? she wondered. Would he want to kill me? He must have doubts about us, or he'd ask me to marry him. Maybe it's a sign we should stay single. If Ted asks me today, I'll tell him no. I'll have a nice, safe life with my daughter. I'm happy the way I am.

Josie felt relieved now that she'd made her decision. Exhausted from her eventful day and early-morning worries, she shut her eyes. Just for a moment . . .

Josie's sound sleep was shattered at six ten by a ring-ing phone. As she grabbed for it, she felt a stab of fear. Early-morning calls heralded death and disaster.

She heard Jane shouting, "Josie! Josie! Wake up!"

"What's wrong?" Josie was wide-awake now.

"Nothing's wrong," Jane said. "Everything's right. Tillie's going free. I just heard from Lorena. That Henrietta woman confessed. She blamed everything on the chef."

"Of course she did," Josie said.

"But she's still guilty. She's the one who took out that insurance policy on Clay. Two million dollars. Imagine."

Josie's mind flashed on Jeff, breathing heavily as he clutched Henrietta in the hallway at Tillie's. Was he lusting for the new widow or a new restaurant?

What made Henrietta turn on her lover? Did she finally realize Chef Jeff's plans for the insurance money didn't include her? Sitting alone in the River Bluff lockup could give a woman second thoughts.

"There's a bunch of evidence," Jane said. "The police found the broken rosary hidden in Henrietta's insurance office and it was made out of castor beans. It was missing a full decade of beads. That's what happens when you desecrate a rosary." Righteous wrath sizzled through the phone line.

"They got those two for the other murder," Jane said. "The chef said Henrietta killed that junk lady."

"You mean Gemma Lynn?" Josie asked.

"That's her," Jane said. "Lorena told me everything the police found out. Clay wanted to cash in his life insurance policy when he couldn't find another job, but Henrietta wouldn't let him. She even sold her new car to keep up the payments on her husband's policy."

"And Gemma knew about Clay's life insurance?" Josie asked.

"Yes. Gemma figured out that the chef and Henrietta were—you know—going together."

Going together. Josie got another vision of the two killers in each other's arms. That scene was burned into her brain.

"Clay wanted to cash in his life insurance policy when he was out of work, but Henrietta wouldn't let him. She sold their Lexus instead and bought something cheap. The police think Clay complained to Gemma about losing their car."

Jane bulldozed through her story, too excited to wait for Josie's reaction. "After Clay was killed, a customer from Hartford Street came into Gemma's store. That's in South St. Louis."

"Yes, I—"

"Gemma didn't get many South Siders in River Bluff," Jane said.

"She didn't get many customers at all, Mom."

"Right. Well, the man was a regular, so Gemma let him pay by check. His Hartford address must have jogged her memory. She remembered Clay telling her his wife took out a big insurance policy on him.

"If Gemma had gone to the police with her information, she'd still be alive," Jane said. "Instead she called Henrietta and demanded half the life insurance money. That Gemma was no good."

"So which one killed her?" Josie asked.

"The police say Jeff and Henrietta did it together. Both their fingerprints *and* their footprints were in Gemma's shop."

"Lots of fingerprints are in that shop," Josie said.

"Not bloody ones," Jane said. "They're both guilty."

"Good," Josie said.

"Mom?" Amelia was leaning against Josie's bedroom

doorway, rubbing the sleep out of her eyes. Harry was perched on her shoulder like a big owl.

"Did the phone wake you up, sweetie?" Josie asked.

"No, you did," Amelia said, her mouth set in a pout.

"Go back to bed, honey," Josie said. "It's Saturday. You can sleep late."

"Not with you yelling." Amelia stomped off to her room and slammed the door.

"Josie?" Jane asked. "What was that?"

"A look at the future," Josie said.

"You're not making sense," Jane said.

"We woke up Amelia."

"And she's just as sweet as her mother in the morning." Jane's voice dripped sarcasm.

"What else did you want to tell me, Mom?" Josie asked.

"Tillie's story is going to be on TV at six thirty this morning," Jane said. "I thought you'd want to watch it."

"I've already heard it," Josie said, then realized she sounded as surly as her daughter. "Thanks, Mom. I'm happy for you and Tillie. But I think I'll go back to bed."

Josie slept until the next call woke her at nine o'clock. "Hello," she said, her voice husky with sleep.

"Damn, Josie, you sound sexy," Ted said. "I wondered if you'd like some food before our walk. What are you hungry for?"

"Not Italian," Josie said. "I wore it yesterday."

Ted laughed. "Let me guess—you've also had your fill of local grease after your TAG Tour work."

"Congratulations! You win a date with Josie Marcus," she said.

"Then let me take you to one of the city's best restaurants. We can go to Saturday brunch. There's a wait, but it's worth it. The *New York Times* says so."

"What do I wear to a restaurant that makes the *New York Times* wait?" Josie asked.

"Same thing you'd wear for a walk in Tower Grove Park," Ted said. "How soon can you be ready?"

"Give me half an hour," Josie said as she hung up.

Before she could start dressing, her phone rang again.

"Alyce," Josie said. "What are you doing calling on a Saturday?"

"Jake's still asleep," she said. "I'm finished prepping the filled pancakes. Justin and I are eating apple slices until Daddy wakes up.

"Congratulations. I saw the morning news. Tillie's free. They showed her leaving the county jail. She looks ten years younger. That detective claimed good police work solved the case, but I suspect you had something to do with it."

"A little," Josie said, and told her friend about Henrietta and Jeff's capture. "Mom and Stuart Little came in like the cavalry. Ted was there, too."

"Do I finally get to congratulate you on your engagement?" Alyce asked.

"No," Josie said.

The silence stretched all the way from Maplewood to Alyce's home in Wood Winds.

"What aren't you telling me?" Alyce asked. "Have you two broken up?"

"Not yet," Josie said. "I think he may ask me today. But I'm going to tell him no."

"Why? Josie Marcus, you'd better have a good explanation. You said you love him."

"I do," Josie said. "But Henrietta loved Clay."

"You don't know that," Alyce interrupted.

"Well, she married him and she killed him. I'm safer being single."

"That's why you're saying no?" Alyce's anger roared down the phone line. "You're afraid? Josie, when you were pregnant with Amelia, did you ever think your baby would grow up and kill you?"

"Of course not," Josie said. "I was worried about a lot of things, including whether I'd be a good mother. But I never imagined my baby could be a killer."

"But it happens," Alyce said. "How many times have you seen on the news where a child kills his parent? But you had Amelia, and she's a beautiful daughter."

"Yes, but—"

"You've known Ted for more than a year. He's a gentle man, Josie. He's never hurt any creature, human or animal. I've known you for years. When your love life goes sour, you don't kill the guy. You walk away. That's what you'll do this time, except it won't happen. Have the courage to be happy, Josie. Please?"

Josie didn't say anything.

"Josie?"

"I promise," Josie said.

"Good. Now promise me I'll be your matron of honor," Alyce said.

"He hasn't asked me yet," Josie said.

"He will. Trust me. Justin! What are you doing? Bruiser doesn't like apples. Take that slice out of his mouth right now. No, don't eat it! I've got to go," Alyce said.

Josie was laughing when her friend hung up. She still had to get dressed for her date. Josie saw the sun pouring through the hall window, turning the white walls a warm gold. Outside, a woman was walking her miniature poodle. She wore a T-shirt, so the day wasn't too cool. Josie wondered if Amelia had pegged that dog owner as a potential customer.

Amelia! What am I doing, making a date like a single

woman? I'm a single mother. Who's going to watch my daughter while I run around like a giddy teenager?

Jane can watch her, Josie decided. She owes me.

Jane must have felt the same way. She happily volunteered to take care of Amelia. "We'll have a cooking class," Jane said. "Amelia wants to learn how to brine a chicken."

"Do you have a chicken?" Josie asked.

"No, we'll go to the store and pick out a nice plump roaster," Jane said. "Amelia can tell me what else she wants to cook. We'll do some serious grocery shopping."

"Good," Josie said, and meant it. If Jane was spending money on groceries, she couldn't give it to bogus charities.

As if she'd heard Josie's thoughts, Jane added, "I called Mrs. Mueller and Mrs. Gruenloh. They both got those government letters. I'm glad it wasn't just me. When do you need to leave, Josie?"

"Ted will be here in fifteen minutes," Josie said.

"I'll be right down. We'll work on a shopping list together."

Josie heard thumps, giggles, and growls coming from Amelia's bedroom. She leaned against the open door and watched her daughter drag a catnip mouse across the floor by its tail. Harry pounced on it, then attacked the pretend mouse with real ferocity. Amelia laughed.

"Morning, Mom." Amelia's sullen mood was gone. She was Josie's little girl again, but her mother knew that stage was nearly over.

"Grandma wants to teach you how to brine a chicken," Josie said.

"Good. That deviled egg casserole was gross."

"It was a little heavy," Josie said. "Grandma wants to go grocery shopping this morning. She says you should think about what meat you'd like to cook."

"Where did Grandma get the money for meat?" Amelia asked. There it was, that sudden shift into adulthood. Soon she would cross that border and stay there.

"I don't know, but she'll be here shortly. I'm going to brunch with Ted. Have a good time."

Josie decided on dressy casual for her date. She put on her good black pants, a white knit top, and a blue-and-white silk scarf. She brushed her hair until it shone and noticed the stab wound in her shoulder didn't hurt. She felt good, better than she had in a long time. She'd finished a tough mystery-shopping assignment. She'd solved a murder. She'd outwitted two killers.

If you're so smart, why can't you find your purse? she asked herself. Josie searched her bedroom and her bathroom, then the kitchen, before she unearthed the purse behind the couch. She heard a car pull up outside the flat, peeked out the window, and saw Ted.

Josie didn't wait for him to walk to her front door. "Bye!" she called to Amelia and ran out into the sunshine.

Ted met her halfway and kissed her while Mrs. Mueller scowled at them. Josie waved at the old sourpuss.

They drove off into a day bright with possibility.

Chapter 39

Many outsiders saw St. Louis as one more redbrick city interested in those Midwest staples—beer, beef, and baseball.

Baseball, yes. St. Louis was definitely a baseball town, especially when the Cardinals were going to the play-offs.

Josie liked a cold beer, too. Like many St. Louisans, she never forgave the Busch family for selling their brewery to a Belgian company. She joined the city's growing trend toward craft beers. Schlafly was now the city's largest homegrown brewery. Tom Schlafly and his Bottleworks hadn't deserted Maplewood, so she remained faithful to his beer.

Josie was proud that her city was a foodies' hidden paradise. It didn't matter that she could barely scramble an egg. St. Louisans loved good restaurants and believed in recreational dining. They spent long evenings over dinner, savoring new dishes. They debated who had the finest northern Italian food, which restaurant served the best grilled skate wing, who had the most innovative locally grown food.

In its quiet way, St. Louis had places that catered to locavores. Winslow's Home was one. The refurbished 1920s brick storefront had stained glass panels over its long windows and a bicycle rack out front.

"Nearly every slot in the bike rack is taken," Josie said. "Are we going to get a table?"

"It's ten o'clock. We shouldn't have to wait more than fifteen or twenty minutes," Ted said. "This is probably the last sunny fall Saturday left. There's supposed to be a hard freeze tomorrow."

Ted opened the door for Josie and said, "So what do you think?"

Josie had never seen a place like this. She liked the gleaming wood floors and pressed-tin ceiling. The old-fashioned glass cases and shelves were crammed with crockery, children's books, coffee beans, laundry soap, and pasta sauce. There was a cooler of craft beer and an entire room of wine.

Josie saw interesting oddities everywhere, from tiddlywinks to Belgian linens. Freshly baked cinnamon rolls, brownies, and chocolate chip cookies called to her. The air was perfumed with coffee and syrup and thick with kitchen clatter and diners' chatter.

"What is it?" she asked. "It looks like part restaurant and part variety store."

"It's supposed to be a new American general store," Ted said. "That's what they call themselves." He was as proud of the place as if he'd created it.

Blackboards advertised "fresh-squeezed lemonade" and "Winslow's Eggs."

"Those are farm-fresh eggs, too," he said. "From Winslow's Farm out in Augusta. That's where the restaurant gets its organic fruit, vegetables, herbs, and chickens."

"Wow," Josie said. "I guess I sound like a hick, but wow."

"Hicks are supposed to go to general stores," Ted said. "I think our table is ready."

They studied the menu. "The cinnamon rolls are tempting," Josie said, "but I want the brioche French toast. And coffee. Lots of coffee."

"I want the same with an espresso," Ted said. "We place our order at the counter."

The waiter brought their caffeine. Josie inhaled it, took a sip, and said, "Strong but not harsh."

Josie poured extra dollops of warm maple syrup on her thick slab of French toast. She was feeling virtuous since she'd ordered hers with bananas instead of bacon. *"Mm,"* she said. "This is heaven."

"I didn't have to coax you to bite into that French toast," Ted said, and grinned.

"It doesn't look as fearsome as pig ears," Josie said.

"What name is Amelia going by today?" Ted asked.

"I think she's still A," Josie said. "Tomorrow, I expect her to adopt an Egyptian pictograph and I'll have to call her the Person Formerly Known as Amelia. You're awfully good-natured with her whims."

Ted shrugged. "Kids all go through that phase. I did. One week I was Ed, then Eddie, then Edward. Teddy lasted the shortest time—once some dude called me Teddy Bear, I dumped that name. I drove Mom crazy. She was big on monogramming, and she couldn't figure out if I was ES or TS."

"I'm glad you settled on Ted," Josie said.

"It was my grandfather's name. I liked him and kept his name." Ted checked his watch. "It's nearly noon," he said. "Ready for that walk in the park?"

Ted seemed distant and preoccupied on the twenty-minute drive to Tower Grove Park in the south part of St. Louis. Ted parked the Mustang and they walked hand in hand through the Grand Avenue entrance, which lived up to its name with pillars topped by lions and griffins. The afternoon sun set the trees ablaze.

"This is perfect," Josie said.

"It's a gift," Ted said.

"It sure is," Josie said.

"No, I mean it's a real gift. To us. To the people of St. Louis. Henry Shaw gave the city this Victorian walking park. He made his pile by outfitting the pioneers, then retired young enough to enjoy his money. He commissioned all the statues and the crazy pavilions. I like the red Chinese pavilion with the dragons on the roof."

"My favorite is that gaudy red-and-white striped Turkish pavilion." A homemade banner between the pavilion supports said WELCOME HAYES FAMILY REUNION.

Boys screeched and chased one another through the grass. A blond man played Frisbee with his dog. A couple rode by on a bicycle built for two.

Josie and Ted took the short path to the Music Stand, a delicate domed pavilion surrounded by the stone busts of Shaw's favorite composers on tall pillars. They heard a string quartet playing. The bandstand was garlanded in white and blue flowers. A bride and groom stood before a minister. A playful breeze caught the bride's long veil and turned it into a silk sail. Her maid of honor held the unruly veil in place and tried to control her own blue chiffon gown. Seated on benches around the pavilion were guests in party clothes.

Ted and Josie watched until the minister pronounced the couple man and wife. She lingered a moment, hoping Ted would ask her now.

"Shall we walk toward the fountain?" he asked.

Josie nodded, too disappointed to say anything.

They strolled toward the tiered fountain in a pond.

Alongside the pond were what looked like ruined palace walls.

"Why would your Mr. Shaw build fake ruins beside this pond?" she asked.

"It was the thing to do back then," Ted said. "Besides, those aren't fake ruins. They are the real ruins of the old Lindell Hotel. It burned down more than a hundred years ago and Shaw moved it here."

Josie crunched through the fallen leaves toward the edge of the water. They watched the fat orange carp swim, then sat together on a stone bench.

Josie took Ted's hand and said, "I love your hands."

"What?" He raised one eyebrow.

"They're strong, but gentle. I've seen you with Harry. When he turned skittish, you were firm with him, but you didn't hurt him."

"My technique needs some work," Ted said. "I've still got the scratches from Dina's ferocious feline."

Josie kissed the healing wound on his cheek.

A horse and carriage clip-clopped to the edge of the pond and halted. White ribbons were woven in its mane and the carriage was decorated with bows and flowers. The groom helped the slender blond bride in a billowing white dress out of the carriage. She was laughing and trying to juggle her filmy skirt and a bouquet of white roses.

A white limousine pulled up behind the carriage, and a rainbow of bridesmaids spilled out, all bows and bouquets. The groomsmen, a photographer, and a videographer followed in a third car.

"Look at the ring bearer in his little tux," Josie said. "He's adorable. He can't be more than three. I think the bridesmaid in yellow is his mom."

While the wedding party posed for photos by the ruins, the ring bearer broke away and dashed toward the fountain pond. "Fish!" he cried. "Big fish!"

He was about to dive in after the carp when Ted jumped up and caught the boy. He restored the squirming ring bearer to his grateful mother.

Josie rewarded Ted with a kiss when he returned to their stone bench. "Quick reflexes," she said.

"Comes from years of catching puppies about to tumble off the exam tables," Ted said.

"What a beautiful wedding," Josie said. "I wonder how many St. Louis brides have had their wedding pictures taken here."

"Want to be one?" Ted asked her.

"What?" Josie's heart was beating fast. The breeze stopped. Ted seemed to move in slow motion. He pulled a dark blue velvet box out of his pocket.

"Josie, I love you. I'll try to be a good father to Amelia. I can't replace her real father, but I'll love her like she's my own daughter. Will you marry me?"

Josie was too stunned to answer.

Ted opened the ring box and said, "It's two diamonds. Together. Like us."

The ring sparkled, catching the orange and yellow fire of the fall leaves. Josie stared at it.

"Still no?" Ted said. "Okay, I'll throw in free vet care for Harry."

Josie had waited for so long for this moment. Now she couldn't say anything.

"You drive a hard bargain," Ted said. "I'll give you lifetime care for your mother's dog, too. I'm serious, Josie. I love you. Please marry me."

Josie heard a chorus of "Marry him!" The wedding party was watching.

"Marry him! Marry him! Marry him!" they chanted.

"Yes," Josie said. "Oh, yes."

Ted kissed her—or she kissed him. Josie wasn't sure. The wedding party cheered when Ted slipped the ring on Josie's left hand.

The bride ran over and threw her white rose bouquet to Josie. "Catch!" she cried. "And live happily ever after."

Epilogue

Missouri is a death penalty state. Henrietta and Jeff were both eager to avoid a rendezvous with the lethal injection table. Henrietta claimed that Jeff had plotted and committed both murders, but the River Bluff police had found enough evidence to prove Henrietta had willingly cooperated in the murders of her husband and Gemma. The insurance company pledged its considerable resources to help get Henrietta convicted. They didn't want her to cash in that two-million-dollar life insurance policy.

When Tillie had threatened to kill the drunken Clay, Jeff decided it would be easy to make the police believe she'd poisoned him. Henrietta said Jeff went to Tillie's prepared to kill her husband. Jeff heard Tillie call Henrietta, who had rushed over to the restaurant. Jeff had suggested that Clay order toasted ravioli. While Clay and Tillie traded insults, Jeff had slipped back to the kitchen. Mitchell was busy bringing in tubs of dirty dishes. Chef Nancy was cooking and plating the food as fast as she could make it. Lorena was racing back and forth delivering dishes. In the sweat, steam, and lunchtime confusion, no one noticed Jeff in his chef's whites.

Jeff grabbed a platter of toasted ravioli that was up

and ready to go. He'd brought finely chopped castor beans in a ziplock plastic bag, concealed in his cargo pants, along with a pair of gloves. He dipped Tillie's own gloves into the poison, so they'd have traces of castor beans. Then Jeff made a small slit in the cooked raviolis and slipped in some six or seven poisonous beans. He waited until he heard Tillie barging through the door, and put the doctored ravioli back on the pass-through shelf by the stove. Then he slipped back into the restaurant and talked to the diners.

Tillie told Nancy, "I'm taking this ravioli here to get rid of Clay. I'll fix more. You go out front."

Nancy did. Tillie whipped up some sauce and served the ravioli. The bar was dark and Clay was too drunk to notice his ravioli had been doctored. He demanded extra hot sauce, and Tillie gave it to him. That's when Clay started screaming and collapsed.

For her cooperation, Henrietta's charges were reduced to second-degree murder and she was sentenced to thirty years in prison.

The court also accepted a plea bargain for Jeff. The one-time chef was sentenced to life without possibility of parole. He works in the prison kitchen. His restaurant was sold to pay his attorney.

Police found the remnants of the Mexican rosary that Clay Oreck gave his mother. Once Clay's murder case was closed, the rosary was returned to Olive. She keeps it in a cedar chest, along with photos of Clay.

Olive Oreck kept Henrietta's crystal rosary. She says she uses it to pray for her son's soul and also for his killers. God knows if that is true.

After Tillie was released from the St. Louis County Jail, she went back to work at her restaurant. Her remarkable story was featured on every St. Louis channel and on a truTV show. The publicity brought back old customers and attracted new ones who wanted to get toasted at Tillie's. The *New York Times* mentioned Tillie's Off the Hill in an article called "Hearty Heartland Fare." *Gourmet* did a color spread on Tillie's toasted ravioli.

A month after her release, Tillie had to hire another chef, two more waitresses, and extra bus help to keep up with the demand. Diners waited more than two hours for a table at Tillie's—all except Renzo Fischer. The lawyer was always given the best table when he showed up.

Desmond Twinings upped his offer for Tillie's restaurant to five hundred thousand dollars. Tillie laughed. Desmond doubled the amount to one million dollars, his original offer. Tillie gave him a copy of the *New York Times* article. The next time he made an appointment to see her, Tillie said she was being interviewed by the Food Network.

Desmond no longer sat at his table in the shadows. Tillie said she didn't have room for the developer's scout, no matter how long he waited in line.

Desmond patched things up with Lorena and begged her to forgive him. He proposed to her and Lorena accepted. Her diamond ring was even bigger than Desmond's. Tillie refused to see her future son-in-law, either at the restaurant or at her home. She didn't believe Desmond wanted to marry her daughter.

"Mark my words," Tillie told her daughter. "If I ever sell this place, he'll drop you the minute I sign the papers."

Lorena wept and told Tillie that she was ruining her last chance for marriage.

"If Desmond marries you within one year of your engagement, I'll eat my words. I'll not only get down on my creaky knees and beg his forgiveness, I'll personally cater your wedding."

But after six months of nonstop cooking and publicity, Tillie was tired. Her restaurant was now a local legend with a national reputation.

"I want to retire on a high note," she told her friend Jane.

Tillie accepted Desmond's offer, which was now up to four million dollars. She gave healthy retirement packages to Mitchell the table busser and Nancy the chef. The newer staff got six months' severance pay and good references.

Jane, Josie, Amelia, and Ted were among the two hundred people who attended the final party. Then Tillie's Off the Hill shut its doors forever.

Once the sale was final, Desmond broke off his engagement to Lorena and started dating a twenty-two-year-old exotic dancer. Lorena did not return her engagement ring. "It was the only genuine thing about him," she told Josie at the party.

Josie noticed Lorena's bare left hand was free of eczema. "That went away after Mom went back to our old soap brand."

Even though Desmond put the land package together, the developer was unhappy that he'd had to pay more than four times the projected costs for the casino land. Desmond never again had a deal on that scale—or another good payday. The exotic dancer dropped him. Desmond is still seeing dermatologists for his stress-related skin condition.

Tillie treated her hard-working daughter to a complete makeover and manicure at a St. Louis salon. Before Lorena and Tillie retired to Fort Lauderdale, they went on a cruise on the *Queen Mary 2*. Tillie said it would help a rested and revitalized Lorena recover from her disappointment in love. She was right. At dinner, Lorena was seated next to a Fort Lauderdale accountant who was two years younger. By the end of the fourteen-day cruise they were good friends.

Richard proposed at Christmas and he and Lorena were married on Valentine's Day. Tillie catered the meal for one hundred guests. For many, that was their first taste of toasted ravioli. One man was so smitten, he offered to back a restaurant, but Tillie said those days were over. Richard and Lorena's wedding was the last time Tillie made toasted ravioli. Lorena loves her new home in Florida and visits her mother often.

Amelia was thrilled when her mother flashed her engagement ring. Jane hugged her son-in-law to be and cried. Ted and Jane both give Amelia cooking lessons now.

Two weeks after his engagement, Ted was teaching Amelia how to make chicken cacciatore. "So how's the dog-walking business, A?" he asked.

"I've got four customers and a Chihuahua on the waiting list," Amelia said. "Mom says that's enough for now. If I keep up my grades, I may be able to take him on, too."

Amelia paused, then said, "My name is Amelia. I don't go by A anymore."

"That's cool," Ted said.

"I had to change it back. The kids at school were calling me Mel Gibson or A-Hole. I was named for Amelia Earhart. She has her own movie with Hilary Swank and Richard Gere. That's amazing. So I want to be Amelia."

"And so you are," Ted said.

Ted made a deal with the mayor of River Bluff that he would bring the clinic's van to do free spays and neutering for the town's pets on a Saturday if Stuart Little would receive a medal for bravery. A TV station did a feature about Ted's volunteer day in River Bluff. The free publicity got the St. Louis Mobo-Pet Clinic more paying customers.

The mayor of River Bluff presented Stuart Little his medal in a ceremony at City Hall. Ted made sure the shih tzu had been clipped and groomed for his appearance. Luckily, Stuart was honored on a slow news day. Jane attended the morning ceremony with Ted, Josie, and Amelia, who was allowed a half day off from school. That night, Jane watched her dog get his medal again at six and again at ten p.m. and taped the ceremony. Stuart wears the medal on his collar.

A third cousin inherited Gemma Lynn Rae's estate. The woman closed the shop and sold the building and its contents at drastically reduced prices. Alyce found a Rose Point gravy boat. Josie bought the FRIENDSHIP, LOVE & TRUTH sampler for five dollars and the Royal Crown Cola sign that Ted liked for ten.

She plans to hang them in her new home, after she and Ted marry. They haven't set a date yet, but Josie and Ted are looking for a house. The search is so intense, Josie even dreams about it. In some of the dreams, she and Ted and Amelia are barbecuing on their back deck, surrounded by frolicking cats and dogs.

In all the dreams, they are happy.

Shopping Tips

This is my chance to brag about my hometown, St. Louis. I challenge you to find a city east of California that is more interested in dining. It doesn't matter if you love grease or granola, locally grown and organic, or offbeat and ethnic. You'll find it in St. Louis.

Somewhere Between Mayberry and Metropolis Is Maplewood

That's how Josie's town describes itself. If you're visiting the St. Louis area, Maplewood is worth a trip. If you already live in St. Louis, rediscover this inner-ring suburb with the old-fashioned downtown.

Josie buys beer from Schlafly Bottleworks. During the winter, Amelia and her grandmother shop for locally grown food and baked treats at the indoor Maplewood Farmers Market at Schlafly Bottleworks. About April, it becomes the outdoor farmers market, but it is still at Schlafly Bottleworks, located at 7260 Southwest Avenue or online at www.schlafly.com.

Vom Fass, where Alyce buys exotic oil, is another foodie attraction. The German-based franchise also ships its fruit, vinegars, and oils. They have unusual oils, like porcini, orange, or truffle. Visit the Maplewood store at 7314 Manchester Road or online at www.vomfassusa.com.

Goshen Coffee's organic, locally roasted coffee is served at many St. Louis restaurants. You can also order it online at www.goshencoffee.com. Goshen Coffee is also sprinkled on some Kakao chocolate, but that's another subject.

St. Louis's Sweet Life Started in Bed

Putting chocolates on hotel pillows began when screen legend Cary Grant stayed at the Mayfair Hotel in St. Louis. The debonair Grant used chocolate to send a sweet message to a woman friend.

Is that story true? I sure hope so.

Lauren Bacall, another star, asked a *Vanity Fair* interviewer to open a box of Bissinger's chocolate bark for her. Bacall confessed that she's gotten free chocolate from the St. Louis chocolatier ever since she said, "Bissinger's is the best chocolate" onstage when she toured the city in the Broadway musical *Applause* in 1971. I like Bissinger's chocolate-covered raspberries, but I've never gotten freebies from them or any other business mentioned in these shopping tips. Visit them at www.bissingers.com.

Merb's Candies is another venerable city chocolate shop. St. Louisans crave Merb's chocolate-covered strawberries in the spring and monster Bionic Caramel Apples in the fall. You can buy those treats at the three Merb's locations, some St. Louis supermarkets, and online at www.merbscandies.com.

Lake Forest Confections has been tempting St. Louisans with molasses puffs, chocolate-covered lollipops, and pastries for generations. They are online at www.lakeforestconfections.com.

Lindsay's Chocolate Café and Coffee House has the best chocolate chip cookie in the Midwest according to *Midwest Living* magazine. Lindsay's Chocolate Café is at 1120 Technology Drive in suburban O'Fallon and online at www.lindsayschocolatecafeandcoffeehouse.com.

There's German chocolate, Dutch chocolate, and Belgian chocolate. Is there St. Louis chocolate? St. Louisan Brian Pelletier at Kakao Chocolate says no. "We're all so different. Bissinger's, Merb's, and Lake Forest have their own traditional approaches and familiar flavors."

Brian sees these trends in St. Louis chocolate lovers: Customers want "all-natural ingredients. We don't use any artificial flavors, colors, or preservatives," he says. "Our truffles and caramels use real cream and we give them a shelf life of three weeks at room temperature."

St. Louisans also like "local ingredients. We use local honey, lavender, fruit, coffee, and locally blended tea in our confections. We buy a lot of inclusions from Vom Fass down the street in Maplewood (liqueurs, flavored oils, and vinegars) and use Schlafly beer, too. Our customers enjoy a lot of unique flavors in our creations—honey, balsamic vinegar, Earl Grey tea, smoked tea, absinthe, stout."

Kakao has two St. Louis area shops, one in Josie's Maplewood and the other in South St. Louis. You can also visit their Web site, www.kakaochocolate.com.

Are you drooling for St. Louis chocolate? I've barely taken a bite out of the subject. If you choose to order some online, be aware that many candy makers do not ship chocolate during the hot weather months.

Farm and Home

Winslow's Home, a restaurant and general store at 7213 Delmar Blvd. caters to locavores. Much of the food is grown at Winslow's Farm, in Augusta, Missouri, about forty miles from St. Louis. Winslow's has offbeat items for breakfast, lunch, and dinner. At breakfast, it might be a quiche with duck confit, mushrooms, and brie. Dinner could be trout baked in parchment paper. The espresso bar is open all day and the pastries are baked at the restaurant. Visit their Web site: www.winslowshome.com.

Get Toasted in St. Louis

Toasted ravioli is actually breaded fried ravioli, dipped in marina sauce and sprinkled with grated cheese. In the Midwest, toasted ravioli is often stuffed with beef or veal, although inventive cooks use fillings ranging from artichokes to cheese. Several restaurants on the Hill in St. Louis claim to have invented toasted ravioli. "T-ravs" may have come from Sicily.

Ask a dozen St. Louisans their favorite place for toasted ravioli, and you'll get twelve different answers. Here are a few local recommendations: Cunetto House of Pasta (www.cunetto.com) and Talayna's (www.talaynas.net). A pub with the fine old Italian name of McGurk's (www.mcgurks.com) has spinach-and-artichoke toasted ravioli in a garlicky butter sauce. Zia's serves toasted seafood ravioli as well as the traditional ravioli Josie sampled. It sells sauces, salad dressings, and other items at their online store: www.zias.com.

Many restaurants get their toasted ravs from Mama Toscano's store on the Hill. Mama's handmade raviolis have been featured in major magazines and on Mario

Batali's Food Network show. Mama ships her ravioli, which you can order from www.mamatoscano.com.

St. Louis's Sweetest Mistake

Gooey butter cake supposedly started as a mistake, but no one knows which baker created this delicious deviation. Best guess is that it happened during the Depression, when a cake was overloaded with butter or sugar, or both. The bungling baker doused it with drifts of powdered sugar and the confection sold. Boy, did it sell.

Now there are endless artery-clogging versions of gooey butter cake, including cherry, pineapple, brownie, and chocolate chip.

For years, it was believed that only St. Louisans loved this caloric miscalculation. Then Gooey Louie started shipping its wickedly sinful creations all over the country. *Martha Stewart Living* drooled (genteelly) over those cakes. Gooey Louie was featured on *Road Trips for Foodies*.

Gooey Louie has about a dozen flavors, from key lime to "Hog Wyld." That's gooey butter with bacon. When a major St. Louis traffic artery was clogged by construction, Gooey Louie soothed frustrations sweetly with "Hwy 40: Driving Me Nuts." The roadwork is over, but the flavor survives. Gooey Louie has two St. Louis locations. For more information, go to www.gooeylouiecake.com.

Now some traditional St. Louis bakeries ship their gooey butter cakes, including Lubeley's Bakery & Deli, located at 7815 Watson Road and www.lubeleysbakery.com.

If you're in St. Louis, stop by one of these bakeries: Helfer's Pastries, 380 St. Ferdinand Street, Florissant, and www.helferspastries.com; Federhofer's Bakery, 9005

Gravois Road, and www.federhofersbakery.com. Josie gets her gooey butter cake at Jessie Pearl's Pound Cakes, Etc., in the heart of Maplewood, at 7322 Manchester Road. They can be reached at (314) 776-3051.

Pie Are Square

St. Louis pizza pie, that is. St. Louis thin crust pizza may be baked round, but it's cut into squares the size of Post-it notes. Traditional wedges cannot support the many ingredients piled on that thin crust.

A thin crust is a hallmark of St. Louis pizzas. They're also heavy on oregano. But the true sign of St. Louis pizza is Provel cheese, a sort of Italian Velveeta. Provel is a processed cheese, a fusion of provolone, Swiss, and cheddar rarely found outside the city.

St. Louis pizza is a city comfort food. Outsiders are often puzzled why the locals love it, though some visitors develop a taste for it. On my trips back from St. Louis, I pack a couple of frozen half-baked St. Louis pizzas in my checked luggage. The pizzas arrive safely, but it takes about a week to air the pepperoni perfume out of my suits.

I'm addicted to Imo's Pizza, which has outlets all over the city. Imo's ships pizzas, if you crave this taste of St. Louis (www.imospizza.com).

Elicia's Pizza (www.elicias.com) is another popular local chain.

Even the mighty Domino's Pizza made a thin crust pizza for St. Louisans, topped with Domino's pizza cheese and a provolone mix that insiders say tastes like Provel. Those in the dough claim Domino's brought in a team to study Imo's pizza. The popular chain supposedly bought precooked thin crusts from Imo's supplier until Domino's produced a St. Louis-style thin crust pizza. That pizza was so successful, it went nationwide as Domino's Crunchy Thin pizza.

Many local restaurants serve St. Louis–style pizza made with Provel. One exception is Pi Pizzeria. In fact, their waiters wear shirts with the classic red slash and circle banning Provel. Pi served pizzas to Barack Obama when he was on the campaign trail. Pi's Chris Sommers and Ryan Mangiarlardo, were invited to the White House to make the president more pizzas. Sommers concocted the Hyde Park with chicken and hot sauce. George Clooney and the cast of *Up in the Air* reportedly ate Pi pizza when they filmed the movie in St. Louis. Find out more at www.restaurantpi.com.

St. Louis Brain Drain

Deep-fat fried brain sandwiches are a St. Louis specialty from a time when city people ate every possible part of a cow. Traditionally, they're served with fries, beer, and plenty of ketchup. Brain sandwiches have become a dying art. Ferguson's Pub is one of the few bars that still serve this local delicacy. If you're not brave enough to chomp a brain, Ferguson's has fried chicken and toasted ravioli. This neighborhood pub is at 2925 Mount Pleasant Street in South St. Louis, (314) 351-1466.

Pigging Out in St. Louis

Dining at the best barbecue joints does not mean eating in upscale splendor. You don't want to get sauce on your sequins. Some of these neighborhoods may scare sheltered suburbanites like Alyce. True 'cue lovers assemble a pack of friends and slather themselves in sauce.

The *Economist*, a magazine that expects readers to know Joseph Schumpeter was an Austrian economist, decreed that St. Louis's "unique contribution to barbecue is the snoot sandwich." When this high-class magazine sticks its nose into barbecue, you know it's important. Once I got past the idea of eating pig ears and snoots, I liked them. Crunchy snoots and ears make one sloppy sandwich.

Big-time African-American celebrities as well as local folks of all colors love the pig ears and snoots at C & K Barbecue Restaurant, 4390 Jennings Station Road, St. Louis, (314) 385-8100. C & K used to be a gas station. Now it pumps out first-rate barbecue. The ribs, rib tips, chicken, and pulled pork are good, too.

Smoki O's, 1545 North Broadway, is tucked away in an industrial neighborhood in the north St. Louis Riverfront. It serves ears, snoots, pulled pork, and rib tips, which are supposed to be meatier and juicier than standard ribs. You can buy sauce, meat, rub, and other items online at www.smokios.com.

Roper's Ribs, 6929 West Florissant Avenue, won the Steve Harvey Hoodie Award for Best Barbecue and the *Travel and Leisure* 2009 America's Best Barbecue. Roper's has snoots, ribs, and more (www.ropersribs.com).

It would take another book to list all the St. Louis barbecue places. St. Louis barbecue sauce is tomato-based and thinned with vinegar. Brown sugar often adds sweetness. Horseradish or red pepper may spice it up. Many St. Louisans buy Maull's Barbecue Sauce (www.maull.com) and doctor the sauce with their own ingredients, including chopped onion, spicy mustard, or beer.

Beer is a major ingredient of backyard barbecues. Some beer goes into the sauce and the rest goes into the chef. Many St. Louisans brush sauce on the meat while it cooks, then keep the cooked meat in a pan of sauce on the grill. St. Louis–style ribs are specialty cut spareribs. Locals also love pork steaks, which are cut from the pork shoulder blade. The meat tends to be tough, so it helps to slow cook it.

Want more tastes of St. Louis?

Check the local magazines, including *Sauce* (www.sauce-magazine.com), *St. Louis Magazine* (www.stlmag.com), and *Feast* (www.feaststl.com).

Another good place to find St. Louis restaurants is the *St. Louis Riverfront Times*. Pick up a free copy or go to www.riverfronttimes.com.

How could I leave out Ted Drewes Frozen Custard and its iconic concrete? What about Dad's Cookie Company? Or Gus' Pretzels, with its hot dogs on pretzel buns? Or Tony's and the city's other gourmet restaurants?

I gave you some clues to the city's fine eating. You'll have to discover the rest yourself.

TURN THE PAGE FOR THE NEXT
EXCITING DEAD-END JOB MYSTERY,

FINAL SAIL

COMING IN HARDCOVER AND E-BOOK
FROM OBSIDIAN IN MAY 2012.

"That woman is murdering my father," Violet Zerling said. "We're sitting here while she's killing him. And you—you're letting her get away with it."

Violet Zerling jabbed an accusing finger at attorney Nancie Hays. Violet was no delicate flower. She was twice the size of the slender lawyer and obviously upset.

Nancie wasn't intimidated by the large woman. The lawyer was barely five feet tall, a hundred pounds, and thirty years old, but tough and adept at handling difficult people. She had faced down—and successfully sued—a slipshod homicide detective and the small South Florida city that employed him. She'd fought to keep an innocent woman out of jail. She didn't back away from Violet.

Nancie was all business, and so was her office. The carpet was a practical dark blue. Her plain white desk was piled with papers and folders. A workstation with a black computer, printer, and fax machine was within rolling distance of her desk. Seated next to the workstation were two private investigators, Helen Hawthorne and Phil Sagemont. Nancie had called in the husband-and-wife PI team to help her new client.

Helen felt sorry for Violet, sitting rigidly in the lime

green client chair. Her beige pantsuit was the same color as her short hair. The unflattering cut and drab color turned her face into a lump of dough.

Violet's clothes and shoes said she had money and spent it badly. Despite her sturdy build, she seemed helpless. Helen thought Violet could be pretty. Why did she work to make herself unattractive?

I'm not here to solve that mystery, Helen told herself. We have to save a man's life.

Nancie did not humor her client. "Violet, we've discussed this before," she said, her voice sharp. "Your father did not leave any medical directive or sign a living will. In fact, he doesn't have any will at all. Your stepmother—"

"That witch is not my mother," Violet said. "She is Daddy's second wife. She married my father for his money and now she's killing him. She wants his ten million dollars. He'll be dead soon, unless you do something. I need to save Daddy. Please. Before it's too late."

Violet burst into noisy tears. Helen had seen women turn weeping into an art form, shedding dainty droplets as if they were Swarovski crystal. Violet's tears seemed torn from her heart.

Helen would bet her PI license those tears were genuine. Nancie, Helen, and Phil waited out the tear storm until Violet sat sniffling in the client chair. Then Phil handed her his pocket handkerchief. Helen loved her husband for that old-fashioned courtesy.

Violet liked it, too. She dabbed at her reddened eyes, then thanked Phil. "You don't meet many gentlemen these days," she said. "I'll have this laundered and return it to you."

"Keep it," Phil said. "That's why I carry one."

Violet stuffed Phil's handkerchief into a leather purse as beige and shapeless as its owner. The ugly bag was well made. It would probably last forever. Unfortunately.

"May I ask a question?" Phil asked.

Violet nodded.

"How does the rest of your family feel about your fight to keep your father alive?"

"There is no one else," Violet said. "I'm an only child. Daddy is the last of the Zerling family. He doesn't even have distant cousins."

"And you're not married, I take it?" Phil asked.

"I'm divorced," Violet said. "My husband married me for my money and the marriage was not happy." She looked down at her smooth, well-shaped hands. They belonged to a woman who did not work for a living.

"I might as well tell you," Violet said. "You and Helen are detectives. You'll find the whole sordid story of my divorce on the Internet. My marriage was miserable. My ex-husband drank and beat me. I had no idea he was like that when I fell in love with him. I was only twenty-one. Daddy opposed the marriage, but I had a trust fund from my grandmother, and I was determined to marry. My ex slapped me around on our honeymoon, and the marriage went downhill from there.

"I tried to hide the bruises, but I couldn't fool Daddy. He knew why I wore heavy makeup and long sleeves in August. He never said, 'I told you so.' He was there for me. It took me more than a year to walk away from my marriage. After my ex put me in the hospital, I got the courage to leave him.

"He wouldn't let go of his meal ticket without a fight. He accused me of living a wild life. We were tabloid material for months. I couldn't have made it through without Daddy. I changed my name back to Zerling after the divorce.

"My family's money never brought me happiness, and I can't trust my judgment about men. I've set aside that phase of my life."

"Oh!" Helen said. She was a new bride and couldn't imagine life without love, though her first husband had been a mistake.

"It's better that way," Violet said. "I can't make any more mistakes."

Now Helen understood Violet's dowdy appearance. It hid a badly wounded woman.

"We aren't here to talk about me," Violet said. "My father helped me when I needed him. Now I have to help him."

"Violet, I wish I could do more," Nancie said. "Legally, Blossom is your father's next of kin. She has the right to refuse treatment for your father. Brain surgery is risky at his age."

"He's only eighty-four," Violet said. "That's not old, not in our family. His father, Grandpa, lived to be ninety-seven. Grandma passed away at a hundred and two. Daddy could go on for another ten, twenty years, if he hadn't married that woman. She murdered him for his money."

"Mr. Zerling is still alive," Nancie said gently.

"He won't be for long," Violet said. "He's on a ventilator. My father is unconscious, wrapped like a mummy in tubes and wires. That machine makes the most horrible sound. I tried to see Daddy in the ICU, but that woman won't let me in his room. She says I give off bad vibes."

"That's her right," Nancie said. "Unfortunately, the law is on Blossom's side. I've petitioned the court to hear your case. The hearing is tomorrow."

"It won't do any good," Violet said. "She's young and pretty and I'm a dumpy middle-aged woman. I know I look ridiculous, but I'm worried about Daddy."

"It wouldn't matter if you looked like Angelina Jolie," Nancie said. "Judge Jane Curtis only looks at facts."

"Then I hope she sees Daddy was strong and healthy until he married that woman," Violet said. "Now she's killing him."

"Mr. Zerling has a heart condition," Nancie said. "He used nitroglycerin pills."

"He took Viagra," Violet said.

"That's not recommended for a man with a heart problem," Nancie said.

"His doctor in Fort Lauderdale would not prescribe it," Violet said. "He got the blue pills from India. That woman told him he was a stud and he believed her. No wonder he had a hemorrhagic stroke."

"It's not illegal to encourage your husband to take Viagra," Nancie said.

"You didn't see the way she flaunted herself at him," Violet said. "I did. Daddy was taking twice the recommended dose when he had a stroke. Now blood is leaking into his brain. If that woman would let the neurosurgeon operate, I know he'd pull through. Daddy is a fighter."

"Even the surgeon says your father only has a thirty percent chance of recovery," Nancie said.

"That's better than no chance at all," Violet said. Helen saw tears welling up in Violet's eyes again.

"Blossom said your father didn't want to linger," the lawyer said. "She told the surgeon that your father said, 'If anything happens to me, pull the plug. I don't want to be a vegetable.'"

"Look at him! Is this the photo of a man who would give up?" From the depths of her beige purse, Violet pulled out a photo of a white-haired man on a glossy black stallion and handed it to Helen. She saw a square-jawed older man with a straight back and strong hands gripping the reins. He looked fit and muscular.

"That's my father on his eighty-fourth birthday, three months before he met her," Violet said. "He barely looks sixty. Blossom has reduced him to a thing on a machine. Soon Daddy will be nothing at all. He'll be dead. She's murdering him so she can have his millions."

Violet's eyes burned with fanatic fire and her pale skin was tinged with pink. For a moment, Helen got a glimpse of the vital woman she could be.

"Violet," Nancie soothed, "you must be careful what you say. That statement is actionable."

"I'm saying it to you in your office," Violet said. "I'm saying it in front of these detectives, but they work for you, right?"

"Yes," Nancie said. "When Helen and Phil are working for my firm, their investigation is protected by attorney-client privilege."

"Well, I want to prove she's killing him," Violet said. "If you can't save my father, I want her in jail for murder. I have the money to get what I want. His millions may kill my father. I want my money to save him."

The Crime of Fashion Mysteries

by Ellen Byerrum

Killer Hair

An up-and-coming stylist, Angie Woods had a reputation for rescuing down-and-out looks—and careers—all with a pair of scissors. But when Angie is found with a drastic haircut and a razor in her hand, the police assume she committed suicide. Lacey knew the stylist and suspects something more sinister—that the story may lie with Angie's star client, a White House staffer with a salacious website. With the help of a hunky ex-cop, Lacey must root out the truth...

Hostile Makeover

As makeover madness sweeps the nation's capital, reporter Lacey Smithsonian interviews TV show makeover success story Amanda Manville. But with Amanda's beauty comes a beast in the form of a stalker with vicious intentions—and Lacey may be the only one who can stop him.

The Bestselling
Blackbird Sisters Mystery Series
by

Nancy Martin

Don't miss a single adventure of the Blackbird sisters, a trio of Philadelphia-born, hot-blooded bluebloods with a flair for fashion—and for solving crimes.

How to Murder a Millionaire
Dead Girls Don't Wear Diamonds
Some Like It Lethal
Cross Your Heart and Hope to Die
Have Your Cake and Kill Him Too
A Crazy Little Thing Called Death
Murder Melts in Your Mouth

water in the backseat, just in case. Matches. Flashlights. Batteries. He'd tried to sneak in a hibachi and some charcoal, but Halliwell had vetoed them. Cassandra Belle, he ghost, wouldn't approve.

Here he was, Samuel J. Archer, a prominent criminal defense lawyer, being treated like a twelve-year-old caught with candy bars at summer camp.

"Well, that does it," Halliewell said when Sam had heaped his supplies onto the front porch. "I'll be off now. If you change your mind, it's a five-mile walk into the village. You have my number."

"I won't change my mind. I wouldn't give Uncle Dryden the satisfaction. Are you sure the old codger's dead? I think he'd have tried to figure out a way to be around for this one."

"I scattered his ashes myself."

Ashes. With Dryden Archer, Sam would have preferred to see the body.

A gust of wind off the rolling, overgrown grounds penetrated right to his bones. Or maybe it was just dread that had him shuddering. Eaton Halliwell seemed unaffected by the chill in the air. He climbed back into his car. "Will there be anything else, Mr. Archer?"

Sam glanced dubiously at the house, its gabled mansard roof in desperate need of repair. A wonder if it didn't leak. "No. Nothing."

"Then I'll be off." He gave Sam a dry smile. "Enjoy Cassandra Belle."

"Well, Halliwell," Sam said, "if I've got to put up with a ghost, it might as well be female."

From her second-floor window, Cassandra Liberty watched with deep consternation as the expensive sedan [illegible] back down the driveway.

Why had it left the dark-haired man behind?

[illegible] was standing in the middle of the driveway, his arms [illegible]d on his chest as if he, too, were wondering why he'd [illegible] left. He wore a black roll-neck sweater and jeans, and [illegible]med tall and strongly built. Just what she needed.

1

THE FOG, THE WIND, AND THE DAMP COLD WERE NOT, IN SAM Archer's mind, a sign of good things to come.

He kept silent as the car made its way up the long, meandering, utterly decrepit driveway. Eaton Halliwell was at the leather-covered wheel. He was an old-fashioned confidential assistant to Sam's rich uncle, very correct in manner and bearing, upright, ethical, of an indeterminate age. Sam had tried to talk him out of this ridiculous escapade up the California coast. He had failed.

"You cannot bring a vehicle of any kind," Eaton Halliwell had told him in the elegant front parlor of Dryden Archer's San Francisco home. "Not a car, not a truck, not even a motor scooter or a bicycle—or Rollerblades, for that matter. Of course," he had gone on, a rare glint of humor in his old eyes, "you wouldn't be able to Rollerblade where you're going."

Halliwell swerved to avoid a crater-sized pit in the gravel driveway. Ancient oaks and shrubbery grew wildly on either side, their branches swirling and shifting in the wind and fog, contributing to a feeling of eerieness Sam immediately dismissed as absurd. He was up in wine country, within half a day's drive of downtown San Francisco. Any sense of isolation was in his head.

But two weeks without a car. Without a telephone or a fax machine or a computer. Without, for the love of God, a simple transistor radio.

The ghost, apparently, disapproved.

"It—er—only seems to tolerate running water and minimal electricity," Halliwell had explained.

"Does it?" Sam had replied mildly. He did not believe in ghosts. He wouldn't, however, be the least surprised if his late uncle did. Dryden Archer had always been something of a kook, although still an Archer to the core and thus a man who looked after his own interests.

"The terms of Mr. Archer's will are very precise," Eaton Halliwell had continued. "You must stay at the old Liberty House for two weeks—fourteen full days—without modern transportation or conveniences before you are permitted to sell it. If you refuse or renege, the house and vineyards will be donated to one of Mr. Archer's favorite charities."

Halliwell had declined to specify *which* charity. Dryden Archer had had a variety of fruitcake causes he supported, and his definition of charity and Sam's were two entirely different things.

Sam had accepted the challenge. Come fifteen days from now, the house and vineyards would go on the market.

Halliwell eased the car around an overgrown mass of something, and Sam sat forward, peering through the fog as his home for the next two weeks came into view.

He shuddered.

The Liberty House was a sagging, peeling, cracked Victorian monstrosity. Lord, but it would be an interminable two weeks. His uncle was probably up on his cloud having a hell of a laugh.

If he were dead. Sam already had his doubts. It wasn't like Dryden Archer to arrange something he would find as entertaining as this knowing he wouldn't be around for the

show. Sam hadn't attended the funeral: his uncle's
stipulated there was to be no funeral.

Halliwell pulled the car up to a dilapidated fron
Steps and floorboards were missing. Others appeare
The front door itself . . . well, Sam could see he w
need a key.

No wonder people said the place was haunted.

The ghost even had a name. Cassandra Belle Libe
had founded Liberty Vineyards a hundred years ago
of the first women wine makers in California. She
her vineyards to an Archer. Sam didn't know the
Until his uncle's death last week, he hadn't even real
old vineyards were still in family hands. He did
however, that Cassandra Belle hadn't been the first
wronged by an Archer. Or the last.

Halliwell turned off the engine. "You could chan
mind," he said.

"That's what Uncle Dryden expected, isn't it?"

Halliwell's refined features remained placid. If h
he would never say what Dryden's intentions were.
two had remained friends for more than fifty ye
ceased to amaze Sam. Eaton Halliwell was eve
upright and honorable as his employer and frien

"I'll stay," Sam said. "Just be here two weeks fr
pick me up."

The old man shrugged. "As you wish."

Sam climbed out, the cold and dampness of t
a relief after the drive north from San Francisc
flight up from San Diego. Civilization. He live
and worked in a modern building with telec
on the cutting edge of technology. He could
anywhere in the world through computer
messenger services, telephones, even the

But not from here, of course. He could
this place. No one could reach him.

Halliwell got the trunk open. Sam re
his boxes of food and drink, his books
camp-style cooking utensils and sup

Suddenly he turned and stared up at her window, and Cassandra shot backward, startled by his quick movement and the intensity of his narrowed eyes.

And by an uncomfortable prick of familiarity. His angular features, his probing expression, his arrogant stance reminded her of someone. She couldn't say who.

She frowned, thinking. No. She'd never seen him before. She would have remembered.

Dropping to her creaky iron-framed bed, she debated how she should proceed with a visitor on the premises. Should she trot downstairs and greet him? Grab a poker in case he was not of the best character? Grab what she could, slip out the back, and go home to San Francisco and forget this whole business?

Of course, she had no car. Dryden Archer had insisted.

Was her visitor his doing?

"What to do, what to do."

It was midafternoon, cold, damp, dreary, as it had been since her arrival the previous evening. She had been relatively unconcerned about Dryden Archer's conviction that the house and vineyards were haunted. The ghost, after all, was supposed to be one of her ancestors—her namesake, the turn-of-the-century wine maker Cassandra Belle Liberty.

She had slept peacefully and spent much of the day exploring the rambling house, and, despite the bad weather, had ventured outside. Long-neglected and abandoned by their Archer owners, Liberty Vineyards lay in a remote but picturesque part of the warm, narrow valleys of California wine country. Cassandra was eager to explore the rest of the property.

But now, exhausted by weeks of overwork, she'd put on a nightgown of flannel-backed white silk, feeling quite feminine and Victorian as she anticipated a long afternoon nap to the soothing sounds of the wind and the rain.

She hadn't counted on a strange man venturing into her midst.

"Maybe you should have," she muttered aloud.

It had been dangerous even to talk to Dryden Archer,

much less *like* him. He had the Archer roguish charm, the Archer arrogance, the Archer zest for risk and adventure. He'd had a proposition for her. A business proposition, he said. He wanted her to catalog and appraise a wine cellar he had recently discovered at her great-great-aunt's old house and vineyards.

With Dryden Archer, of course, there had to be a catch. She had to agree to spend two weeks there, alone, without transportation or modern conveniences or communication with the outside world, not even a newspaper.

If she did, in addition to her regular payment for her work and expertise, she could claim five bottles of Liberty wines, if any remained in good condition. He must have known money alone wouldn't have persuaded her to agree to such a bizarre arrangement, especially with an Archer.

She heard footsteps pounding up the front porch. Rising carefully so as not to make any noise, she sidled back over to the window. The porch roof, however, blocked her view of the front entrance. She tiptoed to her door and listened. Hearing nothing, she pushed the door open and ducked quietly into the hall. She was barefoot. Her long, copper hair hung down her shoulders. Ordinarily she kept it pinned up or pulled back, but not when napping, not when she was supposed to be alone in an empty, hundred-year-old house.

She went down the hall, across a threadbare floral runner, and, holding her breath, peered over the balcony.

The front door creaked, banged open, and a duffel bag was hurled onto the entry floor.

Cassandra froze. Surely the dark-haired stranger wasn't moving in. *Surely* he wasn't.

Her heart thumping, she tiptoed back into her room, grabbed the wrought-iron poker from her marble fireplace, and quickly returned to the balcony. Dryden Archer hadn't said anything about a housemate.

The front door opened. The man from the driveway stood on the threshold with a box of groceries in his arms and stared up at her. His eyes were probing, narrowed, suspicious. "What the hell?"

Cassandra gasped, about-faced, and fled down the hall and into her room. She shut the door firmly behind her and pushed a chair in front of it and collapsed on the bed, poker still in hand.

No. It couldn't be. Dryden Archer *wouldn't.*

"The place is cursed, Cassandra. Only you—Cassandra Belle's youngest descendant—can change that. If you go out there and find eternal love within the boundaries of Liberty Vineyards, she'll lift the curse and finally rest in peace herself. And we Archer men will have a chance at happiness for the first time in a hundred years."

Dryden Archer talk. More of his babble. Cassandra had barely paid attention.

She should have known better. Dryden Archer was a rich eccentric—an adventurer and a scoundrel with a knack for making money, like all Archer men. If he felt her falling in love would lift some crazy curse, *naturally* he would have a candidate in mind.

She simply never would have imagined it would be Samuel J. Archer himself.

Nah, Sam thought. *No way.*

First the window, now the balcony. It must have been a trick of his imagination. Something with the light. Fatigue. Given the prospect of two weeks alone in a purportedly haunted house, without the amenities to which he'd become accustomed, it was not beyond reason that he'd conjure up a copper-haired woman in a lacy white nightgown.

Of course, the poker had been a bit of overkill.

"She was a figment of your imagination, Sammy my boy," he muttered, dumping his sleeping bag atop the rest of his stuff. "She was not a ghost."

A pity, in a way. That copper hair and creamy skin, that slim body, its silhouette clearly visible beneath the nightgown. He'd conjured up worse images, for certain.

The entry was huge, in the center of the rambling house. To his left was a drawing room, done in a large, faded floral print in shades of rose, burgundy, and deep green. Lacy, dingy curtains hung on the windows, and there were lots of clunky, overstuffed chairs and sofas. To his right was a living room, dark and dreary, largely unfurnished.

Leaving his stuff for the moment, Sam ventured into the tattered drawing room, through an archway leading to a dining room with more floral wallpaper and heavy furnishings. The feminine decor must have been to appease the ghost, since none of Liberty Vineyards' Archer owners could have had a woman long enough to make her mark.

"Ghosts," Sam muttered, disgusted with himself for having forgotten for a moment that they didn't exist. The floral decor was probably just in keeping with the house's Victorian style.

He headed out into a hall that, if he turned left, would take him back toward the rear of the house, where he saw glimpses of a bathroom and kitchen. There'd be time enough for that. If anything could send him screaming back to San Diego, it would be the kitchen and the variety of vermin that could congregate there. He knew how to cook. He'd done a lot of it in college and law school. He just hadn't done much since.

He went back to the entry, checking out the living room. There was a fireplace, a window seat, and double doors that led to a wood-paneled library. He lingered in the doorway. No floral wallpaper, no lace curtains. Just a couple of leather chairs, a leather couch, library-type wooden tables and bookcases, and a fireplace. He could carve out a corner for himself here, bury himself in one book after another.

Uncle Dryden, God rest his soul, had insisted Sam carry no cash or credit cards. Halliwell had checked. "There's nowhere to spend money in any case," he had added, as if that would make Sam feel better.

Returning to the entry, he decided he ought to venture upstairs—copper-haired woman or no copper-haired woman—and choose a bedroom.

He grunted to himself, grabbing up his duffel bag and hoisting it over one shoulder. "It's going to be a long two weeks."

He started up the stairs.

A door creaked behind him, off toward the living room, and he thought he heard footsteps. A cold shiver ran right up his back, and he whirled around, nearly dropping his duffel bag.

She was there, in the living room doorway. The shining copper hair, the creamy skin, the lacy white nightgown, the bare feet. The beautiful figment of his imagination.

He could see the outline of her nipples under the white fabric, utterly real.

Her eyes were teal-colored, wide and black-lashed. Intelligent. They fastened on him.

She spoke. "So you're Sam Archer." Her voice was throaty, as if it hadn't been used in a while. "I should have been expecting you."

Not since he was eight years old and had inadvertently stepped on a snake had Sam been so damned close to screaming and running. He tightened his grip on his duffel bag. *You don't believe in ghosts.*

"Who are you?" he demanded.

"Cassandra Liberty."

That was all he needed to hear. He wasn't going to scream and he wasn't going to run, but damned if he was going to stand there and talk to . . . to whatever she was. He had to get his wits back. He about-faced and marched up the stairs, determined not to look back until he was absolutely certain he was beyond seeing things. He didn't believe in ghosts. He hadn't *seen* a ghost. Either Eaton Halliwell's drivel had affected him the wrong way or the copper-haired woman was his uncle's doing, part of some elaborate scheme of his.

Cassandra Liberty.

"Uh-uh. That woman's been dead a hundred years. She is not downstairs in the goddamned entry."

He didn't stop until he'd reached the second floor. There, he glanced over the balcony. If he'd conjured her up, he'd be all right in a few minutes. If not—well, he'd see to it she quit her ghost act.

But he saw nothing but his gear and the eerie light angling

in through the filthy windows, heard nothing but the sound of the wind, howling now, outside. Sam steadied himself. What the hell kind of coward was he, running from some damned alleged ghost.

He grunted. Running wasn't the problem. *Seeing* a ghost was the problem. Of course, if anyone could go to his reward and talk some poor bastard on the next cloud to haunting this godforsaken place, it was Dryden Archer.

But Cassandra Liberty? She'd been a premier wine maker late in the last century, a rare woman in the business. An Archer had ruined her. She'd promised to haunt the lot of them—at least the males. For a hundred years, every Archer man who'd encountered trouble in romance had blamed Cassandra Liberty.

And Archer men *did* have a way of making a mess of their romantic lives. Uncle Dryden, himself the son of an Archer not known for his monogamous nature, had never had an enduring relationship. Affairs and the occasional near marriage, but nothing that he could sustain. Sam's own father was no better. He'd left his mother when Sam was in grade school and never was able to settle down with one woman. Still, Sam was less inclined to blame some long-dead wine maker than some innate Archer quirk. He had promised himself he would be different. But he wasn't sure he was.

He would have to find an old photograph of Cassandra Liberty. There had to be one around here somewhere. He'd see if she had copper hair and teal eyes and skin like fresh cream. Even if the photo was black-and-white, he'd be able to tell if she and the woman downstairs, in the window, on the balcony, bore any resemblance to each other.

Then he'd deal with his "ghost."

"Well, Halliwell," Dryden Archer said later that evening, drink in hand, "I must say, it's never felt so good to be alive. The deed is done?"

Eaton Halliwell nodded, matter-of-fact as always. "Miss Liberty and young Mr. Archer have both arrived at Liberty Vineyards."

"Sam can't wait to get these two weeks over and sell the place, can he?"

"I expect not."

Dryden sipped his Scotch. He knew he'd asked a lot of Halliwell, a straight arrow if there ever was one. But, then, he always had asked a lot of Halliwell. "He shed any tears for me?"

"Not in my presence, I'm afraid."

"The man's not in touch with his emotions," Dryden said with conviction. "Well, maybe the next two weeks will change that. I've got plans for Liberty Vineyards and that damned ghost is interfering with them. I want her out."

Halliwell settled back in his bone-colored leather chair, gazing into his untouched drink. "Mr. Archer—"

"Dryden. For God's sake, man, it's been fifty years."

Only the faintest of smiles. "Yes, I suppose it has. But I must say—I must say, sir, that your nephew and Cassandra Liberty are a most unlikely pair."

Reluctantly, Dryden had to agree. But he was a gambler and an optimist—and he owed Sam a chance at real happiness, never mind that Dryden himself stood to make a profit if all went well. And all *would* go well. If the curse wasn't broken within the year, the ghost—that relentless witch Cassandra Belle—would take over the house for all time and there'd be no getting rid of her.

And no hope for Archer men.

Dryden Archer fervently believed in ghosts.

I curse the lot of you. May not one of you find romantic happiness, ever.

She'd meant it, too.

Dryden supposed an argument could be made that he was using his nephew. Scheming and manipulating, as was the wont of Archer men. Yet surely, he thought, Sam would thank him in the end.

The doorbell rang. Halliwell got it, returning to the study in a moment. "It's your architect, sir."

"Good, good. Let him in."

All inhibitions about manipulating his nephew and young Cassandra Liberty vanished as he eagerly greeted the man who would help him transform Liberty Vineyards into a profit-making enterprise, once Cassandra Belle's curse was lifted.